CHAIN REACTION

by

JENNIFER JANE POPE

GW00580202

CHIMERA

Chain Reaction first published in 2000 by
Chimera Publishing Ltd
PO Box 152
Waterlooville
Hants
PO8 9FS

Printed and bound in Great Britain by
Omnia Books Limited, Glasgow

CHAIN REACTION

Jennifer Jane Pope

Part One

1.1

The face that swum slowly into her vision seemed vaguely familiar to Hannah, but as she fought to clear her brain, the name of its owner remained frustratingly just out of her grasp. One thing she did realise immediately, however, was that she was in deep trouble, for she was naked, laying on a cold flat surface and her wrists, arms, thighs and ankles all appeared to be secured by thick leather straps.

'Welcome back to the world of the living, Miss Levy.' The tall blonde was standing over her, peering down at Hannah's prone body, her expression smug. 'Remember me?'

Hannah blinked, tried once more to focus her brain on 'memory' and decided it was safer to play dumb, at least for the moment. 'I – I don't think so.' Her voice sounded harsh, dry inside her skull, and speaking made the backs of her eyes hurt. Whatever they had given her, it was powerful stuff, she decided. 'Who are you?' She coughed, painfully, trying to clear her throat. 'More to the point, what the fuck's going on here?'

'My name is Kristin,' the woman replied evenly, 'but you will address me as mistress, on those rare occasions when you are able to, that is. As to what's going on – and please don't struggle you stupid little whore, those restraints would hold a bull elephant – as to what's going on, I'm only too pleased to explain.

'You may not remember me immediately – our acquaintance was, after all, only a fleeting one – but I work for Master Rafe. Better known to you as Ralph Hancock, I believe?'

Hannah's expression remained fixed, but inwardly she cursed. Ralph Hancock. Dennison Hall. Yes, she remembered and now she remembered this bitch, too. Hancock was possibly the worst sadist she had ever encountered, but Kristin was not far behind him.

'You seem to be still having some difficulty, Hannah dear,' Kristin said. 'However, don't think it will do you any good to play dumb. We know all about you and your little band of female mercenaries, believe me, and we also know that you led them in an outrageous attack on Dennison Hall, causing Master Rafe a certain amount of inconvenience.'

'More than just inconvenience, I hope,' Hannah retorted. It hardly seemed worth trying to make any pretence and she had no intention of letting this bitch frighten her. 'So now,' she added, pursing her lips, 'I guess he wants his revenge on me, is that it?'

'Yes, indeed,' Kristin purred. 'On you and on as many of your band of Zionist whores as we can track down – track down with your help, of course.'

'In your dreams,' Hannah snorted.

'In *your* nightmares, more likely,' Kristin said. She leaned over Hannah, her face close. 'And we're in no great rush, either,' she whispered. 'I don't mind if it takes a year, though I doubt it will be anything like that.' She half straightened and now Hannah saw the gleaming studs in her sleeveless leather bodice, saw that they had been sharpened to wicked points.

'No doubt your Israeli army training prepared you to resist torture?' Kristin said. 'However, I doubt even *your* teachers could imagine some of the methods I can dream up.'

'Me too,' Hannah said. 'However, some of us are tougher than others.'

'Oh, I know all about your toughness, *Major* Levy,' Kristin snapped. 'And I also know all about your various preferences, including the fact that you are a confirmed lesbian. Quite a few of your unit share the same tastes, I believe? Yes, including at least two girls you've enjoyed affairs with.

'Amazing what a combination of love and loyalty will make some people do. We already know where both your former paramours are, you see, and we could have brought them in at any time,' Kristin continued, apparently savouring every word she was saying. 'However, we wanted you first and you fell straight into quite a simple trap.

'Now we have you, we can use your two whores to help us round up the rest of your little band and then we can put their fitness training to a far more suitable use than breaking into people's private premises.' She turned away and Hannah heard her picking something up. When she turned back again, she was holding a small syringe in her right hand.

'This is just the start,' Kristin smiled, her blue eyes diamond hard, pupils dilated. 'This is a recently manufactured compound that drains much of your ability to control your body. There are drugs that actually affect the muscles directly, but they are self-defeating for our purposes. This compound is much more efficient; you retain most of your bodily strength, but you cannot co-ordinate it properly. Simple tasks like walking and running can be mastered with sufficient practice and you'll be able to eat and drink, if a little messily, but beyond that-' She laughed and jabbed the needle into Hannah's upper arm.

'Beyond that, Hannah dear,' she sneered, depressing the plunger fully, 'you'll be little more use than an animal, except that unlike an animal, you'll still retain your intelligence and awareness, so you'll *appreciate* everything that little bit better!'

Concentration.

Isolation.

Subjugation.

Crazy nation.

'Teddy,' Alison mused, shaking out the rubber dress on its hanger, 'has it ever occurred to you that we're probably both quite mad?'

'What's that, darling?' Lord Edward Blank lowered his copy of the *Financial Times* and peered over the rim of his reading glasses.

'Mad, sweetie,' Alison said. She hooked the hanger onto the picture rail and turned to face him. 'Mad,' she repeated. 'Bonkers, crackers, touched – call it what you will. I mean, just look at me!'

'Gladly,' Edward said, grinning. 'Don't need asking twice, you know that.'

Alison sighed. She turned away from the dress and stalked elegantly across the room, her five-inch heels making no sound on the thick-piled carpet. Planting her booted feet apart, the wall lights glinting on the tight fitting rubber leggings and polished leather corset, she folded her arms beneath her barely concealed breasts and frowned.

'I'm being serious here,' she said. 'I mean, I spend all my time in this house walking around like some sort of fetishistic Barbie doll, something I wouldn't have considered even six months ago, and then get strung out when we have guests who don't share our particular tastes in fashion.'

'Well,' Edward said, folding the paper carefully and laying it aside, 'I suppose I could do something about the guest list, but these things do take time. Can't just cut off decades of family connections at a stroke.

'People would talk, old gel – not that I give a tuppenny ha'penny for gossip, you understand, but some of the connections are useful and the old family business relies

8

on goodwill.'

'No, Teddy.' Alison's sigh was laden with exasperation. 'You're missing my point. *They're* not the problem, we are.'

'We are?' Lord Edward frowned. 'How'd you make that out?'

'Well,' Alison replied, deliberately, 'how many other households do you know where the lord and lady spend most of their free time the way we do?' She looked pointedly at him, in particular at the pink latex jump-suit that had lately become his favourite evening wear when they were alone. Edward inclined his head.

'Well, seeing as you ask,' he said, 'I can think of a few – and those are only among the people I know well enough, if you know what I mean?'

'Teddy, please be serious,' Alison said. 'We both know you have some very unusual friends, but what about the rest of the world, eh? Do you really think that this is the "norm" for British households?'

'Ah,' Teddy replied, 'but just what is normal, eh? For a start, living in a forty room mansion, complete with servants, seventeen acres of grounds, five cars, two orchards and a cellar converted into a medieval dungeon certainly wouldn't be normal for your average English couple. Too bloody expensive, for a start!'

'Well, yes – obviously,' Alison said. 'And maybe that's part of my point.'

Edward shook his head, smiling up at her. 'Lost me now, I'm afraid,' he said. 'Getting too damned pissed to get too obtuse.' As if to emphasise his words, he reached out to the occasional table alongside his armchair and scooped up his brandy glass. 'Not too pissed to know that something's troubling you, though,' he added, before swallowing a generous mouthful of the glass's contents.

'What's troubling me, Teddy,' Alison riposted, 'is the fact that since I met you, I haven't done a decent day's work, nor earned a brass bloody farthing I can call my own.'

Edward raised his eyebrows in genuine astonishment. 'Work?' he echoed. 'But you don't need to, not any more. I told you, I'm stinking bloody rich – not that I can take any credit for that – so why bother killing ourselves?'

'I'm not talking about killing myself,' Alison insisted, 'but I would like to regain some sort of purpose to my life. At least when I was with the paper I had a reason to get up and go for something every day.'

'But you've got me now,' Edward protested. 'Aren't I purpose enough?'

Alison closed her eyes and began to laugh, softly. 'Teddy, darling,' she said at last, 'much as you know I love you, simply attending to your particularly unusual needs is hardly what I'm talking about. I can play "nanny" to you as often as you like, you know that, but I need something more. And no,' she added hastily, seeing the look of doubt rushing across his features, 'I'm not talking about another man, you know that.

'I need a *purpose*, something that I can take pride in, something I can say I've *achieved*. Fine, you've got enough money to keep the pair of us in utter decadence for ten lifetimes, but if I just goof around here and accept that, a little voice deep inside keeps asking me if I'm not just being some sort of glorified prostitute.'

'Oh, never!' Edward stared at her, aghast. 'Oh no, my darling, you're never that!'

'Aren't I?' Alison made a face and turned away from him. 'It feels like that sometimes,' she said. 'Not that I don't enjoy what we do together, but I keep thinking that I should be using my brain more. If I don't, I'll end up as some sort of latex covered vegetable.'

'And a prettier vegetable I couldn't imagine,' Edward said.

Alison rounded on him, her eyes flashing. 'That's

exactly it!' she stormed. 'You won't take me seriously, will you? As long as I play "nanny", as long as I cane your bloody arse now and then, as long as I do everything else you like, you'd willingly give me every last bloody penny you have!'

'I'd give you every last penny anyway,' Edward said, soberly. 'Surely you know that? I'd give you anything, whatever.'

'Then give me a bit of support and understanding,' Alison cried. 'I'm going to go mad otherwise.'

Speech was still possible, or at least the ability to form individual basic words, but the concentration and effort required to achieve even that was no less than what was needed even to stand up and walk, and Hannah was determined not to give her captor any more satisfaction than she was plainly already deriving from the situation.

The drug had taken effect rapidly and its effect was startling, worse than Hannah had anticipated, for true to Kristin's promise, her mind remained fully alert, her vision crystal clear, her thoughts sharply defined, but when it came to translating her will into actions, it was like trying to send a radio message through fierce interference.

Unbuckling the restraints, Kristin had hauled her to her feet and stood her upright against the bench on which she had first awakened. Hannah had expected to fall when she was released, but her ability to retain her balance evidently remained unimpaired. Walking, however, was another matter and it took several seconds before she was able to place one foot in front of another.

'Like a baby,' Kristin mocked. Hannah planted both feet firmly and glared at her, but when she opened her mouth to utter something suitably defiant, all that came out was garbled nonsense. Kristin laughed at her efforts.

'You'll have to try harder than that,' she said. 'We don't have slaves using big words around here, slut.'

'B-b-bitch!' Hannah finally managed. The crop in Kristin's hand blurred through the air, scything against Hannah's unprotected flank and drawing a wail of pain from her lips before she could prevent it.

'Well!' Kristin exclaimed, her eyes shining with pleasure. 'The tough soldier girl can't take pain the way she thought she could, eh?' She flicked the crop in a backhanded swing, cutting across Hannah's other hip and again the agonised howl rang out, seemingly of its own volition. Kristin's eyes narrowed and her lips curled into a sadistic snarl.

'The drug not only dampens certain mental functions,' she said, 'it sharpens others, such as your body's reaction to outside stimuli. You'll find your pain threshold is now considerably lowered, but there are compensations.' She reached out with the crop, probing between Hannah's thighs, the stiff leather braid pressing up between the lips of her sex. Instantly, Hannah felt something akin to an electric shock surging up through her spine and took an involuntary step forward, trying to bring her hands around to ward off this intimate invasion.

Instantly the crop came out and up, swishing twice and delivering searing cuts across both Hannah's forearms.

'Rule number one, whore,' Kristin sneered. 'Your cunt is now my property, or the property of anyone I decide. Not that I want it particularly, but there are plenty who will pay well for the dubious privilege.' She stepped close, seizing Hannah's jaw between forefinger and thumb of her free hand.

'And don't think we don't know all about your personal preferences, bitch,' she hissed. 'I know you'd rather have a nice soft pair of female lips between your legs. But take it from me, that isn't going to happen, at least, not as often as you're going to find yourself wriggling on the end of some nice, fat, juicy male cock.

'And where you're going it won't be all paying

customers, my dear, not by any means. Mistress Rose has recruited several very lusty grooms at the new farm stables. Most of them aren't very bright, it's true, but they know how to follow orders and they know how to fuck a feisty filly, believe me.' She released her grip on Hannah's jaw and stepped back again, focusing her attention on Hannah's naked breasts. She flicked at one nipple disdainfully, ignoring Hannah's gasp of pain.

'Small tits,' she said dismissively, 'despite the big nipples. I suppose that was an advantage to you as an action girl, eh? Well, you'll be training for a different kind of action from now on, and these pitiful things just won't do.' She laughed and this time her touch on the stinging teat was far more subtle, generating a lower-voltage version of the first spinal shock.

'Very sensitive now, aren't they?' she said. 'And they'll stay that way, I promise you. Once upon a time breast implants reduced nipple sensitivity by up to eighty-five percent, but some of the new laser techniques are quite astonishing. A week from now it won't even be possible to tell your new tits aren't completely natural, apart from a couple of tiny scars that won't be visible – most of the time, anyway.'

'Wha-what… you… m-mean?' It required every ounce of concentration to voice the three small words, but Kristin was still not satisfied. The crop hissed and a thin red weal appeared across Hannah's stomach as she staggered backwards, screaming once more.

'I told you, bitch!' she grated. 'You address me as mistress.'

Blinking away tears of frustration and agony, Hannah stared back at her, still defiant. 'F-fuck… you…' she groaned, steeling herself for the next assault. Kristin, however, remained where she was, the weapon dropping to her side.

'You'll never have that pleasure, you lesbian whore,'

she smirked. 'However, I can see that you need a proper induction before you go down to have your nice new tits fitted.' She turned away and moved towards the door.

'I'll send for you when I've attended to a few other things,' she said, 'and when you've been more suitably prepared for your new role. Someone will be along for you shortly.'

And with a grating laugh she was gone, the heavy door slamming behind her.

1.2

'How long have you been with your Teddy now, Alison?' Marcia Davenport extended one elegantly manicured hand and helped herself to another scone. The little café by the river was in mid-afternoon spate, but Marcia was the sort of female who would have stood out anywhere. Tall, with raven black hair, dark piercing eyes and wearing clothes that would have cost any ordinary working girl a month's wages, Alison still did not know her exact age, only that she had been at university with her former editor, Mike Hallet, and that he was approaching fifty now, whereas Marcia looked at least ten years younger than that.

Alison stirred her coffee pointlessly, staring past her older companion and out towards where the quiet waters of the River Arun meandered slowly down towards the

English Channel, the occasional hired motor-boat chugging back and forth carrying tourists eager to reaffirm their English ancestral ties with the water.

'I said,' Marcia repeated, more deliberately, 'how long have you and Teddy been together now?'

Alison jerked herself back to awareness and stared across the table. 'You know exactly how long,' she replied. 'Ever since we were at that bloody nightmare mansion of your ex-husband's.'

'Precisely,' Marcia said, evenly, 'and that is now more than a year, isn't it? During which time,' she added, 'I haven't had the pleasure of seeing you properly, have I?'

'You have!' Alison exclaimed. 'You've spent two weekends at Teddy's with us and we've been to dinner at your place at least four times. Then we all went to Mike and Honey's for Sunday lunch and spent another weekend out on that yacht of Honey's friend.'

'All of which was most enjoyable,' Marcia agreed. She paused, spreading a thin layer of butter across the scone, which she had meanwhile cut open without apparently looking at it. 'But that's not what I'm talking about,' she said.

'Tell me, how much do you see of Honey and Mike?'

'Well, now and then,' Alison replied. She wrinkled her nose, concentrating. 'We see them about once a month, on average,' she calculated. 'Of course, since I stopped working for the paper full-time I don't see as much of Mike as I used to.'

'And you regret giving up your career?'

'Well… yes and no,' Alison said. 'I mean, yes, I was always so sure of what I was going to be and I was getting to be a bloody good journalist, but then Teddy happened and, well, you know how it is. That ancestral pile of his is miles from anywhere and the London flat is just as bad.'

'How about Fleet Street?' Marcia suggested. 'I know Mike would give you an excellent reference.'

Alison shook her head. 'No,' she said. 'It's still too much of a male thing there. You'd never think we were nearly into the nineteen-seventies, would you? If you haven't got anything dangling between your legs, then you're only good for the women's pages, fashion articles, or little interesting snippets about old dears who've qualified for the telegram from Buck House.

'In any case,' she said, peering down at the now unappetising brown syrup in her cup, 'I still want to write my novel. I have done quite a bit of research work,' she added, defensively. Marcia reached across and patted her forearm.

'I'm sure you have, dear,' she said, soothingly, 'but there's just that little something missing, isn't there?'

Alison regarded her suspiciously. 'Like what?'

Marcia's ruby-red lips curved into a delicate smile. 'I don't think you need me to tell you, do you?' she said softly. 'And you're not unique, you know. That's why I asked how much you saw of Honey. I'm willing to bet you didn't know that she still comes to my place every few weeks or so.'

'Well, of course – oh!'

Marcia's smile grew slightly wider. 'Yes,' she said, 'oh! Honey and Mike are as happy with one another as you and Teddy are and, I don't think I'm betraying any state secrets when I tell you that they much enjoy playing the sort of games we all enjoy so much.

'However,' she said pointedly, 'even Honey needs that little extra something occasionally, and she's got herself a basically dominant partner.' Marcia leaned back, the scone now apparently forgotten. 'You, on the other hand,' she said, 'have dear Teddy, who is very much a submissive.'

'He has his moments,' Alison tried to smile and lighten this particular moment, but she knew Marcia had struck straight to the nucleus. The elegant dominatrix nodded.

'I'm sure he does,' she conceded, 'but have you ever

again experienced that feeling you felt when you first came to me? No, I thought not. Nor that feeling when that bastard Rafe… well, there's no need to go on with that,' she muttered. 'That was something different again.'

'Yes, it was horrible,' Alison said, lowering her eyes. 'But, at the same time…'

'I know,' Marcia said, patting her arm again. 'I do know.'

A woman with less self-control than Hannah would have burst into tears at the sight of the figure they showed her in the mirror, but then, she reflected, the vast majority of women would probably not have been so badly shaken, for the transition would surely not have been so total.

Yet, even though the image was so horrendous, it was a long time before she could tear her gaze from it, turning her head with some difficulty, to where Kristin stood waiting just to one side of her.

The blonde was grinning widely, though her pale eyes, above the sharply defined cheekbones, remained as humourless as ever.

'Much better, Tits, don't you think?' she mocked. 'Even your own mother wouldn't recognise you now, would she?'

Hannah's mother was long dead, killed in the Israeli War of Independence two decades before, but the statement was nonetheless accurate had she still survived.

The breast implants were, as promised, realistic and undetectable, only the fact that the skin was still stretching to accommodate them giving a slight clue. And the injections they'd been giving her three times every day since her abduction had already begun to take effect, so that her formerly rakish hips and buttocks were beginning to fill out.

In addition, they had shaved off her short dark hair, replacing it with a long wig of blonde curls and then tattooing a permanent makeup into her face, highlighting

17

her eyes and the lips that they had also somehow contrived to make fuller and more inviting.

'Quite the little bimbo now, aren't we?' Kristin hissed. 'No more action girl stuff for you, Tits.' Kristin ran one hand down Hannah's right flank. 'No, you're now quality merchandise, and no mistake.'

Hannah's breasts felt heavy, cumbersome and painful, though not from the tiny scars that were already well on the way to healing, concealed as they were beneath each of the impressive globes. She lowered her eyes, trying to control her breathing, take command of herself, not show any weakness.

'Do your… worst!' In the days since her capture, she had slowly begun to come to terms with the incapacitating drug they kept pumping into her. She would never be able to exert full control, either over her body's movements or over her speech, but she was at least able to put together basic sentences and could manage to walk without feeling as though she must overbalance at every step.

'I'd rather prefer to think that we'll do our *best*,' Kristin retorted. 'After all, we don't want to waste all the doctor's marvellous efforts, do we?' She stepped forward and began buckling a studded collar about Hannah's throat and Hannah made no attempt to try to stop her.

'No, Tits,' Kristin concluded, clipping the chain leash into place, 'we'll definitely do our best work with you. By the time I'm through you'll be a very obedient little whore, eager to serve and please and do just about everything your kind mistress tells you.'

Mike Hallet leaned against the rail that ran around the sun decking and smiled down at the kidney shaped pool, some fifteen feet below the level of his feet. The sleek female shape, sleeker still in the all-enveloping white rubber skin, slid through the blue water like a pale eel, wriggling and curving, almost as if she were boneless, a thin stream of bubbles flowing out behind her and mingling with the mane of blonde hair, the only part of her not encased within the latex.

Every so often the figure would rise to the surface and the mouth would open to suck in a fresh lungful of air, before the featureless head would once again duck beneath the water and she would be off again at her aquatic gymnastics.

Honey.

The colour of her hair had given her that name, for she had been born Sally Anne – Sally Anne Crichton-Thomas, with the proverbial silver spoon in the mouth that now so often preferred a gag. Mike's grin grew broader as he watched her; he could still scarcely believe he had only known her a year. Nor could he believe his luck in that they were still together, for she was, with the possible exception of Alison Katt, the most lovely female he had ever encountered. And the Alley Katt did not really count, anyway.

Or maybe she did, he reflected, reaching into his pocket for the ever-present cigarette packet. Twelve months had wrought a lot of changes in Alley's demeanour, especially those few days she had spent in the clutches of Ralph Hancock and his twisted cohorts. Where she had once been something of a tomboy – if it was possible to describe a grown woman in her mid-twenties as such – she now seemed far more inclined to concede her femininity.

Of course, there was also Teddy's influence to consider and the fact that Alison had, for reasons none of them seemed quite able to fathom, fallen very much in love with the young aristocrat. So far, from what Mike had been able to glean during their infrequent socialising, she had resisted his pleas to marry, but Honey, at least, seemed convinced that it was only a matter of time before the former reporter did agree to become Lady Folchester.

Down at the far side of the pool Honey was finally

pulling herself out of the water, the early afternoon sunlight dazzling as it reflected off the glistening white rubber. She shook herself, still on all fours like a dog, and then slowly rose to her full slender height, turned and peered up at Mike through the mirrored lenses that covered her eyes.

'Hi, darling!' Even her voice was honeyed and Mike felt the familiar shivers as he watched her beautifully sculpted body rippling inside the artificial skin that somehow made it appear more available than if she had been completely naked. 'I hoped you might come in and join me,' she called, 'but I can see you prefer to stay unhealthy.'

Mike waved away the wreaths of smoke that encircled his head.

'Maybe this evening,' he replied, 'though I prefer to take my dips in the buff.'

'Except when you're dipping me?' Honey's laugh was like velvet and Mike knew he would need all his willpower as he felt himself beginning to harden within the temporary sanctuary of his trousers and underpants. Lenses or no lenses, those blue eyes could give a hawk a run for its money and he knew that Honey was only too well aware of the effect she had on him, even when she was apparently making little or no effort.

'You had a phone call,' he said, changing the subject.

She raised her head towards him, the damp ponytail and red lips the only really human features in an otherwise humanoid appearance. 'Oh?'

Mike nodded. 'Alison,' he said. 'Said she needed to talk to you urgently. Wanted to know when you were going up to Marcia's for one of your weekends again.'

'Did you tell her?' Honey was reaching behind her neck, rubber covered fingers feeling for the zip that held the all-encompassing helmet in place.

'Well, I said I thought you were intending to go up this

20

Friday,' Mike said. 'You are still going, aren't you?' There was a blur of struggling activity and suddenly the mask came free, revealing a rather flushed face and a head that was furiously shaking itself, causing the sodden tresses to whip back and forth across her shoulders. Honey took a deep breath, tossed the limp rubber onto the grass, and grinned.

'That's better,' she sighed. 'Do you know, Michael, I've had that thing on since last night?'

'And the rest of the suit,' Mike laughed.

Honey began fumbling for the zip at the rear of the suit proper. 'I thought about stripping off first, but you know how I love swimming like this.'

'I told Alison you'd call her back,' Mike said, 'but there's no hurry. Apparently she's in the middle of disciplining her naughty little boy and he has to stay in isolation for a couple of hours.'

'Which means she's probably bored,' Honey retorted, beginning to wriggle her shoulders free of the cloying bodysuit. 'Not to worry, I'll just have a quick dip and ring her back. I spoke to Marcia last night, so I think I know what it's all about.'

Wherever they had taken her, Hannah was certain it was not the same estate that she and her all-girl commando group had raided a year earlier, for she recognised nothing outside the house. Her brain was still having great difficulty in linking with her body, but her memory was as sharp as ever and nothing about the woods, the rough pasture and the nearby hillsides was familiar.

Seen from the outside, the main building was Victorian, as had the original house been, but there all similarities ended, for where Ralph Hancock's first mansion had been exactly that, this structure was far less pretentious, probably built initially as a farmhouse, plain and functional and devoid of any decorative additions.

The outer door led straight into a rectangular courtyard, which was enclosed on two sides by a barn and a much lower outbuilding, linked by a high brick wall which then extended to run along the final side of the space, broken only by a gateway that was protected by a pair of heavy timber gates. Underfoot, the ground had been levelled, the mud covered by a layer of gravel that had evidently been rolled into it over a period of years and worn down by a combination of weather and traffic, for there were few sharp edges to cut into Hannah's bare feet as she was led across to the lower building.

'This is going to be your new home, Tits,' Kristin said, bringing her to a halt outside the open door. She indicated the interior, which looked dark and gloomy. 'It doesn't look too comfortable, does it?' she sneered. 'But don't worry, because it isn't meant to be. This is the stables, first built around a hundred and twenty years ago and, as you can see, not much modified since.'

She tugged on the leash again and led the way inside. After the harsh sunlight the gloom was at first almost impenetrable, and Hannah peered into it for several seconds without being able to make out very much. However, as her eyes grew accustomed, she saw that they were standing in a long passageway that ran the length of the front of the structure, off which were set a series of split level doors. Some of these stood completely open, others completely closed, with two more with just the lower section of door closed, the top half latched back against the adjoining wall. Kristin drew Hannah towards the nearest open doorway.

As they stepped into the enclosed area, Hannah's nostrils were filled with a mixture of heavy aromas; leather, rubber, straw, and she quickly saw the sources of them all. Most of the floor had been strewn with the straw, in places to a depth of nearly two feet, whilst along one wall a wooden rack was covered with dozens of items made from the first two materials, some of which Hannah recognised from the short period she had spent in Hancock's first premises after he and his cohorts had fled. Her eyes grew wide as she realised the implications of this, and Kristin was not slow to notice her reaction.

'Yes, Tits,' she hissed, 'this little lot is all for you, and there's even more where this came from.' She turned and jabbed a finger hard into Hannah's cheek. 'I've even fixed for a very special vet to take care of your teeth,' she said. 'He's going to remove two teeth, top and bottom from the back, just so your bit will fit better and you won't have to take it out to eat. Isn't that just too kind of me?'

Hannah opened her mouth to make some sort of reply, but quickly closed it again, recognising the futility of saying anything. This woman, and presumably her mentor, Hancock, held all the trump cards at present and any show of defiance or rebellion would, Hannah was certain, bring her nothing but further grief. Kristin, however, was enjoying herself, deriving as much sadistic pleasure from the promise of what she had planned for her captive as from the forthcoming actuality of it all.

'You see, Tits,' she explained, pushing Hannah towards the far end wall, 'you're going to be a pony girl here. I expect you saw our pony girls the last time, but we've somewhat refined the procedure since then and Master Rafe has invested quite a lot in some of the very latest technology.' She patted Hannah's bulging breasts to emphasise her words.

'These are just the start of it, too,' she assured Hannah. 'Once your skin has stretched and grown to accommodate these implants, they'll be enlarged even further. Eventually you won't be able to see your own feet – or should I say, hooves?' She cackled hideously at her own joke and then suddenly pulled hard on the chain leash, dragging Hannah towards her until their faces were only an inch apart.

'And by that time,' she leered, 'your cunt will have

become so big that it would take a cock the size of a real stallion's to fill it properly. You'll be just a caricature by then, you meddling whore, and not much real use to anyone with any taste. But you'll still have to work for your keep, believe me.

'This is a very big place, Tits, much bigger than Master Rafe's old estate, and there are dozens of different cottages for the guests and plenty of baggage to be hauled back and forth. You'll become our own little dray horse in time, trotting between the shafts from dawn till dusk, and later. Everyone will look at you and see nothing but a beast of burden.

'But long before then,' she said, her eyes narrowing into two slits of pure venom, 'you'll be wishing you could just die. You'll even beg for it, I guarantee.' She relaxed her grip on the chain and withdrew a pace, letting out a deeply satisfied sigh.

'The problem is,' she concluded, 'that you won't die. Not now and not for a good many years. You'll keep on working, trotting, cantering, dragging your loads, until finally your bones and muscles can't take it any more. And then, because we're not after killing you, you'll spend the rest of your days tethered in a pasture, with nothing but the birds and the hares for company.'

1.3

Alison had always been fascinated by Marcia's maid, Melanie, and even now found it hard to believe that the diminutive creature was in fact a male beneath her exaggeratedly female appearance. And not just a male, but an extraordinarily well endowed one at that. Usually clad in either a rubber or PVC parody of a French maid's outfit, today Alison was surprised to see the demure blonde walking across the lawn dressed in an extremely smart, tailored skirt and jacket, even her heels somewhat less extreme than usual.

'Hello, Mel,' she called, easing herself out of the lounger and standing up to wave. 'Come on round and have a drink. Long time no see.' The maid picked her way carefully around the poolside, avoiding the other sun loungers and tables and stepping over Alison's discarded towel that had slipped half into the water. Alison reached for the jug of chilled lemon juice and a glass and began to pour.

'Didn't expect to see you until tomorrow,' she said, holding out the drink. Melanie took it and sipped, gratefully. 'Nothing wrong, I hope, only I'd made arrangements with Marcia...'

'No, nothing's wrong, miss,' Melanie replied, lowering the glass. 'Just a small change to the original arrangements.' She placed the glass down on the table, opened her small handbag and withdrew a folded sheet of paper, which she passed over. Alison opened it, turned it up the right way and read the few typed lines it contained.

'I see,' she said, refolding it once more. 'And when is this supposed to start from?'

Melanie smiled, took another sip of the cold juice and held out her hand for the note. 'From now, I'm afraid,' she said, but her smile was far from apologetic. 'Lord Edward has already left for the day – mistress phoned him last night to explain – and Douglas is waiting in the house with the necessary things.'

Alison returned the smile and shrugged. 'I see,' she said. 'Well, the note was very clear, so I shan't ask any questions, just one small favour.'

'Yes?'

Alison reached out and scooped up the packet of cigarettes that lay next to the jug. 'Five minutes,' she grinned. 'Just five minutes before we go in, seeing as I shan't get a chance for another fag until after the weekend.'

The leather was stiff and unforgiving, encircling Hannah from just below her breasts to a line just below her navel, the corset-come-girth designed to be laced cruelly tight, and the woman who now had charge of those laces determined to ensure that it was employed to its savage limit.

Rose – Mistress Rose, Head Groom as Kristin had introduced her – was not as tall as Kristin herself, but was much more solidly built, with arm and shoulder muscles that would have been equally at home on the body of a middleweight boxer. Dark haired and square featured, her strength easily matched her determination and, whilst under normal circumstances Hannah would have backed her own training and speed against her, these circumstances were far from normal and any fight would have had but one inevitable outcome.

'My ponies all have tiny waists,' she grunted, hauling another fraction of an inch off the corset's circumference. 'A month from now yours will be no more than eighteen inches, and before we've finished I'll have that down to sixteen.'

'Impossible!' Hannah gasped. Her normal waist measurement was twenty-three and the idea that anyone could reduce that by twenty-five percent seemed ludicrous. Rose, however, was adamant.

'Sixteen inch waist, forty inch tits and thirty-eight hips,' she insisted. 'And your tits will be at least a double D, once your medication and stuff kicks in properly.' She hauled on the laces again, drawing a breathless squeal from Hannah, and let out a grunt of evident satisfaction.

'Not bad for the first time,' she announced. 'This is a nineteen inch girth and that's it fully closed.' She began knotting off the laces and, when she had finished, produced a small knife and cut off the trailing ends.

'Can't… can't – breathe!' Hannah managed, her head beginning to spin. She reached out one hand and Rose took it, grasping her upper-arm to steady her.

'Easy, girl,' the groom cautioned. 'Just don't panic. Take smaller breaths, from the top of your lungs. I've got you, so just concentrate. You ain't gonna suffocate, believe me.'

To Hannah's surprise and relief this proved to be so and, as she followed the big woman's instructions, slowly the buzzing in her ears faded and her vision returned to normal, though her ribs still felt as though they were being crushed between two very large rocks.

'Takes practice,' Rose told her, releasing her grip and stepping back. 'Takes practice, but it comes easier than you'd think. I'll soon have you trotting between the shafts as if you'd been born to it.'

'You're… mad,' Hannah wheezed.

Rose's eyes darkened. 'Just you watch your lip,' she warned. 'There's more than the bit to still a pony's tongue, I can tell you. And Mistress Kristin is as like as not to order yours cut out, if you gets too sassy. You're a pony girl now, Tits, and you'd best not forget it.

'Mind you,' she added, her sun-tanned features splitting into a deceptively friendly grin, 'by the time I'm done with you there ain't too much likelihood of that.'

Douglas was waiting for them in the library, standing at ease before the window that looked out towards the orchard on the east side of the house. Alison had not met him before and her first impression was of a giant of a man, with a bulk that seemed to block out most of the light from outside.

He was easily six and a half feet tall, with features that were so harshly defined they might almost have been taken from the pages of a comic book, and eyes that were startlingly blue. His short black hair matched the tight leather trousers and loose fitting silk shirt he wore; his age, Alison guessed, was anywhere between mid-twenties and mid-thirties, and she did not feel disposed to pursue the matter any further.

'Good afternoon, Douglas,' she said, extending a tentative hand as she approached him. He made no move to reciprocate the gesture, simply appraising her with a swift up and down glance before speaking.

'No talking unless given permission,' he said curtly. 'Just get out of that swimsuit and present yourself for inspection. I assume you are already correctly shaved?' Alison gulped and nodded automatically, her fingers already scrabbling for the shoulder straps of the one piece. Quickly she wriggled out of it, kicked the still damp material to one side and stood before him naked, her arms limply at her sides, making no effort to cover her modesty, knowing only too well the response this would elicit.

'I see you've removed your nipple rings,' he said, pursing his lips. He reached into a pocket and withdrew two heavy gold circles, which he passed to Melanie. 'See to her teats, cock-sucker,' he snapped. Alison cast a sideways look at the maid, but Melanie showed no sign of reacting to the insult. Instead she simply opened the first ring, took Alison's left nipple gently in her free hand,

and deftly threaded the first ornament through the pierced flesh, closing it again with a faint click.

'In future,' Douglas said, as Melanie attended to the other nipple, 'you will not remove your rings without the mistress's express permission, do you understand, slut?'

Alison swallowed. Already she could feel the heat beginning to build within her and her knees felt shaky. 'Y-yes, sir,' she stammered.

Douglas nodded. 'Good,' he said. He stepped over to one of the heavy fireside armchairs and pulled it into the centre of the room with no more effort than had it been made of papier-mache. 'Now,' he said, pointing to the leather upholstered back, 'get yourself over there, and be quick about it. I like to make sure my instructions are remembered.'

He turned away, stooped down and, when he turned back, he was holding a slender bamboo cane in his right hand.

'I mean *now*!' he growled, and Alison stumbled to obey, throwing herself over the chair back, the cold leather pressing into her stomach. 'You, bitch,' she heard him say, presumably to Melanie, 'get round in front and hold her wrists. I want her fully stretched, and if she's not you'll take her place when I've finished.'

As Melanie scurried to obey, crouching in front of the chair and seizing Alison's wrists in a deceptively strong grip, Alison gritted her teeth in anticipation, for this position, wherein her arms were being pulled downwards as well as out, meant that her buttocks were stretched taut, a perfect and painful target for his aim.

Douglas took his time – and he was an expert. One by one, unhurriedly, the six strokes of the cane descended upon her upturned rear, the thin bamboo whistling through the air to deliver cuts that made little sound, yet sent a searing pain through her entire body. Without a gag it was impossible to maintain the stoic silence Alison had determined, and by the fourth stroke she was howling unashamedly, air whistling in and out of her flaring nostrils, tears stinging her eyes and rolling onto her burning cheeks.

'Six will do for now, slut,' she heard him say through the red mist that had descended, and she only vaguely felt the touch of his fingers between her legs as he probed for evidence of the effect of his assault upon her.

'Wet already,' he grunted, breaking the intimate contact and delivering a stinging slap on her left buttock with the palm of his hand. Alison bucked and squealed, but the pain was already yielding to another far more pleasurable sensation.

'And now for your hooves,' Rose grinned. She had backed Hannah against one wall and easily secured her wrists to two ring bolts, using simple lengths of cord that forced her to stand with her arms akimbo. But they both knew that the restraints were little more than symbolic, a largely unnecessary precaution against any reflexive action on Hannah's part.

Rose turned away to where a long cardboard carton had been stood against the opposite wall, tearing apart the brown tape binding and extracting a pair of the longest boots Hannah had ever seen. They had been fashioned from stout, gleaming black leather, a perfect match to the corset, and designed to be fastened and tightened by means of D-shaped steel rings set in twin rows up either side of the length of the front openings.

However, it was not so much their length that caught Hannah's attention, but the height of the heels and the fact that those heels had been encased to form a one piece base with the thick soles, the whole shaped and splayed to form a perfect replica of a horse's hoof. They looked heavy enough to make walking in them difficult, but the angle at which the foot would be held would surely multiply that difficulty.

Taking the first boot Rose knelt before Hannah and carefully eased her foot into it, forcing the instep to bend until her toes slipped completely to the end. The lacing was a painstaking process, but she appeared in no hurry whatsoever, threading, adjusting, tightening, gradually closing the leather so that it hugged the flesh in every part, finally tying off the laces at the very top of Hannah's thigh and then buckling a retaining strap over the knot, so that it could not easily be interfered with.

'These lock, see?' she said, with an air of triumph. 'You can tighten the buckle, but without the right key you can't loosen it again.' She retrieved the second boot and bent to repeat the operation.

'There now,' she said at last, standing back to survey her helpless charge, 'don't you look pretty now? Pretty hooves and pretty pony legs. All we need do now is fix your arms properly and then we can take you to the barn. The vet should be here shortly and the sooner we get your teeth seen to and your piercings sorted, the sooner it'll all start to heal up again.

'But don't worry, Tits, I'll start you with a nice soft bit, at least while your gums are still sore. I don't believe in unnecessary suffering – just the necessary sort, and I reckon there'll be plenty of that coming your way soon enough.'

'Put these on her.' Douglas handed Melanie what appeared to be two wide silver bracelets, but as the maid snapped them about Alison's wrists it became clear that they were for more than ornamental purposes, and that they were actually made of strong steel and locked automatically in place. Once on, only the person who held the appropriate key could remove them, and whether that person was Douglas or not, Alison knew only that it was not herself and almost certainly not Melanie.

The two circlets were plain and undecorated, but each had a semi-circular staple set almost opposite the locks. The purpose of these was obvious to Alison, but the way in which Douglas actually put them to use came as something of a surprise.

As soon as Melanie had secured them he stepped forward, pushing her unceremoniously to one side and seized Alison's left wrist in his powerful grasp. Quickly he turned the bracelet so that the staple was sitting in line with her thumb, then raising her arm, he brought it level with the ring in her left nipple and deftly connected the two by means of a small padlock. Before Alison had time to react he repeated the operation on the right side, so that she was now forced to stand with her hands and arms held in a position that was a parody of a dog begging.

If she let her arms drop, Alison realised that the drag on her teats would quickly become more than just uncomfortable. But in keeping her arms raised high enough to ease this strain, she knew her elbows would soon begin to feel a strain of a different, yet no less painful variety.

'I see you have kept the rings in your clitoris, whore,' Douglas smirked. 'Does that mean they are permanent fixtures?'

'Yes, sir,' Alison replied meekly. 'They would need to be cut off.'

'Quite so,' he said. From his pocket he produced two more small padlocks, which he once again handed to Melanie.

'Lock the slut's cunt up,' he ordered. 'Both sets of rings, but first there's a little something for her in that case on the mantelshelf.'

It came as absolutely no surprise to Alison that the 'little something' turned out to be a fat vibrator. It slipped easily inside her saturated tunnel, leaving a short length of cord dangling between her thighs; a cord she knew could have only one purpose. She heard the two clicks as Melanie closed the locks and knew it was only a matter of time before the device was turned on.

'I ought to plug your whorish arse, as well,' Douglas snapped, 'but I think we'll leave that for now. However, I still have one or two more treats in store for you.' He jerked a thumb at Melanie. 'You, get your arse out to the van and bring back the black bag that's on the passenger seat.'

By the time Hannah was led back into her stall she was close to tears, all the years of training and resolution swept away by the nonchalant ease with which these people had so rapidly reduced her to such an inhuman status.

The vet, if indeed he was a vet, had been a balding man in late middle age, overweight and florid looking, the sort she would have expected to become easily excited at the sight of a nubile female in such a state of helpless nakedness. Yet he had handled her as dispassionately as if she had been a four-legged filly, with a professional detachment that was as humbling to Hannah as it was unnerving.

First he had removed the eight teeth, after Rose had laid her on her back on the steel trestle-table and secured her ankles with two broad leather straps. Her arms needed no further restraints, for before leaving the stall they had been laced into leather sheaths that ended in fingerless mittens and clipped to either side of the dreadful corset at wrist and elbow.

At least, Hannah thought grimly, he knew something about painless dentistry, for he injected her gums several times and waited for a few minutes before pulling the molars. When he'd finished he offered her a drink of an antiseptic fluid, which she had to suck through the stem of the sort of cup she had previously seen used for young toddlers, who had yet to master the science of drinking from a normal beaker. She swilled the odd tasting mixture around and spat it into the bucket he held for her.

'Nice clean extractions,' he said, speaking to Rose and totally ignoring his patient. 'She'll heal in a few days, but you should keep her mouth rinsed every two hours for the first day or so and four hourly for another week afterwards. And make sure you change her bit when you rinse her, otherwise there's a risk of infection.'

Finally, Douglas seemed satisfied that Alison had been suitably prepared for the coming journey. Her feet were now laced into ankle length boots that forced her to walk on tiptoe, her head encased by an intricate webbing harness that connected to a stiff leather collar that forced her to keep her chin held high. The final addition was a padded blindfold, designed to clip to the straps that framed Alison's face, covering her eyes and blocking out even the faintest chink of light.

As Douglas checked the adjustment and stepped away from her, Alison suddenly felt very alone, completely vulnerable and as totally in the power of another as she'd done the first time she'd visited Marcia. She could feel her heart pounding against her ribcage and hear the beat of her pulse inside her head, the steady rhythm all but blocking out the sounds of the room and now, for the first time in many months, she knew exactly what it was she needed.

It was not what she wanted – Teddy was what she wanted – but it was what she craved and that was something that dear Teddy would never be able to give her, even though she knew the love they now shared was real and enduring. Marcia had known – perhaps since that very first encounter – which was why she had sent Douglas to bring her, rather than wait for Alison to make her own way to the house.

She felt his large hands on her buttocks, flinching as his rough skin abraded the sore globes, but parting her thighs without resistance when one hand circled around and began probing. She felt a finger forcing its way between the two sets of locked rings, easing past the shaft of the vibrator and seeking her clitoris, now an easy target in its swollen and eager state.

'Slave,' he whispered, his mouth close to her ear. 'Just a hot little slave, with an eager cunt. Well then, slut, let's see what else about you is eager.' She felt his hands now on her shoulders, forcing her down. Understanding, she knelt, listening to the soft purr of the zip fastener as she waited, supplicant, begging, her lips parting as the warm flesh was presented to them, already swelling to quickly fill her gaping mouth.

'Show me!' he hissed, hands entwining in the head harness straps and Alison's hair. 'Let me see what a good slave you are!'

The supposed vet had finished by piercing Hannah's nipples and outer labia, inserting large steel rings into the former, and a row of three much smaller rings into the latter. He had employed a freezing spray in each case, but before she had been back in the stall very long the anaesthetic was quickly wearing off, leaving in its wake a series of dull aches, punctuated by occasional stabs of much sharper pain.

Not that she felt much like trying to move about, for she was barely able to move one foot in front of the other, but when she did, in order to suck water from the curious device mounted on the wall, Hannah had to take great care to keep her thighs pressed as closely together as possible, for the two sets of lower rings had finally been joined by means of threading a short, curved rod through them.

One end finished in a T-shape, the other in a slender oval, small enough to pass through the labial rings but large enough for a padlock to be employed through it, so that locked in place it prevented the rod from being withdrawn again. The effect, apart from preventing any access to her vagina, was to exert an agonising drag whenever her legs moved more than a few inches back or forth at a time, or whenever her thighs parted sideways. Presumably, she thought, once the piercings finally healed the pain would be much diminished, but as she stood morosely alone in the half darkness, it did not require much to remind her of what had been done to her.

Apart from anything else, the ring that had been inserted through her freshly pierced septum was only too visible beneath the tip of her nose, and the densely packed nerve-endings in the flesh there transmitted a continual stinging throb.

Slowly, her old self-control began to return, for she had trained for a long time in order to better deal with the sort of tortures that her country's enemies were known to inflict on captured soldiers – male and female alike. Gums clamped around the spongy bit that drew back the sides of her mouth, Hannah almost managed to smile. The tales she had heard back then, the transcripts she had read, the cold details from the instructors – she knew now that those enemy inquisitors could probably learn much from her present captors, but then theirs had been a different kind of fanaticism.

These people were not just fanatical, they were clearly mad, completely amoral and ruthless in the pursuit of their ends, be they personal gain or, as in her own case, simple revenge. Hannah had seen enough in the short time after her team rescued Alison Katt and her friends from Dennison Hall, Hancock's original base, to know that normal was not a word that could ever be applied to anything they did.

Hancock was incredibly rich and powerful enough that there had been no point in going to the police to report the abductions he had masterminded. His deviant operation, the so-called club, had simply been a means to an end, and too many people in positions of influence and authority now owed him an allegiance guaranteed by the fact that they had too much to lose if ever his crimes came to light.

The woman, Kristin – whether she was Hancock's mistress or not, no one had been clear – was close to being unhinged then, from what the rescued trio had said afterwards. Now, with the evidence of her own humiliation, it was obvious that Kristin had gone completely over the edge.

Both she and Hancock were criminally insane, of that much Hannah was convinced, but the knowledge was less than comforting. Rose, the heavy-set groom, was a born sadist – Hannah had seen enough of them in the ranks to know what she was looking at – but without the brains of her superiors. She would carry out their instructions quite cheerfully, whatever they might entail, but little of what she did would come from her own imagination. *Just carrying out orders*. There was a familiar ring to that, but it made Rose no less a dangerous adversary, especially as they all seemed determined to ensure that their prisoner was kept in such a permanent state of helplessness.

Backing against the wall, Hannah slowly let herself slide down into the straw, extending her legs carefully, screwing up her eyes and chewing fervently against the bit in an effort to ignore the pain this manoeuvre created. Finally, legs together and extended before her, she was able to lean back against the timber partition, close her eyes more normally, and try to think.

No position was ever truly hopeless, that's what her tactical instructors had drummed into them at the academy. Well, she thought grimly, they hadn't had this one in their text books, that much was for certain!

1.4

Still blindfolded, Alison nevertheless knew exactly where she was, for there was something about the aroma in Marcia's cellar dungeon that she would never forget. She heard the clanging of the cell door as it was closed behind her, and for a moment or two she thought she was alone. The unexpected cool touch of the hand against her upper arm made her jump back with a sharp yelp.

'Steady.' It was Melanie's voice. 'Take it easy. I thought you realised I was still here.'

'No,' Alison gasped. 'I thought you'd gone with him.'

'I've got to make sure you're properly fed and watered first.' Alison felt the maid's fingers fidgeting with the snaps that held the padded leather across her eyes, and a second later the blindfold fell away. The light level was as low as Alison remembered and her eyes quickly accustomed themselves, even after so long in total darkness.

'Who is he?' she whispered, looking about to make sure Douglas had really gone.

Melanie placed the blindfold on the rack behind her and turned back, a grim smile set on her tight lips. 'Douglas?' she said. 'He's an old friend of the mistress's. He runs his own establishment, somewhere in Cornwall, I think, but they have a sort of understanding. He's been here more and more frequently these past few months.' There was something about Melanie's tone that prompted Alison.

'You don't like him much, do you?' she said.

Melanie shrugged. 'I'm just the maid. My opinion isn't supposed to count, but seeing as how you ask, no, I don't like him. But then, the feeling's mutual. He *hates* me and anyone like me.'

Alison nodded, understanding. Even in her relatively short experience she had come to know a lot of things. Most of the people who were involved in the various networks of sado-masochistic clubs believed in a definite live-and-let-live approach, but there was a majority who suffered from certain prejudices, the most common being an aversion to males who preferred to dress and act like females.

The fact that someone like Melanie could appear so convincingly feminine and yet still possess the ability – and indeed the willingness and technique – to satisfy a woman was anathema to some men. Perhaps it was a form of insecurity, though someone like Ralph Hancock, who had once been about to have Melanie castrated, did not exactly come across as an insecure type.

'Does he make you do what he made me do?' Alison said.

Melanie nodded. 'All the time,' she confessed. 'He puts his cock in my mouth at every opportunity, though he won't actually screw me. It's as though my giving him a blow-job is okay, because that's what women are supposed to do in his book, whereas pulling my panties down and actually fucking me would be admitting he was gay.'

'*Is* he gay?'

'Probably, though I reckon he's spent his life suppressing it,' Melanie said. 'All I know is he goes to great lengths to make sure I don't get any fun with a woman now. He came up with this horrible bloody device that stops me – well, you know – and also makes me look and feel like a real woman inside my panties.

'It's made of some sort of rubber and there's a band that glues it into place, so I can't take it off, not without damaging it. He has a solvent that I'm allowed to use once a week, otherwise I even have to bathe in it. Look, I'll show you.'

She stepped back, raised her skirt and, holding it up with one hand, used the other to draw her panties down at the front, exposing a very realistic female outline, complete with short dark pubic triangle.

'That's incredible,' Alison cried. 'And he won't let you take it off? What does Marcia say about that?'

'I think she thinks I like the damned thing,' Melanie said, readjusting her clothing. 'I've tried to hint to her, but I don't like to complain. When I came here originally I agreed to serve her and anyone she selected, without question and without complaint. Besides, if *he* ever found out I'd said anything, he'd whip the skin off my back.'

'I can't believe Marcia would permit that,' Alison retorted. 'She has strict limits, I know.'

'Yes, but he's very clever. He talked her into letting him take me to his place for an entire week once. Like I say, I think it's in Cornwall, but I spent most of the journey in the back of that van of his, wearing a straitjacket and a full discipline hood with gag, so I didn't see anything.

'I then spent seven days of total misery. I cleaned the entire house from top to bottom, wearing a full corset that reached to my knees, the most awful posture collar, and I had to service every man who visited him while I was there.'

'But not the women?' Alison had good cause to remember Melanie's skilful tongue, and knew that any woman would have welcomed its attentions.

Melanie shook her head. 'No. The women, such as I saw there, simply watched, while he made really nasty comments about me.'

Alison narrowed her eyes. 'So why did Marcia send him to collect me?' she asked.

Melanie gave her a wan smile. 'Because she thought the unexpected would be better for you,' she said simply. 'You were supposed to drive down here tonight, but then you already knew what you were coming in to, whereas this way, well…'

'It was pretty… amazing,' Alison admitted. 'But that was before you told me all this. Now, well, I'm not so sure. I just hope your mistress doesn't decide to let him have a completely free hand for the weekend, that's all.'

It took two of them to get Hannah back onto her feet again. The corset, the high stiff boots and the semi-disabling chemicals that still ran through her body combined to make it all but impossible for her to regaining a standing posture unaided.

As the two youths hauled her upright, Rose stood by, a look of undisguised amusement on her face.

'Ponies sleep on their feet, unless they're ill,' she chortled. 'Thought you knew that. Don't worry, we've got a special harness for you at nights, so you won't fall over while you gets your rest.' She waved the young men aside and stepped forward, examining Hannah's nipple rings and peering at the piercings with a calculating eye.

'Looks good,' she muttered. 'Be healed up in no time. You, Peter,' she said, indicating the shorter male. 'Get some of the new cream from the end stall and rub it into her teats. These rings have got to be kept turned regular meantime.

'When you've done, hitch her up to the yellow sulky in the barn and walk her out into the yard. She's not to be worked fully just yet, but I want her muscles kept loose. A few circuits of the yard should do it, then leave her hitched by the gate. I'll trot her up the hill myself when I've finished a few other things I need to see to.'

She turned and stalked out of the stall, leaving Hannah standing between the two under-grooms. Warily, Hannah eyed them, trying to decide what they might be like, but what she saw was not encouraging.

Peter, who quickly followed in Rose's wake, presumably

41

to fetch the ointment as instructed, looked about nineteen or twenty, stockily built and of medium height, his eyes set alarmingly close together above a flattened nose, his fair hair cropped to within a quarter of an inch all over his skull.

The second groom was even younger, a little taller and much slighter in build, but his hair, too, was severely short and his wide eyes, blue and watery, looked somehow soulless. Like Peter, he was dressed in white leather breeches, tucked into matching calf length boots, his upper body naked except for a thin white collar about his neck and wide wristbands beset with blunt studs. While they waited for Peter's return, he moved around and stood squarely in front of Hannah, openly leering at her.

'Can see why they call you Tits,' he said. He put out one hand, the index finger extended, and gently touched her left breast, just below the ringed nipple. Hannah shivered at the contact, but continued to meet his gaze, defiantly. He gave her a peculiarly twisted smile, reached out and deftly removed her bit.

'Can you talk again yet?' he said. Hannah debated whether to reply was sensible, but concluded there was little point in attempting to hide something he would soon discover anyway.

'Yes,' she slurred. 'Just… just about.' Her tongue still felt thick and without any real feeling in it, her gums sore from the cruel dentistry and her lips, which also felt swollen, brushed against the ring that dangled from her nose. 'Why? I'm… not… not supposed to?' She looked meaningfully at the saliva covered bit he still held. He glanced down at it and laughed.

'No, not normally,' he agreed. 'The ponies here are kept bitted most of the time, but sometimes, when there's no one about…' He did not finish, but the look in his eyes spoke volumes.

'What's… what's your name?'

He cast a look over his shoulder, as if expecting to find that Peter had already returned, but the passageway beyond remained empty and silent. 'Carl,' he said, turning back to her. 'And you're Tits now, whatever you were called before you came here.' His tone was flat, the words spoken almost without emphasis.

Hannah nodded, realising it was prudent to humour him. 'Yes,' she said huskily. 'I'm Tits. You… like Tits?'

Carl cast another guilty glance in the direction of the doorway and then nodded. 'Very pretty,' he said, nodding. He touched her again, this time on the nipple itself, and Hannah steeled herself not to show the revulsion she felt. Somehow, she sensed that this gangling youth might be her only hope of salvation and, whilst that hope was barely even a slim one, any hope was better than nothing at all. 'Big, too,' Carl added at length.

The sudden clatter of boots on hard stone cut short any further conversation and Peter strode in through the doorway, holding up a green jar in one hand. Seeing Hannah unbitted, he stopped and gave his partner an accusatory look.

'You know the rules, idiot,' he snapped. 'You want to put your stupid cock in her mouth, just you wait until they've all finished for the evening, otherwise Mistress Rose will have us both strung up on one of the paddock frames overnight. You ain't never had that yet, have you? And you don't want to, either, 'specially as the blonde bitch has a habit of whipping anyone she finds on the frames.'

'I only took the bit out to clean it,' Carl retorted defensively. 'Rose said we was to make sure her mouth stayed fresh while it's all healing. I thought I'd give her a salt mouth rinse as well.'

Peter looked somewhat mollified. 'Okay,' he agreed, 'seems like you're thinking for a change. Go get some water from the tap, not the trough. You'll find a salt packet and a metal cup on a shelf above the sink. And remember,' he added as Carl began to move towards the exit, 'I'm the senior here, so if the filly's going to pleasure anyone, it'll be me first, okay?'

'You remember your slave name, don't you, Mitzi?' Marcia Davenport was dressed immaculately in a white leather catsuit that covered, yet emphasised, every curve of her magnificent figure, and the top half of her face and head were hidden by a mask that left only her glittering eyes exposed. But there was no mistaking her voice.

'Yes, mistress,' Alison replied. 'Whilst here, I'm Mitzi, your slave.'

'Quite,' Marcia said. There was not the slightest trace of the usual friendliness that existed between them, and once again she was the uncompromising dominatrix who had first introduced Alison to this secret world of plain, pleasure and restraint. 'Well, I've decided that you will remain here for a fortnight.'

Alison's mouth dropped in surprise, for the arrangement had been for two days only. 'But, but I can't,' she protested.

'And why not?' Marcia demanded. 'I've already told his lordship of my decision and he has no objections.'

No, Alison thought, none he would voice, especially to Marcia, who both scared and excited him. 'But I have things to do,' she said.

Marcia shook her head. 'Like what?' she demanded. 'You told me yourself you're bored and can't settle down to anything at the moment. There's nothing needs doing that can't wait, and you'll probably do it better for your little respite here.'

'But what about Douglas?'

'What about him?' Marcia snapped. 'And it's *Master* Douglas to you, slave Mitzi.'

'I – I'm not sure,' Alison stammered. 'It's just that I didn't expect… and the way he treats poor Mel is awful.

Have you seen what he makes her wear – under *there*?'

'Oh, you mean her little cunt?' Marcia laughed. 'Well, she likes to play the slut, so it's better if she has everything a woman should have. She didn't complain at the breast implants.'

'But that's different,' Alison persisted. 'She has needs, you know, same as everyone else.'

'Ah, I see,' Marcia purred. 'Melanie with a cunt isn't much good to a frustrated little slave slut, is she?' She stepped forward and took hold of Alison's shoulders, her grip firm but not cruel. 'Master Douglas has his own methods,' she said gently. 'Some differ from mine, but they are nonetheless effective. For a start, I approve of the pretty begging position he has forced you to adopt. He tells me that you had removed the nipple rings, by the way.'

'I would have replaced them before coming here,' Alison said. 'I'd just removed them while I bathed and forgot to put them straight back in.'

'Which was very naughty of you, Mitzi,' Marcia rebuked her. 'But don't worry, I'll make sure you're suitably punished.' She released her grip and stepped back. 'I'll even speak to Master Douglas about Melanie. It would be a shame to waste her talents, and I know you two girls are quite fond of one another. We all three went through something of a trial together.' She stepped back again and stood in the doorway of the small cell.

'You do make such a perfect picture as a slave,' she said, and there was genuine admiration in her voice. 'You'll be glad I've extended your visit, I promise.'

1.5

The more Hannah walked, the easier it became, at least in so far as she could now automatically place one foot in front of the other without a huge mental effort. However, the extravagantly arched position in which the hoof boots held her feet and the demonic grip of the girth corset meant that there was only one way anyone could possibly walk in them, with or without the influence of the drug she had been given.

The best comparison Hannah could make was with the whores she had seen on the streets of Soho, in London, for even the high fashion models on the catwalks of the world's capitals did not move with such overtly exaggerated sexuality. Even taking short steps, conscious of the rings dragging between her thighs, Hannah knew that her hips and buttocks were swivelling outrageously and she could imagine the effect the sight was having on the two young grooms, though the heavy blinkers they had clipped to either side of the bridle that encircled her head made it all but impossible to see what they were doing unless they were immediately in front of her.

She swallowed, trying desperately not to consider the prospect of finally being left in their complete charge once Rose, Kristin and anyone else in authority had left the stables area for the night. Neither Karl, nor Peter, had bothered to disguise their intentions and Hannah shuddered inwardly at the mental pictures that kept forcing themselves into her consciousness.

The yellow sulky was a small lightweight cart, similar to the sort of vehicle Hannah had seen used in pony trotting competitions, except that this particular sulky had been modified and scaled to be drawn by a two-legged beast, and every effort had been employed to save weight.

The large wheels were made of some sort of metal alloy, rimmed with what appeared to be pneumatic tyres, larger versions of something that might normally be standard on a bicycle. The framework was made entirely of tubular metal, a latticework of struts providing strength without bulk, and even the narrow driver's seat was evidently formed out of some kind of plastic.

The shafts themselves were the only things made from wood; highly polished teak, Hannah guessed; slim yet strong, with a curious metal collar set halfway along each, secured by means of a butterfly screw. As the grooms positioned her between the shafts, lifting them to snap on metal links to either side of her girth, the purpose of these additions became clear.

Designed to run on only the single axle, and with the seat slightly to the rear of the fulcrum this axle provided, the two metal collars were counterweights, so that a particularly heavy driver or a particularly light pony girl would not result in the sulky trying to tip backwards. The shafts themselves provided some ballast, and the two metal weights could be slid backwards and forwards along them, affecting a perfect balance, or at least a sufficient balance for the pony concerned to cope with.

Hannah was quickly attached to the cart, the shafts inserted between her waist and her pinioned arms, the snap links ensuring that the main strain was taken at her waist. But now came the reins, with which she would be driven and guided. Both ended in smaller snap links which were clipped to her nose ring, having first been threaded through her nipple rings, from where they ran back and were left draped over the thin rail that rose in front of the seat.

'Now then,' Peter said, coming back around to stand in front of Hannah, 'I don't think this needs much explaining. A pull to the right means you start turning right and a pull to the left means you go left. When I shakes the reins you walk on, or move faster if you're already walking, especially if I uses the whip on your backside. And when I pulls back, you stops.' He fingered her right nipple carelessly.

'If you don't respond proper, then these teats are gonna get very sore and so will your nose. Don't worry, though. For today all we're gonna do is get you used to the commands and walk you about slow like, otherwise we'll end up tearing all your pretty new piercings and they'll take longer to heal and look very unsightly and none of us wants that, do we?'

He turned, walked back along the line of the shafts, and Hannah felt the weight shift as he climbed up onto the sulky and sat down. A moment later she felt the slight tension as he took up the slack in the reins, and automatically tried to lower her head to relieve the pull on the nose ring. However, the high collar prevented much movement and she found herself forced to stand with her nose proudly in the air, blinking back tears of pain and frustration.

'Walk on, Tits.' She felt the leather traces shake, and despite an initial longing to assert herself by not moving, she found she was already responding, one heavy shod foot moving in front of the other. Behind her the sulky creaked and she had to lean forward to take the weight, wondering if she would be strong enough to move it, but after the first second or so fighting against inertia, she felt it begin to yield to her straining and suddenly they were moving.

'Good girl, steady now,' she heard Peter's voice again. Where Carl was she could neither see nor did she care. Ahead of her lay about fifty metres or so of stony yard and then a section of the high wall, the open side of the yard to her left. She felt the rein on that side tighten, the drag against her left breast and the pull against her nose in the same direction and, like the obedient creature she knew they intended her to become, Hannah began to turn, steel shod hooves ringing against the hard surface beneath them.

'You're filming everything, I presume?' Ralph Hancock, a looming giant of a man, towered over even the tall Kristin, despite the height of her heels. She looked up at him, her thin lips stretched into a cruel smile.

'*Every*thing,' she assured him, her voice dripping with malice. 'I've even had a look at the earlier stuff,' she continued. 'I must say, these video camera contraptions are excellent. No developing, no printing, just instant play back.'

'And better clarity, too,' Hancock added. 'Mind you, for the price of the equipment, it ought to be.'

'And you're going to send one of the player machines to the bitch's friends?'

'If we want them to see what's happening to her, we have no alternative.'

'So we have to make sure we get the machine back again afterwards,' Kristin said.

Hancock gave a loud snort. 'If we can. But that's hardly a priority. A few thousand pounds is nothing compared to the prices I can get for these bitches from our Arab friends. And meanwhile, we get the satisfaction of paying them back for all the aggravation they caused last year.' He paused, looking out towards the distant hills, his mouth set in a grimace.

'I'd like to take a look at these video films myself,' he said at last. 'Not right now, but tonight. Bring them up to my room just before midnight and we can watch them together, in comfort.'

'How about watching Rose and her lads training the slut – in person, I mean?' Kristin suggested.

Hancock shook his head without turning back to face

her. 'No,' he said, 'not just yet. I'll see her when she's better schooled, say in a few days from now. I want her to know she's already been subjugated fully and then have the satisfaction of seeing her eager to please my every little whim. Then, when she thinks she's succeeded, I'll have her strung up in the small paddock and give her a whipping she'll remember till her dying day!'

'I'm told you have the makings of a first rate slave,' Douglas said. Alison made no attempt to reply, for the gag that Melanie had strapped into her mouth an hour or more earlier made coherent speech impossible. Douglas stepped further into the cell, pulling on a pair of heavy gauntlets.

'However, I understand you've also been trying to interfere with the way I treat that queer little bitch maid,' he said, glaring straight at her, his eyes hard. Alison tried to swallow and shook her head, but Douglas was not mollified. He stepped forward, grabbed her wrists and yanked them, pulling her breasts out into two elongated cones as her nipples were forced to follow. Alison let out a muffled squeal and tried to pull her hands back, but he was much too strong for her.

'You see, slut,' he hissed, 'this may be some sort of game to you, but I play by different rules. It was my idea, by the way, to have your stay extended, and I might even suggest moving you down to my own place for part of that time. I know Mistress Marcia has some other commitments during next week, so I doubt she'll have any objections.'

Alison's eyes grew round with horror at this prospect, yet there was another sensation fighting to the surface, one of pure excitement at the thought of being completely at this man's mercy for a while. She suspected there might not really be that much difference between him and Hancock, except that in the latter's case there had been

50

nothing to temper his vicious ingenuity and he felt free to give rein to his every sadistic whim.

'In the meantime, however, while in her house we play by her rules, or at least a version of them, so I've arranged a nice little game we can play with poor, dear, frustrated Melanie. She's waiting for us in the main dungeon room next door and, as you'll see in a moment or two, she now has her cock nice and free.

'Shall we take us a little walk and I'll show you what I've arranged for the three of us? Apparently you two are good friends, but it's funny how something like loyalty can be strained by the most simple of tests, and I'm interested to see how yours stands up.'

Hannah felt as if she had been walking around the courtyard for hours, but the sun hardly seemed to have dipped towards the western horizon, and she guessed it was probably less than thirty minutes by the time Peter finally reined her to a halt. She felt the shafts dip as he moved to alight and then rise again as he dropped easily to the ground.

'Not bad – for a novice,' he said, moving around into her field of vision. 'Still a bit unsteady on your hooves, but then that's normal. Bet your legs hurt by now, don't they?' Hannah almost nodded automatically and, if the drug had not been still slowing her reactions, would have done so, but she managed to check herself just in time, determined not to betray any sign that she was suffering.

'Course,' he went on, 'I 'spect you're still telling yourself this ain't gonna last, ain't you?' He looked at her, grinning. 'I 'spect you think that eventually you'll get out of this, but you won't. You're in harness and in those boots for good now, girlie, so you can forget everything except learning how to be a good pony.

'There's a couple of fillies here that my uncle's been grooming for three years now,' he said, with malicious glee. 'Bet they thought it was only for a few weeks when they first came here, but they're still in the stables, just along from your stall. And it's so long since either of them was in a position to speak even a single word, I reckon they've probably lost the ability to talk properly, even if they wasn't bitted.' He looked up, peering beyond Hannah.

'Ah, now here's Miss Rose, come to take you for a proper little drive, so you just get your back straight and show her what I've taught you. Then tonight, if you've been a good little filly, I'll have a little something for you, after all the others has gone, like.'

Melanie had been methodically prepared, strung up to an overhead beam, arms wide and secured in thick leather cuffs, the chains shortened so that her feet barely touched the stone floor. Her uniform had been stripped from her, leaving her clad in her usual tight corset, stockings, long gloves and a full discipline helmet that covered her head completely, leaving just two small holes behind which her eyes were just about visible, and two even smaller holes set beneath her nostrils.

Her breasts – her pride and joy ever since Marcia had paid for them – now hung like two distended melons, thanks to the two heavy weights that had been attached to her nipple rings. And her penis stood rigidly to attention, kept that way, presumably, by the tight harness that was buckled, not just about its base, but about her hairless scrotum.

'Not exactly at her prettiest, is she?' Douglas sneered, pushing Alison into the centre of the room. 'On the other hand, I understand that some sluts quite like this look, is that so?'

Alison turned to look at Douglas and decided it was better to be truthful, at least for the moment. She nodded slowly, and he narrowed his eyes.

'I'll bet you've had some of that cock, too, eh?' he said.

Again Alison nodded. Douglas laughed.

'Well, I'm not having one bitch fuck another, so you can forget that,' he rasped. 'On the other hand, we've already seen what a good little cock-sucker you are, so now you get the chance to prove that wasn't just beginner's luck.' He stepped across to one side of the room and took down a coiled whip from the heavily laden rack.

'The way it works is this,' he said, letting the coils fall to the floor and shaking the snake-like thong out across the stone slabs. 'I give dear Melanie here one lash every thirty seconds until you make her come. Of course, as she hasn't had much in the way of relief for some days now, that shouldn't take long in the ordinary event.

'On the other hand, you, Mitzi, will receive one lash for every thirty seconds under ten minutes it takes her to come and another one every time I think you're not trying your best.' He grinned and flicked his wrist and the whip sprung into life, cracking like a pistol shot about a foot from Melanie's burgeoning shaft. The maid jumped in her bonds and cringed.

'It's all rather neat, isn't it?' Douglas said. 'If she lasts out the ten minutes, then your arse is spared, assuming I think you're not deliberately shirking, but then Melanie gets twenty with this.' He cracked the whip again, the sound echoing around the cellar.

'It'll be interesting to see who ends up with what,' Douglas said, 'apart from the fact that we know you're going to end up with a mouthful of the bitch's come anyway.' He tucked the whip handle into his belt and reached up to unfasten Alison's gag strap. The pear shaped rubber plug slid out, glistening from her spittle, and Douglas threw it carelessly into the farthest corner.

'Now,' he said, pushing Alison towards the spread-eagled maid, 'let's get started, shall we? Oh yes,' he added, stooping slightly and reaching for the cord that still hung between Alison's thighs, 'I think it's about time we switched this baby on.'

He tugged it, the vibrator hummed into life, and within seconds Alison knew that whatever tenuous grip on reality ever remained in this subterranean complex, it would soon slip from her grasp completely.

The powerful Rose was considerably heavier than Peter, and although she adjusted the counterweights on the shafts, this did nothing to make the task of pulling her and the sulky any easier, even on the level ground. She also seemed far keener on employing the whip, flicking the stinging leather across Hannah's shoulders, back and buttocks at regular intervals.

She guided Hannah around the yard twice and then once more in a figure eight circuit, steering her charge by judicious use of the traces, and then turned her towards the high gate that was set in the centre of the longer plain wall. Carl was already standing there, and as he saw Rose's intentions he quickly lifted the bar and pushed the two heavy timber sections outwards.

'On, Tits!' Rose urged, cracking the whip above Hannah's head. Flinching, Hannah bent her back with even more urgency, trying to ignore the burning pains in her feet and the agonising strictures imposed by the corset girth. Fleetingly, she considered stopping, refusing to go on, telling herself there was nothing they could do to her that had not already been done, but a small voice in the back of her head warned that this was not so and that any show of rebellion would bring the sort of retribution she did not want to even imagine.

Outside the walls a narrow track continued across a fairly level pasture, running between two sets of wooden fences that appeared to be defining two different paddocks. To the left, in the smaller, were set several wooden frames, mostly simple structures comprising two stout uprights and a crosspiece set a couple of feet or so above head height. From two of the nearer frames Hannah could see leather manacles dangling, making their purpose unmistakable.

Among these frames were set a number of plain posts, and at the far end of the paddock, just before the line of trees that indicated the beginning of a woodland, Hannah caught fleeting glimpses of what appeared to be wooden pillories. But she could not study them properly, for the blinkers prevented any peripheral vision and turning her head imposed an immediate strain on the opposite rein attached to her nose ring.

The field on the right was much larger, and among other purposes was clearly intended for some sort of schooling. There were several low fences; none more than two feet high, but which would nevertheless present quite a challenge to a 'pony' wearing the sort of boots Hannah was currently enduring. There were also three or four ramps, the up and down slopes varying in length and gradient, and several sets of short red and white striped posts, set into the grass, presumably for use as a zigzag obstacle course.

However, of the other pony girls there was no sign and, as Hannah forged awkwardly ahead, trying to ignore the sharp stabbing pains between her legs, the way remained deserted and they eventually came to where the track ran into another area of woodland without encountering another human soul. Overhead, birds chirruped and sang in the branches, the sunlight filtered prettily through the foliage and the air was heavy with the aroma of nature at her most peaceful.

Beneath this idyllic canopy, bitted and bridled, the human pony trudged miserably onwards, the occasional tug on nose or nipple and the regular crack of her driver's whip serving only to emphasise her misery and the depths of humiliation to which she had been brought, yet knowing, as she hauled her burden, that it was unlikely that she had even begun to understand the cruelty of which these people were capable.

Melanie was tough, as she'd had occasion to demonstrate in the past, but even she could endure only so much – both of pain and of pleasure, and she finally lost control well before the time limit set by Douglas.

Hanging helplessly from the beam her body bucked and writhed, her thick shaft jerked between Alison's lips and the pent up frustrations of many days exploded in a salty torrent, accompanied by a wail of anguish and release from behind her gag. Alison gagged herself, but refused to draw back, or even to let a single drop of the maid's juices spill out, aware, even through the haze of her own lust, that Douglas would use that as an excuse to inflict even more torment and torture on the pair of them.

Deep inside her the buzzing invader wrought its own insidious, delicious havoc and wave after wave crashed over her as she fought to retain control of her outward actions. Melanie had climaxed just the once and had fought against the inevitable staunchly, but then Melanie was, after all, innately male. Alison's reflexes, however, were governed by an entirely different set of genes, and one orgasm had run into the next long since, and she was only vaguely aware when Douglas's strong hands seized her shoulders and hauled her away from her now limp partner.

'Enough!' he snapped. 'Open your mouth.' Numbly, her body still quivering in the diminishing throes of her final surrender, Alison obeyed, closing her eyes so she didn't have to look at the triumph in his expression as she showed him the evidence she knew he demanded.

'Swallow,' he ordered. Again she obeyed, choking as the contents of her mouth slid easily down her throat. Behind her, Douglas was calculating.

'I make that four lashes you're due,' he said, 'and twenty for Melanie, as promised.' Alison opened her eyes and peered up at the maid, who was gradually regaining some sort of control as she hung in her bonds. The thick phallus was already subsiding, its head glistening from a combination of Alison's saliva and the last of its spending.

'On the other hand,' Douglas said, 'I could commute the bitch's punishment, depending upon you, Mitzi.'

Alison craned her neck sideways, trying to see his face, but all she could see was one shoulder and arm. 'What am I supposed to do, master?' There was no point in antagonising the brute, and Alison knew well enough the form of address he expected. She heard him laugh, and then his boots scraped on the rough stone as he moved around to stand beside her.

'I'm not sure as yet,' he leered, 'but I'm sure I can think of something suitable. Meantime, I'm going to let this aberration of nature take you back to your cell and put you in a position of serious contemplation. I'm sure she knows what will happen if I'm not satisfied with her efforts.'

1.6

'I've just finished viewing the early tapes.' Ralph Hancock leaned back in his high swivel chair, interlacing his fingers in front of his chin. Across the desk, the sharp-featured Kristin looked as impassive as she ever did in his presence, and waited for him to continue.

'The picture quality really is excellent,' he said. 'Much better than conventional film. It's a great shame that the playback machines aren't available over here at the moment – they'd open up an entirely new market for our production side.'

'Perhaps you should consider investing in that particular market,' Kristin suggested. 'One of our American visitors was full of how every home would have one of these machines within a few years, though how they think the average British family could afford such prices is beyond me.'

'Mass production, my dear Kristin,' Hancock chuckled. 'However, I think I'll keep my money where it is at the moment. What your American informant failed to tell you was that there are currently at least three totally different systems in use for video recordings, each incompatible with the other two. To invest in one of the losers now would be a stupid move and one I do not need to take.' He unlocked his fingers and reached down to open the top drawer at his right. 'No, I think we'll let these people battle it out amongst themselves and then think about it again, once we get some solid clue as to who will be the winner.'

'Are you sure there will be just the one winner?' Kristin, unbidden, lowered herself into the vacant chair opposite Hancock's. The big man regarded her for several seconds, his features wooden.

'There are always losers,' he said slowly. 'You have only to look at the evidence on this tape you gave me.' He pulled the black plastic object from the open drawer and laid it carefully on the desk between them. 'This film is all about a loser and she will be just the first of many.' He tapped the plastic sharply with one forefinger.

'Yes, Kristin,' he said, sitting back again, 'there are always losers and always winners – usually just the one real winner,' he added. 'This bitch and her bastard

58

paymasters thought they could beat me, didn't they? Therefore, they have to be taught a lesson; the one real winner is – and always will be – me.'

Kristin nodded in agreement. 'Of course,' she said. 'The Jewish bitch is already finding that out.'

Hancock sighed and slowly rose to his feet. 'And she must never, ever forget,' he hissed. He slapped his hand down on the video tape again, the sharp report of the impact echoing around the spacious study. 'Neither must any of her so-called friends,' he snapped. He looked down at his hand where it lay on the cassette, as if he had only just realised it was there. Brusquely, he pushed it across the polished leather surface and Kristin was forced to make a grab at it as it slid towards her.

'Make a copy of this final edit,' Hancock instructed her. 'Then send it to the address I gave you yesterday, together with something for the whore to play it on. Have one of Madison's boys deliver it personally. We don't want her to be able to trace anything back to us before we're ready for her, do we?'

'I won't allow any further whippings,' Marcia said, 'not unless they're carried out under my direct supervision.'

Douglas glared, but although he towered over her and was physically far more powerful, Marcia refused to be intimidated. She had known him for too long not to understand what made him tick, and whilst he was quite capable of instilling fear and trepidation among natural submissives, Douglas Miller had a problem when it came to dealing with dominant women.

And today, Marcia knew, she was looking at her dominant best, her latest outfit both stunning and severe, contrasting femininity with a gothic stridency that could reduce any male – and even the odd female – to the status of quivering acolyte.

As was her preference, the ensemble was predominantly

black; glossy, opaque leggings under a short flared skirt, calf length boots laced tightly to enhance the curve of her lower legs, the spiked heels making those legs look longer still than they were. The lacy, long sleeved bodice with its plunging neckline, revealed as much as it covered, displaying just sufficient cleavage, her splendid breasts lifted and emphasised by the tightly laced leather corset she wore over skirt and top, like a broad belt.

Her hands were encased in net and lace gloves, her long scarlet fingernails clearly visible through the dark mesh. Over everything she wore a loose gauzy jacket, trimmed with antique brocade, that floated about her like a giant wing, its flimsiness contrasting with the severity of the studded leather collar that sat about her throat.

Her face was pale, deliberately to set off the darker colours she had chosen for her eyes and lips, so that her overall appearance was somewhat vampiresque; alluring yet threatening, with a hint of menace that complemented her overall bearing.

'I examined Melanie's back last evening,' she said. Douglas continued to scowl, but Marcia had only just started. 'You used that whip on her like a bludgeon, you idiot. Those marks will take weeks to fade. I thought you had more finesse than that.'

'I think we may all have got just a little carried away,' Douglas suggested.

Marcia remained unimpressed. 'You mean *you* allowed yourself to become over zealous,' she snapped. 'I haven't said anything before, Douglas, because you seemed able to control your apparent dislike of Melanie, but I cannot and will not allow this to continue.'

'That – that creature,' Douglas snarled, 'is an insult.'

'An insult? To whom?'

'To just about anybody,' Douglas said. 'The way "she" prances around the place is disgusting. It isn't right.'

'Because of what she has in her knickers, you mean?'

Marcia laughed. 'You wouldn't be the first man to be jealous of what our little Mel can offer a woman.'

'Jealous?' The word was almost spat out. 'You think I'd be jealous of that – that *thing*? At least I'm a real man – and proud of it.'

'I see.' Marcia half turned away, trying to hide the smile that had leapt, unbidden, to her face. 'Well, each to his own, as they say. Mind you, Douglas, a week in skirts might open your eyes to a few things.'

'Bollocks!' Douglas turned away himself, moving to the window and peering out through the net curtains at the busy street beyond. 'The day you catch me primping around like that nancy you can cut my balls off and pickle 'em.'

Marcia laughed, shaking her head. 'You should be careful what you say, Dougie,' she warned. 'In my experience, the more someone protests the guiltier they often are.'

Douglas whirled around, his face scarlet with anger. 'And what do you mean by that?' he demanded, his voice trembling.

Marcia shrugged. 'Nothing,' she said, 'not if there's nothing *to* mean. But just you heed what I'm saying, you idiot. Lay off Mel and go careful what you do with Mitzi. She's no different from any of my other slaves. You can go so far – quite a long way, as it happens – but there are limits and I won't have them exceeded.

'Enjoy yourself by all means, but whatever you do at your own place, here we try to ensure that everyone gets something out of their stay.'

Douglas spun on his heel and stalked out of the room without further comment. As the door swung shut behind him Marcia remained standing where she was for several seconds, her eyes slowly narrowing beneath the black false lashes. At last she let out a long breath and moved across to where the small gilt and ivory box stood on the end of the heavy Georgian mantelpiece.

Carefully she lifted the lid and took out one of the hand-rolled cigarettes from within, placing it delicately between her lips and reaching for the ornamental onyx lighter that acted as a paperweight for the three or four envelopes containing as yet unpaid household bills.

The time was fast approaching, she thought, when she would be forced to sever her personal connections with Douglas. Of late he had changed from the man she'd first met in West Germany, a few years after the war ended. There was a difference between control and spite, and he seemed to be rapidly losing the ability to tell them apart.

Of course, there were a minority who might enjoy the sort of discipline he seemed more and more to relish giving out, including the two women who served as his permanent slaves at his house in Cornwall. But that was a matter between them and him and none of her business, whereas Melanie, Alison, Honey and the rest of her little 'menagerie', as Marcia privately referred to them, were something else again.

Douglas wouldn't like it any more than he had liked being told to curb his excesses, but he would just have to accept things as they were, as she wanted them to be. She still held forty percent of his shares in the recording company, security against the additional capital she had loaned him the previous year and, added to the twenty-eight per cent stake she had taken herself, that gave her overall control, if she decided she needed to exercise it.

And not just control over the company itself, for Marcia had little interest in the pop music scene other than the profit her investment might yield. No, control over Douglas was what she had, a control he was clearly beginning to lose himself, if indeed he had ever truly had it in the first place.

Hannah had not realised they'd been filming her ordeals, not until Kristin herself had finally come to the stables to gloat over her helplessness and taken obvious delight in telling her. Not, she reflected as she hung in the sleeping harness, her hoof boots barely touching the straw covered floor, that it would have made the slightest difference if she had known.

Bordering on the insane as they had to be, these people were nonetheless experts in their chosen field, and in the two days since she'd arrived even Hannah had not spotted a flaw in their security. Not only were they apparently miles from anywhere, from what she had seen Hancock's new lair was on a long peninsular, surrounded on three sides by water. And when Rose had trotted her along the cliff path, she had seen that whilst the drop to the shore was not that far, it was sheer and the waves below boiled around treacherous rocky outcrops.

As to exactly where the peninsular was, Hannah could only guess, but her best estimate, based on the position of the sun and the vague purple smudge she had seen on the horizon, far across the water, was that it was somewhere in North Devon. Though she realised it could have equally been a number of other places, and not necessarily even in Britain itself.

Not that the location made a great deal of difference, nor even the inaccessibility of the shoreline, for so far Hannah had never been left alone in a situation where she had any use of her hands or arms, nor did her captors show any indication that she ever would be. If they continued to keep her in the same secure bondage, escape was looking a less and less likely option and she had nothing to look forward to except more of the same degradation she had been forced to suffer during that first afternoon.

Rose had seemed content to allow Hannah to keep going at the same walking pace, even accepting the necessity for slowing when the track began to climb upwards slightly. The whip still cracked at regular intervals, but mostly above her head and just, it seemed, for effect and to emphasise who was the one in control and who was the one being controlled.

After a while Hannah found herself becoming detached from the reality. The soreness in her feet grew less as they became more numb, the stinging from the pulling rings seemed to abate and even the tight girth felt as if it had loosened, though she realised it was more likely that she was becoming used to it and her body automatically adjusting to the new breathing technique it demanded and enforced.

She plodded on steadily, reacting to the guidance of her reins almost before it was given, one part of her mind focusing on the meandering trail ahead, while the remainder continued, unsuccessfully, wrestling with the possibilities of escape. She had just come to the inevitable conclusion that it would take a careless mistake before such a possibility became even remote, when the track began to widen and suddenly opened out into another grassy area, a wide clearing deep in the woods, but still surrounded on all sides by tall trees.

To one side, set back under overhanging branches, was a building not unlike the stable block, although the brickwork and roof looked to be of more modern origin. In front of this structure stood two carts, one identical to the sulky to which Hannah was hitched, the other larger, longer and with just a single central shaft extending from its front.

Away to the side of these stood a hitching rail, a simple timber structure that reminded Hannah of every cowboy film she had ever seen, although the two creatures tethered to it bore absolutely no resemblance to anything that had ever come out of Hollywood.

At first glance Hannah thought she was looking at some

sort of mutant pairing, for although they seemed vaguely human from the neck down, ignoring their high hoof boots, from the neck up they appeared to be completely equine. It was only when Hannah drew closer to them that she realised the truth – the realistic looking horse heads were manmade, constructed from either rubber or leather, encasing the victims' heads entirely and dehumanising them in an eerie and frightening manner.

The two humanoid ponies were also male, very definitely so, despite the fact that their male-hoods were encased in glistening rubber sheaths, for they were both fully erect, the latex stretched to something approaching its apparent limit, the black phalluses standing to sinister attention and bobbing slightly as the two creatures tried to turn to view the newcomers.

Their outfits were not dissimilar to Hannah's, their waists constricted viciously by tight girth corsets, the heels on their hoof boots just as extreme, and their arms held rigidly in leather sheaths that were attached to their sides. Their bridles differed slightly to accommodate their artificially elongated features, but their nipples, too, were ringed, and the reins that ran down from either side of their bits ran through these steel circlets.

As Rose reined Hannah to an abrupt halt, a female figure appeared from inside the building. She looked to be about the same age as the two male grooms, Peter and Carl, but her face and eyes betrayed a far superior intellect, and the manner in which she was attired suggested that she held a position far above that of the two young males.

Like the senior groom herself, she wore high boots, though of red leather rather than black, and a matching corseted bodice with front lacing that, like her footwear, contrasted with the black stretch bodysuit that made up the remainder of her attire. She had sleek black hair, cut to her shoulders, with a severe fringe that touched the tops of her immaculately groomed and arched eyebrows, prominent cheekbones, and full wide lips that had been coated with a high gloss that reflected the leatherwear.

Her eyes, which were emphasised with the sort of meticulously defined precision that had been the mark of female pop singers since the beginning of the decade, yet overly so, as if she feared the effect might fade in bright light, were a vivid green and lit up as she saw Hannah standing between the shafts of Rose's sulky.

'So this is the commando girl I've heard so much about, is it?' she said, swaying arrogantly towards Hannah on heels that were high and sharp enough to be classified as offensive weapons, and which ensured that she towered over the helpless pony girl by several inches. Hannah stared defiantly up at her, trying not to blink, and the two locked eyes for several seconds.

'Well,' the girl said eventually, realising the futility of trying to outstare Hannah, 'I must say, she doesn't look too dangerous to me. I can see why you've decided to call her Tits, though. They're never natural, are they?' She peered down at her own, not insignificant bosom.

Rose laughed. 'No, Phoebe,' she said, dismounting, 'they're a special present to her from Master Rafe and Mistress Kristin. All she had originally were hardly suitable for a pony girl.'

Phoebe reached out and stroked Hannah's right nipple and, to Hannah's horror, she saw the flesh there immediately begin to swell and stiffen.

'You have to watch this one,' Rose warned, seeing the reaction. 'She prefers girls to men. In fact, she prefers them *instead* of men. I thought I'd leave her with you for a while, so you could teach her the error of her ways.'

'Well,' Phoebe said, turning and looking pointedly at the two male ponies, 'neither of these two has been allowed any sort of relief for three days, at least as far as I'm aware. I could start her with them, if you like?'

Rose nodded. 'That would be most suitable,' she agreed.

'I've had orders from Mistress Kristin – says she wants her put to the biggest studs we can find and as often as we can manage it. Where's Hercules today?' She looked around, her gaze travelling swiftly across the clearing.

'He's booked out,' Phoebe said, regretfully. 'The Dutch woman wanted his services for that silly little Spanish girlfriend of hers. Apparently she caught the stupid bitch with one of the house-boys in her bed, so decided she needed teaching a lesson.'

'She'll learn her lesson with Hercules,' Rose reflected. She turned to Hannah, grinning maliciously. 'Hercules is our prime stallion, thirty-two years old, six feet seven tall and with everything else well in proportion.

'Not my own cup of tea,' she added, 'but then I never fancied not being able to walk properly after a good screwing, which is what happens to any filly Hercules is put to. Shame he's not available straight away, but not to worry, there's plenty of time.'

'It'd probably be better to get her started on something a little less extreme, anyway,' Phoebe said. 'If she hasn't had a man before, or even if she has and hasn't had one for a while, Herc would probably rip her open, unless that's what Mistress Kristin wants?'

Rose shook her head. 'No, nothing like that, though she does want her to end up so anything normal would feel lost in there. By that time, so I'm told, they're intending to boost her tit size, too.'

Phoebe's black eyebrows arched even further. 'Poor bitch,' she muttered. 'She'll end up like some kind of freak show.'

'Exactly,' Rose snapped, her face darkening. 'You weren't with us at Dennison Hall, Phoebe, so you didn't see for yourself what happened. This slut and her lesbian bitch friends wrecked everything they could lay their hands on. Months – years – of hard work was ruined and the place is useless as a hideaway now. We even lost five top clients who were there at the time.

'No, there's no need to feel sorry for this one. Everything that's going to happen to her she's brought on herself. Master Rafe is determined that she'll suffer for her interference, so if you need to thrash her, don't worry, just do it. The more stripes on that arse, the better it'll look for all of us!'

Phoebe smiled, but there was no humour in the expression, which failed to reach her cat-like eyes. 'My pleasure,' she purred. 'Leave her to me.'

1.7

Mike Hallet's penchant for blondes was matched only by his memory for faces, and Ruth Goldman's face was not one that could be easily forgotten, even after a year. He opened the door to the front sitting room and stood back for her to enter first, the canvas grip bag she carried knocking against the doorframe.

'As I said, Miss Goldman – sorry, *Captain* Goldman, I should say,' he smiled, 'this is an unexpected pleasure.'

Ruth lowered her burden carefully and turned to face him, her expression pale and concerned. 'I thought about phoning first,' she said, apologetically, 'but then they may have your line tapped.'

'They?' Mike echoed. 'Who are "they"?'

Hannah let out a deep breath, a sigh almost, and glanced towards the window as if expecting to see something or someone there. '"They", Mr Hallet, are a certain Ralph Hancock and his associates. You remember Hancock, I presume?'

Mike nodded. 'How could I forget? But Rafe Hancock went to ground after you and your team raided his place. No one's seen or heard a whisper from him since.'

'The fact that a dog doesn't bark does not mean it isn't on the prowl, Mr Hallet,' Ruth said, sourly. 'You didn't suppose that our little expedition meant the end of someone like Hancock, surely?'

'Well, no, of course not,' Mike said. 'But we inflicted enough damage on his operation to keep him busy and out of circulation for quite some time.'

'Time is relative,' Ruth retorted, 'and I seem to remember Miss Davenport telling you that Hancock would be back in business before you knew it.'

Mike scratched his jaw and moved across to the sofa, lowering himself into its deep upholstery and indicating for his visitor to do the same in one of the armchairs. Ruth, however, remained standing.

'We already knew that Hancock was more than just wealthy and probably had assets all over the place, in different names, as well as his own,' she said.

'He's intelligent and tricky, as well as dangerous,' Mike agreed. 'But he'd have more sense than to give any of us any further trouble.'

'You think so?' Ruth exclaimed. 'Well, whatever definition of "sense" you use, I think Ralph Hancock uses a different one.' She stooped down and began drawing back the zip on the top of the canvas grip. Mike leaned forward, peering at the black box she began extricating from the bag.

'What on earth is that you've got?' he demanded. Ruth looked briefly up at him.

'This is called a video player,' she said. 'They're a smaller version of what the television people use for action replays in the sports programmes, developed in the USA and Japan, though not widely available yet, even in those countries.'

'I've heard something about them,' Mike admitted, 'though I'm not much into electronic stuff. Where did you get that one from, or shouldn't I ask?'

Ruth completed the task of removing the machine from the bag and stood up. 'This,' she said grimly, 'was sent to me yesterday, along with three video tape recordings. I assume Mr Hancock wanted to be sure I could view the tapes.'

'And I assume you've now viewed them,' Mike replied quietly. He nodded towards the large television that dominated the far corner of the room. 'Will it work on that?'

'It'll work on just about any television set,' she assured him. 'It's just a case of having the right cables, which our friend also made certain came with his little package.'

The darkened cell was beginning to feel very claustrophobic, but that, Alison kept trying to tell herself, was a stupid idea from someone who had spent the last several hours encased in tight rubber from head to toe, unable to move more than her head, unable to speak, and breathing only through her nostrils and an additional tube that ran through the centre of the ball-gag that Melanie had strapped into her mouth beneath the all-enveloping discipline helmet.

The trouble was, she knew, that the initial anticipation had long since dissipated, replaced initially by a sort of boredom and now by a mild feeling of panic, generated by a fear that Douglas might have decided to leave her as she was for the remainder of her stay, pinned helplessly like a butterfly against the wall opposite the door, arms and legs held spread-eagled by the thick leather straps.

It was not something that Marcia would ever have sanctioned, but then Alison had not seen Marcia for what seemed like an eternity. The dominatrix appeared to be quite happy to leave everything to her sadistic recruit, of whom Melanie was quite plainly terrified.

In the still silence of the cramped space, Alison listened to the steady beating of her heart and the tortured sound of her own breathing and began to wonder if this venture had been such a good idea after all. Yes, she had definitely missed the thrill, the suspense, the edge that Teddy – dear Teddy – had been unable to provide for her, but there was little in her current situation that offered much in the form of excitement.

Douglas, she was convinced now, was a dyed-in-the-wool misogynist, consideration for Alison's needs very low on his agenda, concerned more, it seemed, with reinforcing his position of absolute authority. In that there was little, if anything, to choose between him and Ralph Hancock and the pair, Alison thought, would be well matched.

She closed her eyes, willing herself not to surrender to the feelings of panic that kept threatening to overwhelm her. Wherever Marcia was, whatever she was doing, there was no way she would permit the bastard to inflict any real harm on her.

Was there?

Mike Hallet sat staring at the blank screen for a full two minutes, chewing on the knuckle of his thumb and wrestling with myriad conflicting emotions. At last he sat back from the edge of the sofa and turned to Ruth, who remained squatting on the carpet between him and the television.

'Are you sure that was her?' he rasped.

Ruth nodded and leaned across to switch off the set.

'Positive,' she confirmed. 'We grew up together in the same kibbutz. I'd know her anywhere, no matter what.'

'But as I remember her,' Mike insisted, 'Hannah was, well, let's say slightly less well endowed. And she wasn't a blonde, that much I do know.'

'The blonde hair was a wig,' Ruth said. 'As for the other, well, I don't know how they've done that, but it was definitely Hannah. I can run the film again if you want?'

Mike stood up, shaking his head. 'No,' he said tersely. 'There's no need. Like you say, you know her better than anyone else, so if you say that was Hannah, then I'll take your word for it. The point is, what the hell are they up to? Was there any sort of demand note?'

'No.' Ruth sat back, stretching her legs across the carpet, and looked up at Mike. 'But then,' she said, 'Hancock isn't the sort of bastard to work things that straightforward, is he? This is his way of making us all suffer – me, you, the rest of our team, assuming I show them this.'

'And will you show them?'

'I don't know,' Ruth admitted. 'I'm assuming he expects me to, but then that would be just sharing out the angst, wouldn't it?'

'Which is what he wants, we presume?'

'I think so.' Ruth pursed her lips, looking very suddenly like a little girl. 'The trouble is, Mr Hallet,' she said, suddenly speaking very quietly, 'is that most of the girls aren't in this country at the moment anyway. Becky's doing something in the States, both Rachel's are back in Israel, and Viv and Mary are doing something in Africa.

'Our little raid on Dennison Hall was the last time we had the original crowd together, and even that was only a last minute thing. I was about to get on a plane for Canada when Hannah called me.'

'Can you not reach any of the team, then?' Mike asked.

Ruth shrugged. 'Even if I could, I'm not sure what good it would do. We don't have any idea where they're holding

Hannah and, even assuming our contacts could establish some sort of trace, it would take weeks, probably months. By that time, who knows what those bastards will have done to her.'

Mike was pacing slowly back and forth across the room, but he stopped, searching in his jacket pockets for the ever elusive cigarette packet.

'Forgive me for being blunt,' he said cautiously, 'but you haven't brought that tape here just to tell me how hopeless the situation is for your friend, am I right?'

Ruth looked up at him for several seconds and then shook her head.

'So,' he continued, 'you must think I can help you in some way. I assume you haven't considered going to the police with this?'

'No.' Ruth shook her head vehemently. 'I think they'll possibly kill Hannah if I did that.'

'You think they'd know?'

'With Hancock's contacts?' Ruth looked at Mike the way a teacher might look at a class of errant infants. 'What do *you* think?'

'Good point,' Mike conceded. 'But we can't just do nothing.'

'We're not expected to,' Ruth retorted. 'Take a look at this.' She reached inside her jacket and withdrew a folded slip of paper, which she passed up to him. Carefully, Mike straightened it out and read the message aloud.

'This is all racist crap,' he said when he'd finished. 'Who's the "Jewish whore" they're talking about? Not Hannah, obviously, seeing as they already have her.'

'No,' Ruth agreed. 'They're not talking about Hannah.'

'Who then?'

'Can't you guess?'

Mike sighed. 'In a word, "no",' he said.

Ruth drew in a deep breath. 'Hancock and his little friends have obviously done their homework,' she said, 'but then it wasn't that difficult. Certain names give their own clues. Mine, for instance. Goldman is unmistakably Jewish, and a lot of people changed it to Gold, but I don't know who they think they were fooling. Gold, Goldman, Goldberg, it's all much of a muchness.

'Thirty years ago, the Nazis were very good at identifying Jews, because we just didn't want to let go of so much of our roots. People fled, migrated, call it what you will, from all over Europe. We Jews had gotten just about everywhere – Poland, Russia, France, Germany itself – let's face it, our culture and our brains were propping up so-called Western civilisation for centuries.

'Then along came mister Hitler and his cronies, looking for scapegoats and, wherever their armies went, there they found Jews to blame for every ailment in that supposed civilisation. About the only place they didn't get to us was here, in Britain, though they had plenty of bastards waiting to help them if they'd ever won.'

'I'm sorry,' Mike interrupted, 'but I don't see where all this is leading us.'

'I know you don't,' Ruth conceded, 'but bear with me. What I'm trying to tell you is this – there are plenty of Jews in this country, Jews you'd never know were Jews and why should most people bother about that anyway?

'Except,' she continued, 'for people like Ralph Hancock. 'Apart from everything else, Hancock is a bloody neo-Nazi. His father was a Moseley sympathiser, in case you didn't know.'

'No, I didn't know that,' Mike confessed. 'But I still don't understand what all this is leading up to.'

'Well, mister investigative journalist,' Ruth said sourly, 'obviously your intelligence isn't what it ought to be. Fair enough, you latched onto the fact that Hancock was using his perverted little set up in order to corrupt the system, but it was, and always has been, far more than that. He and his friends want to see an ultra right wing government established here, or at least a government in which they control enough key figures to gradually usurp the democracy on which this country is supposedly founded.

'Eventually, the way they see things, the country will get fed up with socialism, strikes and all the rest of it, and then they'll work their way into power, the same way Hitler, Goebbels and the rest of them did in Germany in nineteen thirty-three. And it's not just Hancock's money funding this, believe me.'

'But you still haven't told me who this so-called Jewish whore is,' Mike persisted. 'Nor why she's so important to them.'

'In herself,' Ruth said, 'she's not that important, other than that she went into Dennison Hall as a spy, that she's a woman, and above all else, Jewish. Can you imagine what that knowledge has done to Hancock's Nazi ego?'

'Well, yes,' Mike said. 'But who? You can't mean…?'

Ruth raised her eyebrows. 'Can't I?' she riposted. 'The name Katt is, quite often, just a contraction of a variety of names: Katnovski, Katnovich, Katner, Katnov… I could go on, but you're an intelligent man.'

'You mean Alison?'

Ruth nodded. 'Yes, Alison. Her father was a Russian refugee. A Jewish Russian refugee. We made the connection last year and Becky did a trace. Her dad was a very brave man. He and his wife, plus a few cousins and friends, walked more than a thousand miles to get to Sweden around the time the war broke out.'

'But Alison never said,' Mike insisted.

Ruth gave another one of her expansive, dismissive shrugs. 'Few of us ever do,' she said quietly. 'But if Hancock ever makes the same connection…'

The sound of the cell door being unlocked jerked Alison back to full consciousness and she opened her eyes, unsurprised to see the powerful figure of Douglas silhouetted against the light of the corridor beyond. He stood there for several seconds, unmoving, watching her. And she in turn remained just as motionless. Finally, he broke the stalemate and stepped into the room.

'You must be uncomfortable by now,' he said flatly. He reached out a hand and tested the strap holding Alison's left wrist outstretched, but it was no more than a symbolic gesture, for they both knew that the leather was thick and strong enough to restrain a fully grown bull. His hand moved across, fingers brushing lightly against the latex of the discipline hood where it was stretched over the flange of the stubby gag.

'Silence,' he whispered, 'is golden, as the song says.' He took a step back and studied her carefully. 'Very nice,' he said eventually. 'Very nice indeed.' He peered down to where the padded pole projected from between Alison's thighs and gave a smug grin as he saw the tell-tale dampness on its upper surface. 'Keeping yourself warm?'

Behind the mask Alison was already blushing, but then what did he expect, she asked herself? Marcia herself had designed these cells, the short poles with their ridged edges adjustable so that a slave could indeed keep herself on the very edge of anticipation – even take herself beyond that precipice and into the very chasm itself.

Inside her, she felt the lifeless vibrator suddenly start to feel larger and larger, though she knew this was only an illusion. She grunted, trying to shift her position, but succeeded only in causing the horizontal phallus to abrade her sex lips where they protruded through the strategically placed slit in her catsuit, a friction which instantly began to reawaken her libido.

Douglas reached down, his massive hands grasping her hips and he stooped slightly, so that his eyes were looking directly into hers.

'Shall I help?' he hissed, between clenched teeth. Slowly, deliberately, he drew her forward a few inches, before thrusting her backwards again until her buttocks slapped against the wall, all the time keeping a relentless downward pressure on her, so that the cunningly crafted ridges began to do their intended work. Alison gasped, and a stream of air hissed out through the narrow opening in the middle of her gag.

'Marcia was right about you, Mitzi,' Douglas said. 'A few chains and some rubber and you're almost begging for it, aren't you?' Alison wanted to shake her head, to deny what he was saying, but inside she knew the truth only too well, and right now there was only one thing she really wanted.

It had been this way at Dennison Hall, too, even though she had known that Hancock and his cronies were not just playing role games, but meant everything they said and did. Alison had been in genuine danger then – not in danger for her life perhaps, but in danger nevertheless; hours, maybe only minutes away from being sold into a life of real slavery, miles from any help, as she had thought at the time, and helpless to change her fate. And yet, in the midst of the worst horrors, she knew she had never been more than a touch away from surrendering to some inner demon that demanded it be satisfied above and before all else.

Inside her rubber covered head, Alison could now hear her pulse beginning to pound faster and faster. Between her thighs she felt hot and moist and, no longer shamed by what Douglas might think, she began to grind her hips against the protuberance beneath her, groaning through her gag and willing him to either turn on the vibrator, or maybe seek another route to her fulfilment.

'Animal!' Douglas relaxed his grip on her and stepped away again, but Alison continued to work herself towards even greater excitement. Dimly, she was aware that this was probably what he expected, what he wanted; for her to debase herself before him. But she no longer cared.

Inside her latex cocoon, silent, helpless, anonymous, she no longer cared about shame, for he had turned her into a creature designed only for lust, an amorphous female figure he knew only as Mitzi.

'Stop that!' His barked command was ferocious, yet still he had to intervene physically, one hand hooking under the front of her corset to lift her clear of the stimulation, the other seeking and unfastening the bonds that held her upper limbs. Then, no sooner had he released his grip in order to free her ankles, Alison was once again astride the rubber shaft, rocking furiously back and forth in a race to bring herself to the climax her burning body needed, before he could once again turn his attentions towards depriving her of it.

Douglas won the race, but only just, and as he pulled Alison into the centre of the cell, her knees gave way beneath her and he was forced to catch her in his arms. Slumped against his chest, she turned her head and stared up into his face, her eyes imploring him, rippling growls rising from her throat to force their way past the rubber gag and the outer skin of the helmet.

'Shameless bitch.' He forced her upright again, holding her easily at arms length, grinning at the way she still tried to work her thighs together in an effort to bring the lifeless vibrator into play.

'Wait,' he said eventually. He stretched out one booted foot and kicked it between her feet, forcing her legs further apart and keeping it there as a precaution against her drawing them together again. He regarded her with an air of amused detachment and then nodded.

'Let's have you in the appropriate begging position again first,' he said. Quickly, he fastened snap rings to the staples in her ankle cuffs and unzipped the rubber suit where it covered her ringed nipples. Realising his intention, Alison gave a muffled squeal of protest and tried to wriggle away from him, but he was far too strong and very efficient.

Seconds later, she stood once again as she had when he'd prepared her for the journey here, hands and arms half raised in an attitude of supplication.

'Better,' he said, releasing her at last. Instinctively, she pressed the tops of her legs together again, but this time he made no attempt to stop her. Instead, he retreated even further, until he was once again framed in the doorway and slowly dropped one hand to his crotch in an unmistakably provocative gesture.

'Is this what you want, puppy dog?' He rubbed himself and Alison's eyes were drawn, as if by magnets, to the rapidly swelling bulge beneath the tight leather breeches. She hesitated, but only for the briefest second. With a moan of frustration she began to nod. Douglas raised his free hand and crooked the index finger at her, backing out into the corridor as he did so. The implication was obvious.

With Alison tottering after him, Douglas backed along the short passageway until he arrived at the door she recognised as leading to the largest of Marcia's subterranean dungeon area. It swung open easily when he pushed against it and continued his reversed progress inside.

'Come to me.' He spoke flatly and without any apparent emotion, but Alison was now scarcely listening to the words. Obediently, hands still raised like begging paws, she moved towards him until he stopped, raising both hands to indicate she should do likewise. He looked around, apparently seeking something, and his eyes flared angrily when he did not see it.

'Get in here, you whore spawn scum!' His roar echoed around the stone walls and Alison recoiled at the vehemence in it, but his rage was not directed towards her, as she quickly realised when the white-faced figure of Melanie appeared beside her. Douglas pointed at the maid, his lip curling.

'I told you to wait for me in here!' he bellowed. 'I didn't say wait outside, nor in the next room, but in here, right?'

'Y-yes, master,' Melanie quivered. 'I-I'm sorry, but I realised you might need this.' She held out a small jar, presenting it to him. He narrowed his eyes, leaning closer to inspect it, and suddenly his brutal expression twisted into a crooked grin.

'Ah, yes,' he said, his voice dropping several decibels, 'of course. Looking after your little friend's interests.'

'And yours, master,' Melanie hastened to assure him. 'Ease of entry will increase your own pleasure.'

'And you'd know all about these things, wouldn't you?' Douglas sneered. 'Perhaps you'd rather I was going to do this with you, eh? Or maybe you'd rather fuck the bitch yourself, is that it?'

Melanie shook her head, more vigorously than was perhaps necessary. 'No, master,' she exclaimed, obviously alarmed that her intentions had been misconstrued. 'I would never dare to presume.'

'Of course you wouldn't, you heap of useless crap,' Douglas retorted. 'But you may still have your uses, and who knows, maybe I'll let you fuck the whore anyway. Now, hold onto her while I prepare myself.'

'Would you like her gag removed, master?' Melanie suggested, relinquishing the jar to Douglas and turning to steady Alison, who was now becoming decidedly *un*steady. Douglas shook his head, reaching for one of the sturdy steel framed upright chairs that stood together beneath one of the many equipment racks that adorned the wall of the chamber.

'No,' he said tersely, 'leave her mouth plugged. She makes such delightful noises when she's excited. But you can unzip her gusset, though I want the vibrator left in.' He dragged the chair nearer the centre of the floor and placed the jar on its seat, so that his hands were free to wrestle with his belt and the zip that held the front of his breeches closed.

Alison, for her part, barely felt Melanie's fingers as they tugged at the zip that ran back from her crotch opening. As if through a smoked glass screen, she was gazing around the room, remembering it from little more than a year ago, when she had first come to Marcia to be initiated into this bizarre world of pillories, stocks, chains, hoists and whips.

She remembered how she had stood in line with Honey and the other two rubber slave girls, each of them indistinguishable from the other three, and how the bemused Mike had been offered the use of any of them he chose. She could picture the expression on his face and heard again Marcia's voice as she had given her that final escape route.

'Girls,' she had said, in that calm, authoritative tone, 'Master Michael is obviously quite taken with what he sees, but as you have heard, he has certain doubts.' One of which was the prospect of actually fucking his attractive blonde reporter, Alison knew. 'Now, to save a lot of trouble, those of you who would like to feel his stiff rod in your hot little pussy, take one step forward.'

Alison had only to remain standing where she was and that, presumably, would have been that, for Mike Hallet would never have let her then go on to risk herself undercover at Dennison Hall and Marcia had known that only too well. Maybe she had also known, even then, what her ministrations and expert tuition had begun to awaken in her newest pupil, for she had certainly betrayed no surprise when Alison stepped forward, in perfect unison with her sister slaves.

As things had turned out, she never found herself 'wriggling on the end of his cock', as Marcia had so indelicately put it. But she had writhed on the end of a rubber phallus strapped between the thighs of the eager and athletic Poppy, until finally she'd exploded in a crescendo of abandonment and ecstasy that she'd never previously believed possible.

This situation, however, was totally different, for as Douglas drew his swiftly erecting organ from within his breeches, Alison knew she was about to be offered to no artificial phallus, but to a burgeoning, flesh and blood shaft that was as impressive as it was awesome. He held it loosely in his right hand, stroking the flesh that began to glisten beneath the lights as the blood continued to pump into the tissue within.

'Take a good look,' he said, making sure Alison had plenty of opportunity to do just that. His expression had become even more curious and he was watching her eyes for a reaction. Alison tried to stifle a groan, but her body was working mostly without direct instructions from her brain. He turned, picked up the jar and unscrewed the lid.

'You can thank your little friend for this afterwards,' he sneered, dipping two fingers into the translucent goo inside the jar. With slow deliberation he withdrew them, half turning to discard the jar and its remaining contents onto a pile of sacking that was conveniently nearby. Then without taking his eyes from hers, he began to smear the grease over the head of his organ, working it down the entire length and massaging it methodically until he had applied a complete covering, wiping the excess on his breeches and ignoring the white streak it left on the leather.

'Right,' he breathed, stepping forward again. He seized Alison's wrists, jerking them cruelly so that her nipples were forced into a painfully elongated shape, a reminder to her that resistance was futile. He dragged her towards the chair and then slowly lowered himself onto the seat, bending her forward over his knees until their faces were less than two inches apart.

'You're going to enjoy this, bitch,' he whispered, 'so don't even think about struggling.' He leaned forward, straightening her, turning her, until she stood with her back to him, and then he began to draw her backwards, so that she was forced to splay her knees in order to straddle his thighs.

He held her easily with one hand, the other grasping his thick pole and guiding it towards its target. Alison felt the hot, slippery knob pressing against her tight muscles and let out a low yelp, but Douglas either did not here it, or simply decided to ignore it.

'Squat, bitch,' she heard him rasp, one hand pressing down on her thigh to reinforce the instruction. Alison closed her eyes, her teeth sinking into the hard rubber between them. She felt another touch, this time on her upper arm and heard Melanie's voice close to her ear, urgent yet supportive.

'Relax,' the maid whispered. 'Just relax and don't try to fight against it.'

'That's right,' Douglas growled, 'don't fight it, slut. You're going to have it anyway, one way or the other.'

Reluctantly, Alison tried to obey, fighting against every instinct. She had been penetrated in this way before and it had not been unpleasant, but never by anything the size of the monstrosity that now sought entry in this tightly muscled sanctuary.

And then, suddenly, the monster's head was inside her and Alison groaned as she felt her ring distending around it, her sphincter muscles already contracting in their eagerness to draw it further inside. With a gurgled sigh she let her weight fall back and down, oblivious to the potential fate of the invader's owner. But Douglas was ready for her and had two hands steadying her at the waist, controlling her descent, until finally she sat on his lap, impaled and filled as she had never been filled before.

She felt his legs extending forward between her calves, forcing them wider still, until he was able to raise his knees between her thighs and spread them obscenely, the labial rings pulling against their entwining locks as they sought to open with the movement. Douglas moved his hands up, fingers prising a way between her wrists and her distended nipples, seeking out the swollen teats and slowly manipulating them, sending tiny shock waves coursing through her body with inevitable results.

Alison felt her stomach muscles tense, the reflex action transmitting itself lower, her buttocks clenching and back arching. From behind she heard Douglas grunt and his grip on her nipples intensified, eliciting a shrill cry of pain and pleasure from behind her gag. Deliberately, she raised her body a few inches and then, before he had time to react, slammed down with her full weight, gasping as his shaft rammed fully home again and throwing herself forward, kept upright only by his rapid reaction and the firm grip he kept upon her.

'Slut,' he groaned, and Alison knew he was right, but she was long past caring. Only one thing mattered, and she knew she was close. Douglas, however, was more than prepared and suddenly she found herself pinned down, fully impaled but unable to take advantage of the situation. Desperately, she tried squirming from side to side, but he was far too strong and held her easily.

'Not yet,' he whispered, his mouth close to her ear. 'Not yet, bitch puppy. There's more to come.' His fingers were working overtime, kneading, twisting, rolling, and Alison howled into her gag, far beyond caring what he thought.

'Now, you misbegotten whore,' he cried, and for a brief moment Alison thought he was shouting at her, but then she understood, for Melanie was between her thighs, kneeling, head bobbing as her avaricious tongue probed between the interlocked rings, seeking the little bud that was the only trigger now needed.

'Key, you stupid bitch.' Douglas's voice sounded strange and Alison was only dimly aware that he was wrapped in his own struggle. This had become a battle, a trial of wills. Grimacing, fighting against her innermost nature, she fought to gain the only victory now remaining to her, determined to rob him of the satisfaction, knowing that she could reach her own goal the moment she had proved her point.

But now came the final betrayal, for Melanie was already unlocking the rings that sealed her sopping sex, gently prising her swollen lips apart, tongue already lapping furiously. It was an unfair contest, but Alison was on a different planet and no longer cared. She had proved her point, made her stand, and it was time to take her reward.

With a long animal howl she surrendered in a helpless spasm that jolted every bone in her back, and had the final satisfaction as Douglas spurted his pent up frustration deep into her and triggered a second round of multiple climaxes that continued long after she blacked out.

1.8

'I still don't see the point of Hancock sending you this film,' Mike persisted. 'What does he hope to gain from it? He hasn't made any demands yet, has he? In fact, there's nothing on the film to connect him with it at all. The other people involved were all either masked or filmed from behind.'

'Precisely,' Ruth said. 'He'd be far too cute to risk anything that could be used as evidence against him. As to why send the damned thing in the first place, I can only guess he wants to make us suffer. He'd guess I'd try to contact the others and that I'd show this to you.'

'But if he was able to kidnap Hannah, for God's sake, what's to stop him just grabbing the rest of you?'

'Nothing at all,' Ruth replied grimly. 'Hannah's a tough nut with plenty of experience in bad situations, which is why I reckon he's gone for her first, to prove he could. Now he knows the rest of us will be looking over our shoulders every minute of the day and night, waiting, wondering if this is going to be it.'

'You think he will definitely try for the rest of you?' Mike asked, furrowing his brow. 'And Alison?'

Ruth nodded. 'No doubt about it in my mind,' she said. 'For all I know they could be watching us now, right at this minute, though I'm pretty certain I wasn't followed here today.'

'Hancock probably knows exactly where to find me, if he wants me,' Mike said sourly. 'This place has belonged to Honey's family for over a century and, if what you say is right, he'll know that she and I have been together since last year.'

'Oh, he'll know all right,' Ruth agreed. 'He's pretty damned thorough and has excellent intelligence. You saw all those records at Dennison Hall.'

'The thing is,' Mike said, standing up and walking across to the window, 'what are we going to do about this? I reckon the best thing is to go to the police, don't you?'

'And tell them what?' Ruth moved silently across to stand at his side, looking out over the freshly cut grass towards the orchard. 'That film wasn't made at Dennison Hall. I told you, I did some checking and the place has stayed shut up since our little raid. I also had a friend check up for other addresses for Hancock and all he came up with was a small flat in Chelsea.

'I got a girlfriend of mine to call there first thing this

morning, posing as a council official, and the only occupant at present is a young model, who reckons she rents the place from an agency in Fulham. She'd never heard of Hancock and the neighbours confirmed he hasn't been seen there for at least two years, even if the place is still in his name.'

'And there's nothing else?'

'Nothing. The word is that Hancock took off for Spain last year and that he was last heard of in Switzerland. His name has been removed from the list of directors of all the companies he's supposed to own. Dennison Hall is supposedly on the market, though there have been no offers as yet and he hasn't re-entered the country on his own passport.'

'Seems you have a pretty good line in intelligence yourself,' Mike said.

Ruth gave a muffled snort. 'And a lot of good it's done me so far,' she said. 'I've used every contact, called in every favour, but still nothing. To all intents and purposes, Ralph Hancock has disappeared off the face of the earth.'

'We should be so lucky,' Mike growled. 'But meantime, we can't just sit around and do nothing, can we? I've got a couple of pals in the Met; I could ask them to make a few unofficial enquiries.'

'If I were you,' Ruth said, 'I'd be more worried about Alison, and I wouldn't rule out Hancock trying to grab you, too. Everyone who was involved in last year's little escapade is at risk.'

'Yeah, I *had* worked that out for myself,' Mike said. 'Alison should be all right where she is, at least for the moment. The place she's staying at is pretty secure and even Hancock would be pushed to get in there.' He turned back towards the centre of the room, scratching the side of his nose. 'On the other hand,' he continued, 'it's best not to take chances.'

'No,' Ruth agreed. 'Your best bet is to go and get Alison

and then the pair of you take yourselves a holiday. Go abroad. The States, Australia even – the further the better. I presume you can afford to do that?'

'Well, money's no problem, but I've got my work to consider. I'm in the middle of a fortnight's holiday at the moment, but I'm due back in just over a week.'

'Well, go sick, or take a sabbatical,' Ruth said firmly. 'You've got to get out of things, at least until I've had time to think and get some of the girls back together.'

'You think you can take Hancock on by yourselves?'

'I think we're going to have to,' Ruth replied quietly. 'We did it before, but then we did have the element of surprise on our side the first time and this time he'll be expecting something. However, that's not my main worry. Our biggest problem is finding him.

'Before,' she added, 'he starts finding us.'

'The Goldman woman visited Hallet earlier today,' Ralph Hancock said. He moved aside two bulky manila folders and picked up a thinner, pale blue one, which he opened, withdrawing three black and white photographs and a single sheet of typewritten paper.

'Smith had this delivered to me half an hour ago,' he continued, passing the prints across the desktop to Kristin. 'He's had four men on her since the film tape was delivered. She's been quite busy, it seems, though he only knows that she's made a lot of phone calls from a series of public call boxes.'

'You think she knows that you've got her line tapped?' Kristin asked.

Hancock smiled. 'She's probably guessed,' he said, 'but then she'd play it safe anyway. Her kind may be little better than animals, but they're very professional.'

'And you're sure they can't trace us here?'

'Not a chance. I bought this place five years ago, long before there was any hint of trouble, but I used a series of names and agents that had nothing to do with any of the companies. No, this place is as secure as you could want.'

'So,' Kristin said, studying the pictures, which showed a young woman getting in and out of a car outside a picturesque country cottage, 'what's the next move?'

'We wait and watch,' Hancock said. 'The Goldman whore will no doubt start contacting the rest of her Zionist bitches. They'll be only too eager to rescue their beloved leader, so they won't be long in gathering, believe me.

'Once we know where they all are, we can make our move and catch them all in the same net. It saves a lot of unnecessary bother.'

'And the little spy whore?' Kristin reminded him.

Hancock's smile widened. 'We'll have her, too,' he assured her. 'At the moment one of Smith's men is watching my beloved ex-wife's house, which is where the slut is currently staying.'

'Why not move in now?' Kristin suggested. 'Take the pair of them, and the so-called maid.'

'That would be very neat, I agree,' Hancock replied. 'However, it's not the easiest of targets. Dear Marcia has strengthened her security of late. The building is like a fortress and she has a permanent minder living in, not to mention her latest houseguest, who's not the sort of fellow to be trifling with, from what I know of him.'

'It's not like you to resist a challenge,' Kristin smirked.

'There are challenges and there are challenges,' Hancock said. 'And there is little point in wasting time and manpower on something that could prove a little tricky, especially when there will be other, easier routes. No, we'll have them all, in time.

'And then,' he added, with an air of grim satisfaction, 'we shall have all the time we want – time that will seem like an eternity to them.'

Hercules.

He was well named, Hannah thought, as she watched Phoebe leading the prize 'stallion' across the paddock, for he was without doubt the biggest man she had ever set eyes upon, towering even above his handler in her steepling heels and bulging with muscles in places where lesser men did not even have places.

Six feet seven, Rose had said he was, but to Hannah he looked even taller, probably, she realised, because of the heavy hoof boots he wore, which easily added another five inches to his height. At a guess, he had to weigh around three hundred pounds minimum, and not one of those pounds was surplus.

His facial appearance, however, remained a mystery, for like the two smaller 'stallions' who were still tethered to the rail in front of the stable, his entire head was enclosed in a rubber horse mask, his eyes barely visible through wide set plastic lenses.

It seemed impossible that such a huge creature could be subservient, even to the likes of Kristin, Rose and Phoebe, for even the leather restraints that kept his arms close to his sides did not look strong enough to hold him if he was really determined to break free. Besides, Hannah thought, surely they could not keep him bound permanently, any more than they could keep their female charges restrained full-time.

The inference, Hannah realised, was that Hercules was more or less here of his own free will, the pony paraphernalia just trappings to maintain an image for Hancock's perverse guests and clientele. She stared at the leather tube that rose from his loins, held tightly across his stomach by a series of three thin leather straps. Even allowing that the hide itself was not thin, the proportions were unbelievable and Hannah's stomach lurched at the thought that such a massive instrument was soon to be her fate, too.

Phoebe, however, seemed in no hurry to expedite the proceedings; indeed, Hannah understood, she was probably deliberately drawing them out, giving Hannah as much time as possible to imagine and to torment herself with thoughts of the inevitable. She strolled casually across, Hercules' lead rein dangling from her wrist, and tethered him alongside the first two pony boys. Only then did she even acknowledge Hannah, who remained several yards distant, her own rein knotted to a stake driven firmly into the mud.

'Big, isn't he?' she smirked, standing in front of Hannah, arms nonchalantly folded across her chest. 'And he gets even bigger, once that restrainer's off,' she added, with obvious relish. 'They say every female dreams of meeting a man with a huge cock, but I wouldn't want to be on the end of one that size, would you?

'Oh, but of course,' she continued, stifling a deliberate giggle, 'that's exactly where you're going to be, isn't it? Poor Tits is just a pony girl, so she doesn't get any say in the matter. Never mind, Tits, they tell me you soon get used to something that size, though going back to a normal cock afterwards must be something of an anti-climax. In fact,' she laughed, 'probably no climax at all.'

She stooped, gathered up Hannah's rein and began to haul it in, dragging Hannah towards her. Hannah considered kicking out at her. The hoof boots were cumbersome, but even a glancing blow from them could inflict some serious damage and Phoebe appeared to be alone, apart from the three stallions, none of whom were exactly in much of a position to come to her aid.

However, even if she managed to disable the bitch she would be little better off. The bit and the arm restraints left her little with which to work and the stiffness and weight of the boots would prevent her getting very far at any pace, even if she had known the terrain, which she didn't. Any escape would be merely temporary, a stalling exercise that could and would only bring her even more trouble, hard as that was to imagine.

'You'd love to claw my eyes out, wouldn't you, Tits?' Phoebe sneered, pulling Hannah's face close to her own. 'Yes, I can see it in your eyes. In fact, I reckon you'd even kill me if you could, but don't get any ideas.' She turned and nodded towards the trees around the clearing's perimeter.

'There are three cameras up there,' she said, 'all wired back to the main house. Even if you did manage to make a break there'd be help here within a couple of minutes and they'd soon find you. This estate is big, but it isn't that big, and there are high fences all around, plus a bog, a river and an old quarry, and you're not exactly kitted out for one of your commando expeditions, are you?

'No, Tits, you're kitted out to get yourself a damned good fucking by the best damnedest stallion in England – maybe even the best in Europe. Mistress Rose suggested I might like to give you a warm up thrashing first, but to be honest, I don't think I can be bothered. You'll be sore enough after Hercules, anyway.

'Now then,' she said, releasing her grip on the rein, 'just you stand there like a good horsey, while I get a covering frame out here. That's the term used when a stallion fucks a mare, in case you didn't know. Of course, with four-legged mares, when they're in season, a frame's not exactly necessary, but for a reluctant two-legged filly we find it makes things a bit simpler for Hercules.

'I could let him chase you round the paddock, of course, but why waste his energy when we don't have to? Far better to conserve it for the important things. Now, just you wait there. I shan't be long.'

She turned away and strutted across to the stable, pausing long enough to deliver a firm slap across the rump of each of the three tethered males and to look back and grin at Hannah. The performance was deliberate, calculated to emphasise the difference in their stations. She, Phoebe, was the one in control, exercising complete power over the three stallions, whilst Hannah was simply a helpless pawn in the game, waiting in harness to be used at Phoebe's whim.

Grimly, Hannah ground her teeth into the bit, fighting against the feeling of panic that was threatening to overwhelm her. She had known fear before, even the fear that comes with the prospect of imminent death, but that had been different. At least on the battlefield she had been in a position to fight back, to shoot at those who were shooting at her and her comrades, but here, now, there was no possibility of retaliation.

All she could do was submit, but at least, she told herself fiercely, she could try to do that with dignity. That would be a form of victory, albeit a minor one, but then, as her instructors had never ceased to drum into her, even the smallest victory could contribute to a war being finally won.

When Phoebe re-emerged it was not from the fairly narrow door at the front of the stable block, but from a much wider double door that swung open in the left hand end wall. She pushed both doors back, latching them against the stonework, and then came back around to where the three figures still waited at the hitching rail. Walking past Hercules, the first in the line, she stopped at the second male, untied his tether, and led him back the way she had come.

A minute or so later she reappeared for the second time, followed still by the chosen stallion who was now hitched to heavy traces, on the other end of which was a most curious engine. Hannah stared at it as it lumbered out on four tyred wheels, and her eyes opened wider as she understood its purpose, for its various features could be intended for but one thing and one thing only.

The vehicle comprised a flat decking, about four feet

wide and six or seven feet long, sturdy timbers nailed to a frame supported by axles front and rear. A foot or so from the front a single steel pole rose up at right angles, at the top of which was another metal bar, set at right angles and fashioned to form three hoops. As it drew closer Hannah saw that this upper bar was, in fact, two bars, mirrored halves that could hinge open and closed, so that the three apertures were, in effect, a steel pillory.

From just below the point at which the crosspiece and upright joined, a second horizontal projected, this time at right angles to the first and ending in a shorter T-piece. This bar appeared to be able to swivel and to telescope in and out, the length adjustable and fixable by means of a short split pin that hung on a length of slim chain.

Further back on the platform, roughly at its halfway point, two more metal poles were fixed, though these were no more than a foot high, ending in manacles that could only be intended to lock around ankles. As the cart lumbered to a halt, scant feet from where Hannah stood, she could see that these latter uprights were actually set into metal grooves, enabling them to be moved either forward or back.

'Voila!' Phoebe announced, gleefully. 'One covering frame, feisty fillies for the use of. As you can see it's fully portable, but as we don't have a large audience today that won't really matter, unless you'd prefer me to hitch Max up with Zero and give you a little ride while you're giving Hercules a bigger one?'

The bitch was really laying it on, Hannah realised, deliberately prolonging the agony, knowing that her captive could do nothing to avoid what was coming, but wanting her imagination to do its worst before the actuality itself.

'Yes,' Phoebe said, stroking her chin, 'maybe that's an idea – give all the cameras different angles. Hercules isn't a straight in and out stallion, believe me, so there'll be plenty of time to show you both off to your best advantage.

'Now,' she continued, planting herself firmly in front of Hannah, 'let's have you up there first and then we'll hitch up the horses as a pair afterwards.'

1.9

Ruth Goldman turned the nose of the red MGB towards the late afternoon sun and headed steadily towards the motorway that, when finished, would connect London with South Wales. At the moment the blue line on the map was broken in three places, the first gap little more than twenty minutes west of Chiswick. But at least it was a start, and she did not wish to give the car that had been tailing her for the past half-hour too difficult a trail to follow.

Turning off onto the A4 she drove for another quarter of an hour and then pulled off into a service station, cruised up to an empty pump and topped her fuel tank to the brim. Moving slowly around the car, ostensibly checking the tyre pressures, she managed to utilise one of the wing mirrors to get a better look at the blue Jaguar saloon. The driver had pulled up next to another pump, but was making no attempt to refuel. Instead, he had raised the bonnet and was going through the motions of checking the engine.

Smiling to herself, Ruth stood up, reached in through the open window for her handbag and strolled nonchalantly across to the low building that acted as a small shop and café. She pushed open the door and quickly took in the surroundings, including the two telephone booths set between the doors marked *Ladies* and *Gentlemen*.

'Ladies and gentlemen,' she muttered under her breath, 'for my next trick…' Wiping the smile from her face she strolled across to the till, paid for the petrol and then turned back towards the exit. Once outside she paused, looking up at the sky, feigning interest in the passing clusters of white clouds and then, as slowly as she dared, made her way back to the sports car.

Immediately she opened the door she heard the metallic clunk as the Jaguar's bonnet was slammed closed and a quick glance in the interior rear-view mirror confirmed that the driver was already sliding back behind the wheel.

'Not just yet, Tiger,' she whispered, and gunned the motor into life. She sat back, drew out a cigarette, lit it and blew out a stream of smoke, before finally putting the engine into gear and letting out the clutch. The exit back onto the main road was ahead and to her right, but just as it seemed she was about to turn into it, she pulled hard down on the wheel, slued the little car into a tight turn and headed back past the petrol pumps, turning again to guide the nose into one of the parking spaces reserved for the non fuel patrons, resisting the temptation to see what her shadow was doing.

Unhurriedly, she climbed out of the cockpit once more, wound up the window and locked the door, stopping to make a show of checking inside her bag, before finally walking back towards the entrance to the building. As she pushed open the glass door and re-entered, from the corner of her eye she saw the Jaguar pulling into another parking space at the far end of the line and gave a grunt of satisfied amusement.

The coffee was unpromising in appearance, but

surprisingly palatable, and Ruth quickly drained the first cup and returned to the counter for a refill. Outside the Jaguar had not moved, the driver still sitting inside, obviously watching for her to reappear and, as she returned to her table, a new thought occurred to her.

She checked her watch, calculating. Presuming he *had* been following her on route to Mike Hallet's, or even that he had known she would end up there and had simply been waiting close by for her to show up, that would account for at least an hour. She had been inside the house for another two hours, at least, and it was now nearly another hour since she had left there. Four hours.

Leaving her coffee on the table she stood up, tucked her bag under her arm and strolled across towards the toilets. She flickered a sideways glance out of the window again, checking that her unwanted escort was still there, and smirked wickedly.

Her mother had once told her that all men thought with their balls, a statement that Ruth's subsequent experiences had taught her to be not entirely true. On the other hand, one thing she did know was that it was not easy to think straight with a full bladder, whether you were male or female.

She stopped level with the telephone booths, considered whether to make her calls now or afterwards and decided that afterwards was favourite. The more time *he* had to think about toilets, flushing cisterns and such things, the better.

She smirked again. The way to a man's heart might lay through his stomach – sometimes courtesy of a long and wickedly sharp knife, as Ruth was only too well aware – but the way to his stupidity was generally most effectively via his cock, whether that included the contents of his testicles, or those of his bladder.

Phoebe was as methodical and careful as Rose before her, transferring Hannah to the covering frame without once giving her the slightest hint that an escape bid might be feasible.

She kept the reins attached whilst she drew Hannah up onto the raised decking, wrapping them loosely around the horizontal pillory bar whilst she stooped to secure her ankles, dragging her legs apart to effect this, so that Hannah was left standing in what seemed to be a very precarious position, balancing only with a great deal of concentration, even though the initial effects of the incapacitating drug had long since worn off.

'Now, Tits,' Phoebe said, unhitching the reins from the bar and reaching up to detach them from Hannah's nose ring, 'there's an easy way and a hard way to do this.' She discarded the reins, drawing them back and out of the nipple rings and, in their place, produced a length of thin cord, at one end of which was a small snap link that she clipped back to the nose ring.

'If you try to struggle,' she said, wrapping the cord once around her right hand, 'then I'll do this, only harder.' She gave the cord a sharp jerk and instantly the pain in Hannah's nose brought tears to her eyes. Phoebe stared at her impassively. 'Understand?' she said. Miserably, Hannah nodded.

'Good,' Phoebe said, smiling. She moved around and unclipped each of Hannah's arms in turn and then, still keeping a firm grip on the nose cord, moved back in front and began hinging up the top of the pillory, which Hannah now saw was in three sections.

'Neck and wrists, please Tits,' Phoebe said. Their eyes met for a second or so and Hannah saw the challenge there, almost as if her captor was willing her to rebel, but Hannah was not going to make that mistake. Now was not the time, regardless of what was about to befall her – it would happen anyway, one way or the other, and to bring further pain upon herself and to no avail would be stupid.

Obediently, she leaned forward, gripping the bar while she positioned her throat into the central semicircle and then placing her wrists in the smaller grooves. She closed her eyes, listening as Phoebe snapped the top sections shut, trying not to imagine the picture she now presented.

'Just got to get you adjusted, Tits,' Phoebe chuckled. She swung the horizontal T-bar around from the side, so that the crosspiece was now in line with Hannah's lower stomach, and then adjusted the length so that it pressed back into her, forcing her back to straighten and her buttocks to project lewdly. 'That should do it,' she muttered, adjusting the butterfly screw that prevented the bar from telescoping shut again.

She straightened up and walked around to stand behind Hannah, her hands gently caressing the upraised globes and then one hand sliding down, probing between Hannah's thighs and between the two rows of interlocking rings.

'Still dry,' she muttered, prising apart the compressed labial lips as best she could. 'Mind you, that's only to be expected. They tell me you're not over fond of cock at the best of times, but don't worry. I'll lubricate you well before Hercules mounts you, otherwise you'd know all about it. Now, let's get this pretty little cunt unlocked, shall we?'

Two phone calls, three cups of coffee, another visit to the ladies toilet and an hour and a half later, Ruth stubbed out her fifth cigarette, snapped her handbag shut and stood up. Outside, at the far end of the front row of parked vehicles, the blue Jaguar was still there and, as she stepped out into the open and strolled towards the MGB, it was all she could do to stop herself from giving its driver a cheery wave.

'Now then,' she said to herself, as she settled back behind the wheel, 'let's see where we can take you.' The sun was dropping close to the horizon and she estimated that another hour or so would bring darkness. By that time, assuming her tail had not managed to find a way of relieving himself without leaving his car, he would be feeling very uncomfortable indeed; also, by around that time, she needed to be within a few miles of the rendezvous point Becky had suggested. Meanwhile, it was important that she kept her shadow interested – and in touch.

Opening the small glove compartment she pulled out the folded roadmap, turned it over and refolded it to the appropriate section and studied it for a few seconds. Then, nodding to herself, she laid it on the passenger seat, turned the ignition key and gunned the powerful little engine into life.

To Alison's surprise, Douglas remained as hard as ever after ejaculating and seemed determined to keep her impaled on his lap, gripping her hips with his powerful hands, his knees keeping her thighs wide spread for Melanie's attentions between them. She groaned and writhed as the little maid's devilish tongue probed her clitoris, shuddering again and again as one orgasm after another swept over her. Close to her ear, Douglas was upbraiding her, but Alison was beyond being affected by mere words, and if anything his torrent of insults simply added fuel to her fires.

'Dirty little whore,' he hissed. 'Look at you, you shameless bitch. You couldn't open those legs wider if you tried.' To emphasise this, he thrust his own legs wider, stretching Alison's thigh muscles to their absolute limit as Melanie's tongue lapped deeply within her. Then, to her further bemusement, she felt Douglas's hand tugging at the zip over her mouth, drawing it back and then tugging the gag from between her teeth.

'Now,' he said, his own mouth close to her ear as she lay back against him, 'tell me what you are, Mitzi.'

'I-I'm a whore,' Alison gasped. 'A dirty whore, master.'

'And what is it you need, dirty whore?'

'I need to be fucked, master. I need to be fucked by you.' He grasped her hips again, pulling her down hard on his shaft and preventing her from raising herself.

'Then beg for it, whore!' he rasped. As if on cue Melanie drew back and Alison, eyes wide, screamed in frustration. Douglas laughed and dug his fingers deeper into her. 'I said beg, whore,' he taunted. 'Beg to be butt-fucked some more.'

'Oh *yes*,' Alison wailed. 'Yes, please fuck my butt, master!'

'And do you want the slut maid's tongue in your cunt, too?'

'Yes, master.' Alison tried to work herself around his erection, but he was far too strong for her. 'Please, master!' she screeched, desperate to return to the abandoned oblivion she had been on the point of entering just seconds before. 'Please, master – have pity.'

Douglas laughed again, but he lifted her slightly, withdrawing his organ a few inches from her tight sheath, leaving just the tip and first two inches or so still within her.

'Show me,' he said quietly, releasing his hold on her. Alison needed no second bidding. With a low moan she let herself fall, grunting as his throbbing column once more filled her to the hilt. At the same time Melanie bent forward again and her tongue found its target with unerring precision.

As the momentum built up once again Douglas chuckled contentedly, but Alison no longer heard him. Nor did she see anything beyond the blonde head bobbing between her thighs and her own breasts, wrists still cuffed to their nipple rings, bouncing in unashamed and unfettered time as she willingly skewered herself to the accompaniment of a steadily rising howl of pure, animal surrender.

Breathing harshly, saliva dribbling past the bit and onto her chin, Hannah stood bent double, neck and wrists secured in the metal pillory, and waited for the inevitable. But the tall Phoebe did not appear in any hurry to introduce Hercules to her. Instead, the young dominatrix picked up a riding crop that had been placed on the decking beneath the pillory and, swishing it through the air dramatically, stalked back and forth in front of her captive.

Meanwhile, Zero, the male 'pony' who had hauled the apparatus from the stable block, stood slightly to one side, still connected to the front of the wheeled frame by the long leather trace with which he had towed the cumbersome vehicle, waiting patiently until he was required again.

The horse head masked his features and all but his eyes, but Hannah knew that the man inside was watching her intently, his penis rigid inside what appeared to be a thick rubber sheath that enveloped both it and his entire scrotum. No doubt, she thought, the bastard was anticipating the time, which would surely come, when it was he and not the more imposing Hercules who would be put to her in the same helpless state.

'I think,' Phoebe said, eventually tiring of her back and forth promenade, 'that it's time to get things properly under way.' She looked up at the sky and towards the setting sun. 'Damn!' she muttered, and Hannah realised that the girl had plainly become so engrossed in her pantomime that she had forgotten the passing time. In another hour, little more, it would be virtually dark; in half that time there would be insufficient light for the various cameras to record her humiliation.

Shaking her head, Phoebe wheeled away, covering the ground between the frame trolley and the hitching rail at something approaching a canter, no mean feat in her steepling heels. She almost ripped Max's rein from the bar and nearly dragged him to join Zero, who had moved back to stand directly in front of Hannah, though with his back to her, ready to haul the vehicle when ordered.

Zero, understanding what was required of him, dutifully took up position to Max's right, and Phoebe quickly completed the task of hitching him likewise.

'Take the strain!' she called, and moving around to the rear, stepped up onto the back of the decking, just behind Hannah. The two equine humans shuffled forward, the slack traces tightening into a straight line. Hannah felt a gloved hand press between her legs, a finger probing, then another, and finally a dull click as the lock on the end of the securing bar was released.

She felt the slender metal prong being withdrawn, bringing an immediate lessening of the strain on her labia, which now, due to the wide nature of her stance, parted immediately. Hannah closed her eyes, shuddering at the thought of the cameras on her, imagining the image she presented. Phoebe's hand returned again, cupping her sex, pressing, kneading.

'Sweet, Tits,' she laughed. 'Very sweet.' Two fingers insinuated into Hannah's vagina and, to Hannah's horror, she realised she was growing moist, for the rubber covered digits met little resistance. Phoebe, however, seemed most pleased with the result.

'Sweet and tight,' she sniggered. 'But we'll soon change that. Hercules is going to enjoy himself with this little cunt, and before we know it, it'll be a nice big cunt.' She broke the intimate contact and then, before Hannah had time to realise what she intended, there was a hissing sound and the crop slashed across her taut buttocks.

Hannah shrieked, as much in surprise as from the pain, though the braided leather stung like fire. Again Phoebe swung and a second burning line flew across unprotected flesh. This time Hannah ground her gums and teeth hard against the bit and managed to confine her audible reaction to a hiss of air expelled through her nostrils.

'Hup there, boys!' Phoebe shouted, and as she poised to deliver a third cut with the crop, the two steeds leaned forward against the inertial weight and very slowly, platform, pillory, it's helpless occupant and the grinning Phoebe began to move.

'Once around the paddock!' Phoebe cried, adding an open-handed slap across Hannah's left buttock. 'Once around boys, while I warm up this filly's rump and then we'll show her what Hercules is really made of!'

The warm bath water felt like velvet as Alison lowered herself into it. Naked for the first time in she had no real idea how long, the rubber suit had left her sweat soaked, clammy, exhausted and surrounded by an odour that was a combination of her own body smells and the warm latex itself. The atmosphere in the tiny subterranean bathroom felt heavy and oppressive, even though the overhead extractor fan was humming busily.

'I'll take this lot for washing,' Melanie said, scooping up the catsuit, over corset, mask and boots she had peeled from Alison's sticky flesh. 'Master Douglas has apparently chosen a completely new outfit for you to wear tonight, and he's left it laid out on the bed in the bedroom at the very back of the house.'

'Upstairs, you mean?' Alison asked, raising her eyebrows. 'I had the feeling he intended to keep me down here for the duration.' Even Marcia rarely allowed a slave above the ground level, except when Melanie needed assistance with routine chores or maid duties.

'That's what he said,' Melanie confirmed. She clutched the rubber and leatherwear to her bosom with one arm and struggled to get the bathroom door open with the other.

'Now,' she said, 'my instructions are to allow you half

an hour in the tub and then to help you wash your hair. After that, I'm afraid I have to put the cuffs back on your wrists and clip them back to your titties. Sorry about that, but that's the orders. You've also got to wear an ankle hobble.'

'Just to go upstairs?'

'You won't be going straight up to the bedroom,' Melanie said. 'I've been told to take you up as far as the back parlour and leave you there.'

'And then what?'

'I haven't a clue,' Melanie confessed. 'He's said he'll ring for me when I'm needed again. In the meantime, I have to report back to madame and see what jobs she needs me to do.'

The indignity of her position was bad enough for Hannah to endure, but now her recently enlarged breasts were adding their own form of humiliation, as they swung freely beneath her in time to the rocking movement of the cart.

Phoebe, clearly experienced beyond her apparently tender years, lost no time in making sure Hannah could not ignore this fact, using her crop to flick at each nipple in turn, landing stinging blows with an accuracy that quickly had Hannah's eyes filling with salty tears. Surely, she thought, she could not be brought to anything worse than this, but the agonies of her teats had momentarily banished the prospects of Hercules from her mind, and as Phoebe reined the two steeds to a halt in front of the waiting stallion, Hannah knew her greatest trial was still to come.

At last, as the sun began to touch the treetops in the west, Phoebe's approach became more direct, more urgent. With one final backhanded swipe of her crop across Hannah's pulsating buttocks, she leapt down from the wheeled dais, strode across to the hitching rail and began unlooping Hercules' rein. The awesome creature turned obediently at her directing tug, his parody of a head swinging around so that his eyes were looking at his intended victim.

From his groin the carefully laced sheath still pointed directly upwards, but to Hannah's horror, it appeared to have grown since she'd looked at it earlier. The leather, which she had taken to be of a substantial thickness, clearly had a certain amount of give in it and now the black hide positively gleaned from stretching to accommodate its contents. Phoebe walked him up to face Hannah, allowed the two protagonists a few seconds during which to evaluate each other, and then turned her charge about and began unfastening the waist strap that held the top of the intricate webbing that fastened down the penis restrainer.

It did not take her very long and then, as she turned Hercules back around once again, Hannah found herself staring at the most incredible organ she had ever seen. Goggle-eyed, her immediate reaction was to recoil from the monster, but the steel pillory held her as it was meant to, held hypnotically by the sight of something that could surely never penetrate her.

'Sun's nearly down,' Phoebe muttered, almost as if talking to herself. She patted Hercules' naked rump. 'C'mon, cock-steady, time to give this bitch of a filly a good humping.' She shortened the rein and began to lead him towards the rear, but as she passed Hannah's head, she paused and leaned towards her.

'I'll probably leave you in the frame afterwards,' she sneered. 'At least you'll have something to hold you up when Herc's done with you.'

And then the moment had come and there was no more stalling. The decking creaked as the huge male stepped up onto it, shuffling forward until Hannah suddenly felt the heat and weight of his erection pressed against the cleft between her buttocks. Unseen by her, Phoebe reached out to grasp the straining shaft and very deftly repositioned it, placing the swollen head against the labia that revealed an opening that seemed totally inadequate to admit it an entry.

'Mount her, boy!' Phoebe cried, and Hannah heard the crack of the crop landing across Hercules' buttocks to add further encouragement to her command. Hercules began to thrust and Hannah felt Phoebe's hand still there, guiding him lest he might start to slip on the juices that had begun to flow.

Hannah grunted, screwed her eyes shut and willed her muscles to relax. No matter how disgusting she found being taken by a man it was going to happen – was happening – anyway, and anything she could do to ease its passage…

'Nooo-ooo-oo!' Her wail of pain and disbelief forced its way past the gagging bit as her inner labia suddenly yielded, admitting the oversized plum and the first few inches of the shaft itself. Hannah felt as if she was being stretched completely asunder, but this was just the beginning. Slowly, as Phoebe now removed her no longer required guiding hand, Hercules pressed forward, not hurrying in his penetration.

However, studied approach or not, he was still huge, and the air whistled through her nose as he pushed himself fully home, eliciting a final gurgle of disbelief from behind the bit. He leaned against her, the heat of his loins penetrating her crushed buttocks, allowing her to assimilate his size, to fully realise how totally filled she now was. Her fingers clawed helplessly at thin air, two powerless hands scratching at nothingness and, all too late, she realised that she was wriggling against the invasion and that the movement was simply contributing to his enjoyment.

She heard him grunt, felt him withdraw a few inches, pause, and then thrust hard into her, now confident of her ability to take him and aided by the lubrication her treacherous body seemed to be freely manufacturing.

'Nice,' Phoebe trilled. 'Just look at the little lesbian bitch pony now. What a picture for the family album, eh? Your dyke friends will love seeing the rerun of this, I'll bet.'

Hannah drew on her final resources, screaming at Phoebe through the gag, no longer caring that the intended words came out only as garbled nonsense, wishing she were free to tear the bitch's throat out, whilst at the same time detesting herself for the way she was reacting to Hercules. No man had ever managed to bring her to a climax, yet this man – this grotesque parody of both human and animal – was about to do precisely that and she, Major Hannah Levy, former professional soldier, decorated heroine of the state, was powerless to do anything to prevent it.

1.10

'Knowing Ralph the way I do,' Marcia said, shaking her head, 'I doubt this is simply a matter of revenge.' She stood up and walked across to one side of the bay window, looking down into the street below.

'Don't get me wrong,' she continued, speaking over her shoulder, head only half turned towards where Mike was sitting in the other fireside armchair, 'he's vindictive enough to make sure he gets back at anyone he thinks might have crossed him. I warned Hannah to be on her guard after last year, but there's something more to this little lot.'

'You sound very sure about that.' Mike sat, unmoving, watching Marcia's back, her figure little more than a dark silhouette against the fading daylight and the amber glow building up from the streetlights that were beginning to come on outside. She paused, continuing to watch the street for several seconds before continuing.

'I am,' she said eventually. 'For a start, Ralph could have organised a kidnap attempt against any one of us – me, you, the Alley Kat, Honey – we'd be fairly easy targets; certainly easier than the one he's gone for. Hannah Levy is a damned professional, plus she's not exactly the easiest person in the world to track down.'

'Ruth reckons he started with Hannah precisely because she would represent the most formidable challenge,' Mike replied. 'That way, given the fact that Ruth would be bound to contact all the rest of us, including her own group, it would cause us the maximum distress and consternation.'

'That sounds like Ralph all right,' Marcia agreed. 'But what doesn't sound very like him is waiting around for twelve months before eventually striking back.'

'He'd have needed time to reorganise and regroup after the business at Dennison Hall,' Mike suggested. 'That would have taken some doing.' Marcia turned back from the window, her eyes glinting in the reflected lamplight.

'My dear Michael,' she said, with what sounded like a barely suppressed sigh, 'you've known Ralph for nearly as long as I have – maybe not known him so well nor so intimately – but long enough to know that he doesn't leave much to chance.

'When Hannah and her girls trashed the hall, he didn't run off to lick his wounds and set up a new headquarters. No, wherever he's gone, that was already established and was probably always intended to be the real HQ anyway.

Think about it – he had too many guests at Dennison Hall, apart from the targets he was setting up to blackmail. Granted, some of those were too dense to be let out without a nursemaid, but there would have been others he wouldn't have wanted knowing any more about his real intentions.'

'The area where we found all his records was pretty secure,' Mike pointed out. 'That wouldn't have been open to his so-called general public.'

'No, it wouldn't,' Marcia agreed, 'but then there would always be an outside chance that something could go wrong there – as it did – and that's why he would have had a fall back position that was more likely to be the real thing.'

'Ruth suggested something similar,' Mike confirmed. 'Trouble is, even with her contacts, she hasn't got the first bloody idea where to even start looking.'

'Well, Ralph isn't the sort of person to make something like that easy, is he?' Marcia cut off a snort of derision and suddenly wheeled away, crossing to the light switch. There was a click and the room was suddenly flooded with light. Mike looked across to the bay window and nodded meaningfully.

'Didn't you ought to draw the curtains?' he said. 'We'd make good targets from out there.' Marcia shook her head and walked with deliberate slowness back across to the fireside.

'Michael, my dear,' she said softly, 'if Ralph wanted to shoot either of us he wouldn't have waited a year. Oh, he probably wants us all right, but he'll want us alive and kicking. Not to mention screaming, probably,' she added bitterly, and lowered herself into the vacant chair.

'You haven't been taking in what I said, anyway,' she continued, crossing her shapely legs and revealing several more inches of stockinged thigh. 'The revenge thing is only part of it, and if Ralph has waited until now, then he's got a reason for it – a very good reason, too, knowing him.'

'Any ideas what that might be?'

'How long's a piece of string?' Marcia retorted. 'No, I haven't, not exactly, but I've thought about a few possibilities since last summer. For a start, you can narrow things down a bit simply by looking up a copy of his little blackmail lists.

'His regular guests included an awful lot of rich, influential and directly powerful people, right? From his files – from the copies, anyway – we had a rough idea of those who were paying for their "indiscretions" directly, donating large sums of cash to Ralph, selling him a couple of properties on the cheap, that sort of thing.'

'Properties he's since sold off at a handsome profit, according to Ruth,' Mike concurred, 'but I still don't get the point.'

'Well, you obviously haven't studied your copy of the stuff we got from Dennison,' Marcia said, 'at least, not as thoroughly as I have.'

'I read through enough of it to know that no responsible editor would ever publish any of it,' Mike retorted defensively. 'It's one thing to expose a few vices for the odd cabinet minister or peer of the realm, but when you go through that list – well, for fuck's sake Marcia, there'd hardly be enough left afterwards for anyone to form a government with!'

'And not just in this country,' Marcia pointed out. 'We both read through those lists, together and separately. The point I'm making is this – Ralph can call in a lot of favours from a lot of places and he can put pressure in places where pressure really shouldn't be put, not unless we want to find ourselves looking down the barrels of some pretty nasty guns.'

'It had crossed my mind that he was sitting on something of a powder keg, yes,' Mike conceded. 'But he's hardly going to start up a minor war, is he?'

Marcia's immaculately groomed eyebrows arched dramatically. 'No, maybe not a minor war,' she said quietly. 'Just a major one.'

'But what would be the point?'

'What's the point of anything that happens in politics?' Marcia snapped back. 'The point about this, though, is that Ralph is anti-Semitic and has been since he started getting into his neo-Nazi, anti-Communist crap, about a year after I first met him, as it happens.'

'And Hannah and her commandos are all Jewish,' Mike said. 'So, Fuhrer Ralph can't have them getting one over on him, can he?'

'The fact that they're Jewish only complicates things. He'd have had to try paying them back anyway. But the fact that Hannah is Jewish isn't as important as the fact that her father is Jewish also – and before you tell me that's stating something obvious, just shut up and listen or I'll give you a quick lesson on Jewish hereditary and blood lines.

'No, Hannah's father is Joshua Levy. I presume you've heard of him?'

Mike's eyes widened. 'You mean – in the Knesset?' Marcia nodded. 'But Ruth didn't say anything about that.'

'I don't suppose she did,' Marcia said. 'As far as she's concerned, her main reason for calling on you was to warn you and Honey, plus me, Alison and Teddy, to be on our guard. Having done that, the rest of it becomes personal to her and her friends and they've grown used to settling their personal problems, quietly and somewhat permanently.

'The problem apart from that is that there's no knowing where this is all likely to end up, especially if Joshua Levy gets wind of what's going on. There are too many people connected with this, too many people involved in too many volatile global situations and if anything goes wrong, it could set off the sort of chain reaction that the major powers have been trying to avoid since Hiroshima and Nagasaki!'

The Jaguar and its driver stayed faithfully behind Ruth for a further two hours, during which she led a merry dance, heading first towards Swindon, turning off as if to head down into north Hampshire and then veering again, taking the road that she knew would ultimately lead her to Salisbury Plain.

The sun had long since set, the moon rising in an unusually clear sky, but visibility – or the lack of it – did not feature in the plan Ruth had concocted. When the crucial moment came, her shadow could be lost as easily in broad summer daylight as in a thick fog at midnight; it was just a matter of timing and training.

Slowing the MGB to a steady fifty miles an hour, she turned down the volume on the car radio and reached under the seat to retrieve the compact little walkie-talkie, checked that it was on the correct frequency and depressed the transmit button.

'Goldie to Buttermilk.' She spoke quietly and carefully, not bothering to repeat her callsign. These radios were set on rarely used frequencies, but since the days of the first pirate pop radio stations, the Home Office had taken to increasing its random monitoring and the area towards which she was heading was, after all, one of the principal training grounds of the British army.

'Buttermilk. Come in.' The female voice sounded crackly, but clearly audible.

'Buttermilk, Goldie. Approaching point A now. ETA ten minutes.'

'Roger, Goldie. In position. Standing by.'

'Standing by, roger.'

Carefully, Ruth rested the transceiver on the passenger seat and looked into the rear-view mirror, checking that the headlights were still there and nodding when she saw them, one set back from what was probably a mini.

'There's more to it than that, Tiger,' she breathed. 'You watch too many TV programmes and this is the real world out here.' She glanced down at the luminous display on her watch, adjusted Bob Dylan back to a level just above that of the engine and began humming along to the tune.

Phoebe did not bother returning Hannah to the main stable block. Instead, when Hercules had finally withdrawn from her, the young dominatrix simply removed her from the covering frame, fastened her arms back to her sides and led her, weak-kneed and staggering, into the nearby block, where she thrust her into an empty stall, removed her bit and offered her a water bottle, from which she gulped greedily, ignoring the fact that half the contents spilled down the front of her, soaking her breasts and running off to puddle on the floor at her feet.

'I'll leave your bit out for a while,' Phoebe announced, recapping the empty bottle and hanging it on a hook to one side of the split-level door. 'There's some mash in there,' she added, indicating a small steel trough bolted to one of the side walls, just below head height. 'It's not very tasty, but then it's not supposed to be, but it's got vitamin stuff added, so I'd try to get some down my throat, if I were you.'

'Lucky for you you're not, then, isn't it?' Hannah spat back.

Phoebe's top lip curled, revealing perfect white teeth. She stepped close to Hannah, grasping one of the bridle straps at the side of her head. 'Don't get mouthy with me, Tits!' she hissed. 'You're going to be here for a very long time and I could make your miserable life even worse than it's likely to be anyway.

'Take tonight, for instance,' she added, with evident enjoyment. 'I could let those other two beasts in here with you, or I could have done what I said originally and just left you out there on the frame. Hercules gets the run of the paddock at night and he wouldn't need my help to fuck you stupid between now and tomorrow morning.'

Hannah stared at her, tight-lipped.

'The boss man apparently doesn't like you and your kind,' Phoebe sneered. 'From what I've been hearing, his plans are that you end up with tits down to your knees and a cunt you could park a bloody car in, so I doubt he'd give a toss what I did to you in the meantime.'

'I don't suppose he would,' Hannah agreed sullenly.

'I'm glad the message is getting through,' Phoebe said, relaxing her grip and stepping back. She looked Hannah up and down, shaking her head slightly. 'Mind you,' she said thoughtfully, 'it seems a waste, in a way. You've got a very good body. You must keep yourself pretty fit.'

'Goes with the job,' Hannah said.

'Trouble is, Tits,' Phoebe laughed, 'you've got yourself a new job now, haven't you?'

'What's going on now?'

Alison had spent what seemed like an eternity in the back parlour, sitting naked on a high stool, her hands cuffed behind her back, ankles fettered loosely to the wooden legs, her feet kept several inches clear of the carpet. When Douglas had finally reappeared, instead of the expected latex or leather outfit, he was carrying her own blouse and skirt over one arm, together with what appeared to be a set of perfectly ordinary cotton underthings.

Laying his small burden on the table, he quickly unlocked Alison and told her to dress. Getting stiffly to her feet, she stared up at him and repeated the question. Douglas shook his head.

'Marcia will explain,' he said gruffly. 'Change of plans and it sounds urgent, so you'd better get a move on. I'll wait for you outside.'

Alison paused, letting this last sink in, and then laughed. 'Men!' she said, reaching for the white panties that were on top of the small pile. 'Game over, so you start worrying about modesty.' She stepped into the flimsy garment and wriggled it up to her hips. 'Forgive me,' she said, leaning over for the matching brassiere, 'but weren't you the same man who—'

'Shut up!' Douglas sounded embarrassed and his discomfiture added an extra edge to the curt command. He half turned, but paused in the act of reaching for the door handle. 'Obviously,' he said quietly, 'you've never fully understood the house rules.' He turned back and placed his hands on Alison's shoulders, but unlike earlier, his grip was more gentle than firm.

'Mitzi,' he said quietly, 'or whatever your name really is, you and all the others who come here do so voluntarily, knowing near enough what's going to happen to you. I give you something that's maybe missing out there in the real world, but that doesn't mean to say I have to act like a bastard otherwise.'

'No,' Alison agreed. She clipped the brassiere together under her breasts and swivelled it around into position. 'No, I guess not. Though if all that was an act, I must say you're pretty convincing.'

'Would it have been as good if I hadn't been?'

Alison wriggled her second arm through the strap and carefully adjusted the cups into a comfortable position, all the while looking up into his face. At last she smiled. 'No, it wouldn't.' She touched him lightly on the arm. 'Thanks, we must do it again sometime.'

Douglas grinned, and this time did turn away and open the door. 'You can count on it,' he said, stepping out into the passageway.

For Eddie Miller, what had been a 'money for old rope' assignment was fast turning into a nightmare situation and he wished he had risked the few minutes it would have taken to nip out of the car and make use of the toilets at the garage where the girl had spent most of the late afternoon. If only he'd had any way of anticipating the length of her stop.

However, at the time it had looked as if she could go again at any minute – a luxury Eddie himself was currently being denied – and then, as now, he had not dared to risk losing sight of her. The prospect of having to face Smith with that news was not an appealing one; Smith himself was bad enough, but even he seemed scared to death at the possibility of failing whoever it was who was paying for the operation.

'Just stick to the girl,' Smith had growled, 'make a note of everywhere she stops and take photographs to prove it. That shouldn't be beyond even your capabilities.'

Eddie gritted his teeth, shifted his position awkwardly, snatched at the wheel as the road suddenly began to bend right and swore. Why hadn't he used the damned bushes outside that big plush house where she stopped earlier? But then he hadn't felt the need at the time, had he? And the way Smith explained it, the stupid bitch should have been heading for one of the town addresses straight afterwards.

'Bloody women!' he groaned, fighting to ignore the messages his bladder was now screaming in the direction of his brain. 'Bloody – oh shit!'

His foot hit the brake almost before his tortured brain had issued the directive, with the result that the Jaguar's wheels locked immediately, the rear end of the heavy car instantly beginning to fishtail. Automatically Eddie released the pressure, letting the steering wheel whip back through his slack grip and then braked again. This time the result was better, but the road surface now seemed to be covered in a combination of gravel and sand and the bonnet straightened for only a few feet, before it once again slued left and the car went into a wild spin.

The massive outline of the Chieftain tank went past the windscreen three, four times, growing closer with every pass and then Eddie shut his eyes and waited for the impact. But with one final scrunch of scattering grit the Jaguar slid to a standstill, the nearside wing nestling in a clump of bushes that had spent years crawling down the embankment to the roadside.

Heart pounding, Eddie opened his eyes and leaned out of the open driver's window. He saw figures emerging from the top of the tank, heavy boots landing on solid ground and clumping towards him. He reached shakily for the ignition key and killed the motor, at the same time reacting in the time-honoured fashion of the driver who knows he's in the right.

'Fucking idiots!' he screeched. 'Fucking maniac bloody squaddies!' the running figures slid to a halt and he found himself peering up into the faces of two of the biggest soldiers he had ever seen. The nearer one leaned forward, a look of concern on his dye-smeared face.

'You okay there, sir?' he asked. His companion said nothing, but from behind them came another voice, the accent clipped and precise.

'Everything all right there, Corporal White?'

The soldier who had first spoken turned his head slightly in the direction of the sound. 'Sah!' he snapped. 'Seems to be, sah!'

'Jolly good.' The sound of more boots and the officer loomed up alongside the first two men. His face, like those of his subordinates, was smeared with some sort of camouflage paint, but he looked very young for whatever rank it was he held.

'I say!' he exclaimed. 'Jolly nice motor, what?'

'Fuck the motor!' Eddie exclaimed, fumbling for the door handle. 'What the fuck are you doing riding around in that heap of scrap iron with no fucking lights on? That's

118

more to the fucking point!' He finally managed to get his door open and struggled out, hauling himself upright on the reassuringly solid coach-work... except, he realised, staring up at the tank that sat only ten feet in front of him, some things are only reassuringly solid by comparison.

'I say,' the young officer said, reaching out a supportive hand, 'are you okay there?' Eddie stared at him, eyes blazing, and only the presence of the two hulking rankers persuaded him that driving a fist into the pale face might not be a wise move. Instead, he reverted to words to make his case, but vocabulary had never been Eddie's strong suit.

'All right?' he echoed. 'All right? Yes, but no thanks to you wankers!' He pointed with a shaking arm. 'Where's your fucking lights? It's fucking dark, in case you haven't noticed!'

The young officer looked blank. 'Well, yes, I had noticed that, sir,' he replied smoothly, 'seeing as this was scheduled as a night raid simulation exercise.'

'That and the lack o' a bit o' sunshine,' Corporal White offered, though he addressed his contribution out of the side of his mouth and to his original companion, who nodded sagely.

Eddie was slowly recovering something akin to composure. 'I'm going to sue the fuck out of you lot,' he stormed. 'Crashing around in the middle of the night in something that size. What's your name, son?'

The officer, who showed no reaction to being addressed in this manner, other than the merest flicker of an eyelid, looked past Eddie to the Jaguar.

'Captain Roderick Green, Fourth Tank Brigade,' he replied languidly. 'Jolly lucky you didn't hit Bertha,' he added, completing what had evidently been an assessment of the car's condition. 'She's a bit solid, even for a nice bus like that.'

'You don't seem to understand,' Eddie stormed. 'The

fact I didn't hit *Bertha* has got fuck all to do with the price of eggs! You weren't showing any lights!' Captain Green looked at him in the manner schoolteachers had once reserved for Eddie and the rest of his particular bunch of cronies; a look that said, 'If only you'd pay attention you might just learn something useful before one of us dies.'

'Not a good idea to show lights in enemy territory,' he said, 'and this sector is designated as part of the Black Forest for this exercise.'

'But it's a public highway!' Eddie raged.

Captain Green again gave him a pityingly patient look and shook his head. 'I'm afraid not, old chap,' he said, and waved his arm in an expansive gesture that was intended to indicate not just Bertha, the all too solid looking tank, but just about everything as far as the eye could see, or would have seen had it been daylight. 'This is part of the tank ranges, actually. Main road's back that way.' His arm swung round in a wide arc and his finger stabbed back in the direction from which Eddie had come. 'About four miles back, actually. There's a dirty great sign and a barrier across the road.'

'Not when I came through there wasn't,' Eddie snarled. 'There's nothing there at all, not even a red light.'

However, by the time he finally retraced his route, some ten minutes later, sure enough he had to stop the car and get out to drag the barbed wire covered trestles to one side, lacerating his hands in the process and adding, in no small way, to the murderous depths of his mood.

'I suppose you've come to gloat, you perverted bastard.' Hannah stood against the rear wall of her stall, staring up at the massive figure of Ralph Hancock, only too well aware of her own vulnerability, but now past caring. Hancock, arms folded across his silk shirted chest, stood in the doorway and looked at her without replying immediately. Finally, he stepped forward and moved with a speed not normally associated with a man of his build. His right arm shot out, right palm crashing across the side of Hannah's face, knocking her sideways with such force that she would have fallen had not the side wall of the stall intervened to keep her upright.

Hancock stepped back. 'Watch your mouth, whore,' he grated.

Hannah shook her head, clearing the tears from her eyes, and drew herself upright again. 'That's about your limit, isn't it?' she sneered. 'Hit a woman, especially one with her arms tied, who can't even think about fighting back. Go on,' she urged, as Hancock tensed for a second assault. 'Go on, hit me again. What does it prove, eh? Oh yes, you're a big man, aren't you?'

With an effort Hancock restrained himself, but the expression of total distaste did not waver at all. 'You won't be so smart by the time I've finished with you,' he sneered. 'And that tongue of yours can easily be cropped, believe me.'

'Oh, I believe you all right,' Hannah replied, leaning back against the rear wall and breathing as heavily as the tortuous corset girth would permit. 'Your sort will stoop to any level.'

Again Hancock's eyes flared, but this time he did not make any move towards her. Instead, he refolded his arms. 'Nice try,' he said. 'Try to wind me up and maybe I'll kill you, is that the idea? Well, forget it. Dying would be an easy option compared to what I've got planned for you and your friends.'

'Assuming you get to them before they get to you.'

'Ah, but this time around,' Hancock said, 'I'm not only waiting for them, I know who they all are *and* where to find them.'

'I doubt that,' Hannah said. 'Oh yes, I expect you've located a couple of them, or at least found out their names,

121

but I don't think for one minute you know them all. That's why you've brought me here, isn't it? You think that by filming what your perverts are doing to me and then sending the film to whichever of our group you can reach, that'll have them all putting their hands up and throwing themselves onto your so-called mercy in order to save me.'

'Something fairly close to that, yes,' Hancock agreed.

'You don't know people as well as you think you do,' Hannah sneered. 'You don't think they'd take your word for anything, do you?'

'Time will tell,' Hancock replied smoothly. 'In the meantime, I'm not exactly in a great hurry. After all, we've got you to play with and what a good start we've made, eh? I mean, look at you now; just a few days and already a complete transformation. The perfect blonde bimbo.'

'Well,' Hannah said, shuffling her hoof boots deliberately wider. 'What are you waiting for? You've got me and I can't stop you, so why not just fuck me and get it over with, huh?'

'Is that what you think this is all about?' Hancock stared at her with transparent distaste. 'Do you really think I want to even touch a whore like you? Sully myself on something that isn't even fit for a stable?

'No, I don't think so. You're for the likes of Hercules now – all cock and no brains. Just think about that, bitch, whenever you're wriggling on the end of a prize cock. That's all you're good for, something to exercise our stallions on and not even good enough to be a brood mare.

'We have to get back to Teddy,' Alison said firmly. 'Hancock knows exactly where to find him and you know what an inept idiot Teddy can be.'

'But you've got that butler fellow, two gardeners, Teddy's valet bloke and the chauffeur, so-called,' Mike pointed out. 'On top of which, I know for a fact that Teddy had all manner of security alarms fitted after the Dennison

Hall nonsense. The place is like a castle.'

'Not *like* a castle,' Alison reminded him. 'It *is* a castle. Trouble is, it was built to withstand Tudor technology and if Rafe Hancock has managed to snatch someone like Hannah Levy, our would be defences will be woefully inadequate.'

'The chauffeur is some sort of ex-special forces guy, isn't he?' Mike said. 'Teddy told me he recruited him more as a personal bodyguard for the pair of you. I know he was worried about reprisals from Hancock, so he's not as daft as you seem to think, young lady.'

'I know,' Alison replied, 'and I love him dearly anyway, but he needs to be warned.'

'I've already phoned him,' Marcia interrupted. 'He's on his way up as we speak – with his bodyguard driving,' she added, smiling reassuringly. 'And,' she continued, 'as soon as he gets here, I think it's time to do as Ruth Goldman advised; get the pair of you tickets for somewhere like New Zealand.'

'And do what?' Alison retorted. 'Count bloody sheep and skulk around until we think it's safe to come home again?'

'Something like that,' Mike said.

'No way,' Alison said. 'Running never solved anything. All we'd achieve is a stay of execution, if you pardon the terminology. We disappear to the antipodes, Hancock mops up everyone left behind and then, when we come back he'll be waiting, same as before.'

'And I suppose you have a better idea?'

'As it happens, I do. I'm not saying it'll work any better, but it certainly won't be any worse and at least we won't have to run halfway across the globe in the meantime.' She turned to Marcia.

'You had a number to contact Hannah, presumably,' she stated. 'Have you any way of getting hold of Ruth Goldman now?'

There was a moment's silence, broken eventually by Mike. He reached inside the top pocket of his jacket and withdrew the small rectangle of card between two fingers. 'I have,' he said, 'but I'd rather wait until we've had time to discuss this with Teddy. I think he should have a say in this.'

'Fair enough,' Alison agreed, grimly, 'but he'll bloody well say what I tell him to, otherwise he can find someone else to change his nappies!'

Captain Roderick Green stood and watched as the dark Jaguar's taillights disappeared back down the track. Meanwhile, behind him, Bertha clanked and rumbled back into the darkness and mud from where she had come and then, finally, he was alone and everything was silent.

'Neatly done, Roddy.' The soft female voice seemed to drift out of thin air, before its owner slithered down the grassy slope to land a foot or two from where Green was standing. He turned, smiled at Ruth Goldman and blew her a kiss.

'My pleasure, dear gel,' he quipped. 'Not a very well mannered chappie, as it happens,' he added. 'Bit of an oaf. Wet his bloody pants as well. D'you reckon he's got some sort of fetish, only one reads about these things?'

'Who knows?' Ruth said. 'Anyway, the girls will pick up on him back at the main road junction. He'll have to stop to shift the barrier and Becky will pop a bug onto the car while he's otherwise occupied.'

Roddy Green – whose family name had once been Greenberg – knew better than to ask too many questions, but he'd known Ruth since they'd been children, playing in a mutual aunt's orchard and later capsizing a canoe on the nearby river.

'Sure everything's all right now?' he asked. 'I mean, it's just that, well, you know, if you need a bit of extra firepower, that sort of thing, well, you only need to ask.'

Ruth leaned across and kissed him on the cheek, immediately regretting the gesture and remembering, too late, just how foul camouflage make-up could taste.

'Thanks anyway,' she said. 'I don't think this is likely to be your sort of show, Roddy, but if we need the heavy artillery I'll be sure to give you a shout. You can bring Bertha along, if you like.'

Roddy grinned. 'Bertha and her seven sisters,' he said. 'Bloody brass has given me a whole squadron of the beasties to play silly buggers with.'

'Maybe so,' Ruth said, 'but I'm sure they'd have something to say if eight tanks suddenly went missing.'

'You think so?' Roddy snorted. 'This isn't Israel now, you know. This is the *British* army and the day HQ knows exactly where all its armour is, the British army will be in big trouble!'

1.11

For two days Hannah had been left in relative peace. Having savoured the first stage of his revenge and made sure that Hannah knew how much he enjoyed gloating over his victory, Ralph Hancock apparently lost interest in her. And even Kristin failed to appear, leaving her in Phoebe's charge, with occasional visits from Rose, who apparently liked to keep a regular check on all the stable blocks.

On the third day, however, Phoebe announced that it was time to begin Hannah's new regime.

'It's one thing to have your tits getting bigger,' she said, 'but quite another to let you go to fat. Eventually you'll be available for pony duties to all of Master Rafe's special visitors, but first we have to make sure you're properly trained.

'Oh yes,' she added, lifting the bit to Hannah's mouth and then withdrawing it again, 'I forgot. Hercules will cover you three times every day. In between times you'll be kept plugged with a stretcher dildo. The vet reckons it'll take about a month before your vaginal muscles weaken completely and another month before they atrophy.

'At that stage your clitoris will be surgically removed, as Master Rafe has decided that you will then no longer derive any pleasure from the sexual act.'

'Do you think I derive any pleasure from it now?' Hannah asked bitterly. For a moment she thought she detected something like pity in Phoebe's expression and tone.

'No,' the younger girl said. 'I don't suppose you do, any more than I ever did with a man.'

'And *you* call *me* a lesbian bitch?' Hannah snorted. 'Talk about pots and kettles!'

'Maybe,' Phoebe replied, 'but then I've got enough sense to know when to forget my preferences and now I have this job, so the problem no longer arises.'

'I'd call you a hypocrite,' Hannah retorted, 'except that I can think of worse things you are.'

'And I'm the one holding the bit and the whip,' Phoebe reminded her. She relaxed her stance temporarily, placing one hand upon her hip, the bit dangling from her fingers.

'Listen, Tits,' she went on, 'this is going to happen whether you like it, or whether I like it. You fucked the big boss off last year and he's not the type to forgive and forget. Plus, as you may well have guessed by now, he's a bit of a racist, especially towards you people.

'Now, I'm only following orders—'

'Where have I heard that line before?' Hannah sneered, but Phoebe raised a warning hand.

'Following orders,' she continued, 'but I do have a certain amount of personal choice within those orders. For instance, you're going to get well and truly shafted by Herc, morning, noon and night, but I don't have to fix you to the frame every time – not if you co-operate.'

'You mean, if I just bend over and offer myself to that thing like some brood mare in season?'

Phoebe raised a single eyebrow. 'That's about the strength of it,' she agreed, 'and while that might not exactly appeal to you, it's got to be slightly more dignified, hasn't it?'

'Only slightly,' Hannah muttered.

'Plus I can lay off the whip a bit, though the boss says you're to have a dozen strokes on the buttocks every day, even if you are behaving.'

'I see,' Hannah sighed. 'Then I guess I don't have much choice, do I?' She knew that the more she was seen to co-operate, the more likely it was that guards would drop.

'I thought you'd see sense eventually,' Phoebe said, raising the bit for a second time. 'Now, let's have the horsey mouth open, shall we? It's a lovely day and I've a brand new sulky ready for you to pull. Ten miles around the estate should get you nicely toned up for Hercules' lunch time session.'

'What do you mean, you haven't seen the girl for two days?' Paul Madison rounded on the portly figure who trailed forlornly across the car park of the *Fulchester Arms* pub, and the expression on his face would have frozen the blood in many men a lot tougher than Eddie Miller.

'I tried to tell you, Mr Smith,' Eddie whined, 'she

wandered off the main road and I nearly smashed the car into a fucking great tank.'

'In the middle of a tank practice range, you say? And just exactly what do you think she was doing in a tank range in the middle of the night?' Madison, alias Dennis Smith, the name by which most of his hired recruits knew him, clenched his fists, his eyes narrowing and, if there had been fewer people about and it had not been broad daylight, Eddie suspected his current boss and paymaster would have floored him.

'The truth of the matter is, Eddie,' Madison said deliberately, 'that you actually lost her some miles before that, then managed to lose yourself. Someone like the Goldman woman would know better than to ignore all those warning signs and fences they have down there.'

'But that's just the point, boss,' Eddie persisted, 'there weren't no signs, nor no barriers.' He wisely elected not to mention the mysterious way in which both had reappeared by the time he made his return journey; Smith would only suggest that he'd gone back by a different route, or else just had his eyes more on the job following the near collision.

'Either way,' Madison said, 'you've lost the girl and now we don't know where to start looking for her again. You tried the address in Kingston?'

'That's where I've been almost ever since,' Eddie said, nodding. 'I figured she'd have to go back there some time, for clothes and stuff, you know?'

'And what about now? Who's watching the place while you're here?'

'Tommy, my cousin's lad, the one who delivered the package to her in the first place. I rang him to take over from me.'

'Well then,' Madison said icily, 'you'd better get back there and take over again, hadn't you? The woman met your cousin's lad face-to-face, in case you'd forgotten, so if she recognises him hanging around her gaff, she'll leg it before he knows what's happening.'

'I – I know that, boss,' Eddie said, 'but Tom was the only one I could get on the phone in time and the lady who answered on your special number told me you'd already left to come here with the cash.'

'Ah, yes,' Madison said, as if suddenly remembering. 'The cash.' He let the word hover in the air between them for a few seconds. 'I suppose you think I'm going to pay you for your ineptitude.'

'Well, I did get the package delivered and I sent Tommy back with the photographs showing her going into that posh bird's gaff,' Eddie protested. 'Like I said, the rest wasn't my fault, honest.'

Madison hesitated and then reached inside his jacket to withdraw one of the four envelopes he had placed there earlier. He handed it to Eddie Miller, but retained a firm grip on it when Eddie made to take it.

'This is just to cover expenses so far,' Madison said. 'The balance when you pick up with the woman again and start getting me some more addresses – addresses I don't already know, that is.'

That was the trouble with using a certain class of petty criminal, Madison thought, as he watched Eddie shuffling morosely back towards the Jaguar. They were cheap, largely unobtrusive, didn't ask unnecessary questions and knew enough to keep their mouths shut down the pub and little enough to matter if they didn't; unfortunately, they were generally not well endowed in the thinking department, untrained for this sort of operation and quick to blame failure on anything other than their own ineptitude.

But at least they knew better than to expect full payment for failure, even if they felt obliged to try it on, and Eddie Miller's cock-up would save Madison a few bob ultimately, without doing any great harm to the overall scheme. Unbeknown to Miller, Madison had posted a somewhat more skilled operative to watching an address in West Sussex, where the current tenant was reputed to have been a member of the team that had raided Dennison Hall the previous summer. And, sure enough, Ruth Goldman – or someone matching her description with uncanny accuracy – had turned up there the previous evening; leaving after two hours with a brand new tail less than a hundred yards behind her.

Part Two

2.1

Mistress Rose MacAuliffe studied the figure in the mirror, gazing at her reflection critically for several minutes and, not for the first time recently, concluded that Mother Nature had at last seen fit to be kind to her, even if, as a teenager, Rose had considered there to be sufficient cause to see otherwise.

A stocky child she had, at the onset of puberty, shot upwards with a speed that was nothing short of alarming, but where most of her contemporaries had lost what was euphemistically described as 'puppy fat' during these teen years, Rose simply saw her fleshiness converting itself into muscle. And the square jaw and somewhat flat nose had then contributed their parts to give her a mannish air that a height in excess of six feet did little to contradict.

In school Rose excelled at sports, when she chose to, but at nothing else. Her classmates, whilst not quite brave enough to do so openly, taunted her behind her back in ways that ensured Rose knew that she was the butt of their jokes, and when the time came for one of the all too frequent school dances, Rose was the one left standing, not just as a wallflower, but as a neglected sunflower of the most statuesque proportions. Boys looked, evaluated, considered – and then retreated.

Brought up by an aunt, after her parents' divorce and her mother's subsequent death in a skiing accident, Rose suddenly found herself a full orphan at the age of twenty-one, when the father she had never known was killed in mysterious circumstances in the middle east. She also found herself independently wealthy, if not extravagantly so, for her departed sire had managed to acquire a house, a small holding in Wales and several thousand pounds worth of stocks and shares, which came to Rose as his only surviving relative.

Selling the house she had never seen, Rose retreated west of the Taff and set up a solo lifestyle in the two-bedroomed cottage that went along with the smallholding, rented out her puny acreage to a local riding school and settled down with the intention of becoming a writer. With no need to work for an income and a retreat that kept her miles from the humanity that had scorned her so far, everything was set for a successful career; everything, that is, but for one flaw.

Rose as a writer was hopeless, and it seemed far too late to make up for the years she had wasted at school. Embittered, lonely and frustrated, the future did not hold much promise, but then a quirk of fate – as quirks of fate so often do – brought about a change in her life and outlook so dramatic that Rose could hardly believe it was true.

In an auction room in Haverfordwest, she bid for and bought a tea chest full of old crockery, having spotted a jug among the general detritus that was clearly Victorian and which took her fancy. With little competition she secured the lot for the princely sum of three shillings and sixpence, hefted it with her usual ease into the back seat of her Morris Minor and took it home, where the jug was instated above the fireplace and the remainder of the junk consigned to the rickety shed behind the cottage.

And there it might have stayed indefinitely, but for a chance meeting with the wife of the local vicar, who happened to mention that she was collecting for a jumble sale in the church hall. Happy enough to be rid of what she considered to be worse than surplus, Rose offered to donate the china and returned home to sort through it and throw out anything that was chipped or cracked, not wanting it to appear that she was the sort of person prepared only to give things that were completely useless.

To her surprise, the cups, saucers, sugar bowl and two small teapots had survived thus far unscathed, thanks to the fact that they had originally been wrapped in old newspaper and magazines, and only the top few pieces had been unwrapped for the auction. To her even greater surprise, the very bottom layer had been wrapped and padded with pages torn from the sort of magazine Rose had only ever heard of in the Sunday papers.

Her initial reaction was to throw the things out, or to burn them, but a deep-rooted curiosity found her smoothing out the crumpled paper and reading the contents, firstly open-mouthed and then, as the full import of what she was reading struck her, with her square jaw firmly set with new-found determination.

The magazine itself was, of course, some considerable time out of date, but a car journey down to Swansea the following week produced five much newer issues of three different glossy publications, which Rose devoured eagerly once back in her solitary fortress.

Not having a telephone at the smallholding was a potential disadvantage, but this was overcome by the expedient of renting a post office box number and calling back the replies to the advert she placed the next month, using the public call-box at the end of the village. There were six replies in total, three of which Rose immediately dismissed, but of the remaining fifty percent, one in particular intrigued her most.

She had anticipated that her potential clientele would be exclusively male, a chance to extract a little retribution for the way the opposite sex had regarded her up until now sweetened even further by the fact that they appeared eager to pay ridiculous sums of money to be beaten by a six foot amazon. What she had not expected, however, was the short letter from one Geraldine Harper-Gibbs. Perhaps, Rose thought, it was someone's idea of a joke, but the ensuing phone call confirmed Geraldine's enquiry as being genuine and an appointment was made, leaving Rose with but three days in which to make a few preparations that – if what she had read in the magazines was to be believed – were almost mandatory.

2.2

Geraldine Harper-Gibbs looked as if she were somewhere in her mid to late thirties and was petite and blonde, although the colouring owed less to nature than it did to peroxide. She was not particularly pretty, but she was dainty and feminine, everything that Rose was not, a fact that was to guarantee Mrs Harper-Gibbs the soundest and most satisfactory thrashing she could ever have craved. She would also have been astounded to know that Rose would have quite cheerfully administered it even without the inducement of the twenty-five pounds fee she handed over upon arrival at the pub in the next village.

Ordering Geraldine to leave her own car in the car park there, Rose thrust her into the rear seat of her Morris and, when they were suitably far enough along the rather winding back route that she had decided upon, and the last of the daylight now having faded, handed her a simple black linen bag.

'Put it over your head, slave girl!' she commanded, adopting the terminology she believed to be *de rigeur*, and was gladdened when Geraldine obeyed without demur or hesitation. 'Now tighten the drawstring and tie it off in a bow, but don't strangle yourself.' Once again, Geraldine did precisely as instructed. So far, so good.

Back at the cottage Rose's hurried efforts awaited. In the spare bedroom, which she had emptied of the few old pieces of furniture that had been left there, a sturdy carpenter's trestle dominated the centre of the bare floorboards, fixed down with four hefty screws and running parallel to the window. Near the foot of each supporting leg was fixed a broad strap; Rosie had purchased several leather belts and cut down four for the purpose, whilst a fifth belt, uncut, was screwed to the horizontal beam itself.

Along this four inch wide beam, Rose had tacked a strip of carpet, affording some protection against possible splinters, and on the wall opposite one end of the structure, the end she intended Geraldine would be facing, a second-hand mirror would enable the helpless woman to watch herself being punished.

'Get your clothes off,' Rose ordered, without making any move to remove the bag from Geraldine's head. 'Just throw them behind you and then stand and wait till I return.' Leaving her blindfolded client to struggle on as best she could, Rose closed and bolted the door behind her, stepped through into her own bedroom and sat down on the bed with a huge sigh, fighting to control her erratic breathing and the trembling that had suddenly beset her hands.

From the bedside cabinet she took a small bottle of vodka, twisted off the cap and gulped a large mouthful down neat, gasping as the raw spirit burned her throat, but following it with another generous draught almost immediately. Slowly, as she began to remove her own clothing, the shaking began to subside.

She had wanted to buy herself some sort of corset, but the best she had been able to manage at such short notice was an elasticated all in one control garment. At least, she thought, as she wriggled into it, it was black, the colour featured most prominently in all the magazine stories and photographs.

Seamed black stockings came next, clipped neatly to the suspender tabs on the corselet, and then came the shoes. It had taken visits to five shops before Rose managed to find a pair of black stiletto court shoes in her size, and they were a tight fit, as she discovered the previous day when practising the precarious art of walking on five inch heels.

She fastened the gusset between her thighs and took the gloves from the top drawer of her dressing table. These were her favourite item of them all; long, black kid, soft and supple and very expensive, as had been everything else on offer in that so formal dress shop in Cardigan. Next time, she reflected, she would make the return trip to Swansea; it wasn't really that much further and the larger city had to have more choice than anywhere in her part of Wales.

Slowly, lovingly, she smoothed the gloves up her arms. They were long, reaching almost to her armpits, and the supple wafer-thin hide clung to her like a second skin. She stood, savouring the feeling and running kid clad fingers down kid clad limbs, studying what she could see of herself in the too small mirror and realising, far too late now to do anything about it, that she should have thought about make-up, something she never usually bothered with.

'Next time,' she whispered, and found herself grinning idiotically at the awesome figure that looked back at her. 'Assuming you fancy a next time after this, madame muck.'

Back in the spare bedroom Geraldine was standing demurely, head bowed, bag still in place, hands clasped loosely behind her back. Trying not to stagger in her unaccustomed heels, Rose circled, studying her naked body and noting the way the waiting woman was beginning to tremble slightly.

'I hope you haven't tried to remove the bag,' Rose challenged. The bag in question began to shake side to side, the denying motion causing Geraldine's breasts to jiggle enticingly. On a whim, Rose reached out and took a hold of one of the swollen nipples. Immediately, a small sigh came from under the makeshift hood.

'I see,' Rose muttered and released her grip. She walked behind and studied the quite pert buttocks, the soon-to-be subjects of her attentions and, without warning, dealt a firm slap across each of them in turn. Geraldine's only response was to lurch forward a bare half pace and give a muffled grunt.

'I think they need much more severe treatment than that, don't you, slave girl?' This time the bag nodded eagerly, if a bobbing bag could be described as looking eager. 'Right then.'

With some small difficulty, Rose guided her victim forward and finally managed to get her straddling the rear end of the trestle. Leaving her standing in this awkward position, she stooped and secured each ankle in turn, smiling with satisfaction at the way in which the cut-down belts performed the task for which she had prepared them.

'Down!' Rose snapped, and thrust a hand between Geraldine's naked shoulder blades, forcing her to lie along the carpeted beam and drawing her wrists down to the waiting straps. The positioning of everything had involved quite a lot of guesswork and with Geraldine being so small her arms were fully stretched by the time Rose finished buckling the stout leather, but not one murmur of complaint came from within the black linen.

Eager to complete this stage of the proceedings, Rose drew the fifth belt over the small of Geraldine's back and tightened it to the last but one hole, pressing her belly hard against the unsympathetic surface and forcing her buttocks upwards, so it seemed. Stepping back, Rose studied the effect, mentally comparing it with the photographs which had been her inspiration and from which she had derived her design ideas. All in all, she concluded, it wasn't an unfavourable comparison.

Finding a suitable gag had given Rose her final problem. In the magazine photos, most of the victims seemed to be wearing something described as a ball-gag, an item Rose was sure would not be readily available in West Wales. The pet shop in Haverfordwest offered a selection of hard rubber balls for dogs and she duly purchased three in different sizes, together with a thin dog collar which offered possibilities as a means of securing one of them in the mouth.

However, game as she was to try almost anything at least once, a satisfactory means of first securing the leather to the rubber did not immediately spring to mind. On the point of opting, if only temporarily, for a simple cloth gag instead, she was on the way out of the shop when she saw the rubber dog bones from the corner of her eye.

She purchased two and, from the hardware shop next door but one, bought a hank of smooth cord and returned home relatively satisfied. Now, as she picked up the longer bone, a length of cord slipped over the 'joint' protrusion at either end, Rose knew she had made a good choice. Loosening the drawstring around Geraldine's neck, she lifted the bag far enough to expose her mouth.

'Open wide, bitch doggie!' she snapped, unable to stop herself grinning, and forced the foul tasting rubber between Geraldine's teeth when she duly complied. The cords drawn behind Geraldine's neck and tied off, the helpless woman was now effectively gagged, her teeth bared like the ponies who were exercised regularly in the fields behind the cottage. 'Stay, bitch,' Rose grunted, barely stopping herself from giggling, and turned to fetch the selection of bamboo canes that had been her final purchase.

They felt damp to the touch still, evidence of their overnight immersion in a bath of brine, but not as damp, Rose realised suddenly, as the gusset between her thighs. Bending forward she peered down in disbelief, but there was no denying the slightly darker patch spreading in the already dark fabric.

Breathing slowly, she extended a gloved finger and touched herself there, gasping at the sudden shock wave that coursed up through her body at the first contact. For several seconds she stood gazing down, and then a slow smile began to spread across her square features. Revenge and money – and now this? It was too good to be true!

Gathering up the canes in one hand she straightened up, thrust her shoulders back and stalked arrogantly back into the rear bedroom, dropping the bamboos in a clatter and snatching the hood the rest of the way off Geraldine's bowed head.

'Eyes up, bitch!' she thundered. Geraldine raised her head slowly, to find herself staring at her own reflected discomfiture and the sight of Rose standing behind her, hands on hips, legs astride, every inch the dominatrix for which she had travelled so far. A shiver ran along her spine and the damp patch of carpet beneath her sex lips continued to grow, so that even the somewhat inexperienced Rose now noticed it.

'You slut – look at you,' Rose continued, getting into the swing of things, 'dripping your pussy all over my nice new whipping frame. I'd say that deserves a real punishment, wouldn't you?'

The punishment was duly administered. The cane Rose

used was about three eighths of an inch in diameter and perhaps three and a half feet long, supple enough to be slightly whippy, without being thin enough to risk it splintering. Later on Rose was to grow quite expert in the matter of canes, whips and crops, but for this, her first assignment, she preferred to err on the side of caution.

The rod hissed through the air and exploded across both nates simultaneously, the sharp report as cane met flesh sounding unnaturally loud in the echoing room. For a moment Rose wondered if she had overdone it, but to her surprise Geraldine merely twitched and let out a sharp gasp, although, as Rose was eventually to learn, it was only the fifth strap across the small of her back that prevented her from bucking.

Slowly. That was supposed to be the key. Don't rush at it, don't flail. Wait, breathe, aim… *crack*!

Wait, breathe, aim… *crack*!

A fourth time and a low howl reverberated around the walls and tears began to appear in Geraldine's eyes, tears that she blinked away furiously as she screwed her eyes tightly shut. Seeing this, Rose paused, tapped the end of the cane on the back of Geraldine's head and tapped the toe of her right shoe in unison.

'Eyes open, slut slave,' she ordered. 'You watch yourself, understand?'

Slowly, the red rimmed eyes opened and Rose resumed the ritual.

The agreed number had been twelve, but when Geraldine twice exhibited reluctance to open her eyes before further strokes, Rose added an extra cut as punishment and then, for good measure and tidiness sake, delivered a fifteenth cut to finish off. By now Geraldine's chest was heaving and the tears flowed freely, but so did the juices from her displayed lower lips and her clitoris was so engorged that it was clearly visible and obviously ready for the final satisfaction that Geraldine had stated she would give

140

herself.

Rose, however, was not now prepared for relinquishing control so readily. Instead, she tossed the cane aside, unclipped the soaking gusset that covered her own saturated sex, walked around in front of Geraldine, untied the cords at the back of her neck and snatched the bone from her mouth. Grasping a handful of the blonde hair, she hauled Geraldine's head up and back, spread her legs and thrust her crotch towards the saliva coated lips.

'Get your tongue in here, bitch,' she leered, hardly able to believe it was her saying such things and expecting a babble of protest from her victim. Instead, to her complete astonishment, Geraldine stretched out her tongue and when, ten seconds later, Rose exploded into the first orgasm she had ever experienced, the mouth remained firmly there, sucking and massaging until the tidal-wave finally washed back out into the sea of utter exhaustion and bewilderment.

2.3

At last Rose turned away from the long mirror and walked slowly across her room to stand in the high bay window. Looking out into the gathering twilight she smiled to herself, remembering, as she now did with increasing regularity, that first encounter with Geraldine and the subsequent initial encounters with her first two male clients, one a stockbroker from Bristol, the other a gentleman farmer from Herefordshire.

They had paid well and revelled in her scathing treatment of them, even introducing her to another three willing 'victims'.

A rerun of the original magazine advert yielded four more suitable contacts, including a second female named, so she claimed, Gwen, but whom the contents of her handbag revealed, was really the Honourable Gwyneth Morgan, aged forty-six and not the thirty-nine she originally claimed to be.

By now Rose felt disposed towards satisfying Geraldine's needs without payment, permitting the only too willing woman to act as her occasional maid and assistant and letting her sleep overnight as often as practicable, though the need to use the spare bedroom as a punishment chamber created problems in that respect. True, Geraldine happily curled up in Rose's bed and her darting tongue was ever willing to pay suitable homage, but allowing a slave to share one's bed too regularly was not, apparently, the 'done thing'.

Meanwhile, despite the remote location of the cottage, the presence of the riding school horses in Rose's fields and the regular incursions of small batches of pupils and instructors meant that a certain amount of care had to be exercised. Tongues wagged only too frequently in such communities and the bush telegraph meant that the absence of phone lines to many properties was scarcely noticed.

However, two problems were solved in one. The riding school went broke, the horses were sold and Rose was left with a somewhat dilapidated stable building at about the time she first saw the article on human pony training. With a glint in her eye she set off for the town to find a reputable general builder and, a few weeks later, Geraldine was installed in one of the three newly refurbished stalls that now occupied half the space inside the completely renovated stable block.

It was not a permanent arrangement, of course. Geraldine's banker husband persisted in returning to their country home at least twice a month, and expected to find his dutiful spouse waiting upon his return. But there were soon other candidates for the remaining stalls and for the specially designed bridles and harnesses that Rose ordered during an extremely educational and illuminating weekend journey to London. Soon, whether they originally requested it or not, her visitors, male and female alike, would find themselves stabled for a few hours prior to their anticipated punishment session, and then returned to a stall to contemplate again afterwards.

The local builder was engaged once again, this time to erect a high chain-linked fence, together with a secure gate, effectively denying access from the slightly wider lane that serviced the narrow lane leading up to the cottage and stable. Thus relatively secure, Rose acquired her first pony cart, recruiting the long suffering, but never complaining Geraldine to help her get to grips with the finer points of pony driving. A second cart was not long in following the first and very soon the clientele included those who preferred to drive, as well as those who wished to be driven, plus a few who came to be driven whether they wished it or not.

Meanwhile, despite these additional outlays and a few smaller investments that expansion – and Rose herself – deemed indispensable, the balance figure in her bank account never seemed to reduce. In fact, quite the opposite was true and, had Rose thought about this logically at the time, she would have realised that this was not necessarily as good a thing as at first it appeared.

Whereas the long arm of the law appeared to fall short of Rose's cottage and booming enterprise, the longer arm of the Inland Revenue displayed no such oversights. A certain tax inspector of less moral fibre than Her Majesty's civil service would normally have expected from their senior employees, apart from issuing a demand for exorbitant amounts of back tax, also suggested to a cousin who worked at the less salubrious end of Fleet Street that there might be 'something worth sniffing around after' beyond the gate and fence he had encountered on his own one reconnaissance visit.

The resulting publicity had not lasted long, it was true, but the effect on Rose's cosy existence was catastrophic. With the exception of Geraldine – who even kept a low profile for a few weeks – her clients deserted her as one and then, to add insult to injury, the tax office issued a summons alleging that she had evaded even larger sums of tax than those they were already demanding.

Broke to the extent of being declared bankrupt, Rose was in despair. She kept her car by the simple expedient of lending it to Geraldine to hide for her, ignored the summons to appear in person in the local courts and found a small bedsit, using the few hundred pounds she had managed to keep away from public scrutiny.

Alone in her room she counted her funds and did some calculations. If she were prudent, she reckoned, she could survive for maybe six months, but that was all. Once the money ran out she would be in deeper trouble still, for the moment she tried to get a job she would surely be recognised.

Even before that dreaded day came she lived on the edge of her nerves, every knock at the outside door of the house reducing her to a nervous wreck, a knock at the door of her own room sending her stomach into somersaults of terror. Until one day, when she answered such a knock, expecting to find Geraldine standing in the passageway, she found herself confronted with one of the biggest men she had ever met, a man who towered over even her.

'Miss MacAuliffe?' he said pleasantly, extending a hand. 'You don't know me, but I think I might be able to help you. Permit me to introduce myself.' He released his iron grip and stepped past her into the shabby room.

'My name,' he said quietly, 'is Ralph Hancock, and I have a proposition I think will interest you.'

2.4

Interest, Rose thought, smiling in the darkness, was something of an understatement. She had sat on the bed and listened while Hancock outlined his offer, scarcely able to believe what she was hearing. Quite how he had found her was never made clear, though she suspected that Geraldine had been involved somewhere along the line. But that was hardly important and she left that same evening, her few remaining belongings packed in two suitcases, which he stowed in the cavernous boot space of his gleaming Bentley.

Since then, with the exception of the unfortunate business at Dennison Hall, Rose had never looked back and once again her bank account – in a different name and in the Channel Islands – began to assume healthy proportions. And as she learned about things that even she had never believed happened, she took a fierce pride in her new career, dedicating herself to the pursuit of perfection in everything she did.

'My stables,' she told Kristin, 'are the equal of anything in Europe, probably the world.' And Kristin had agreed with her, though the two women never got on in most things, for where Rose's desire for avenging herself upon a society that she considered had treated her badly in her earlier years now abated and was tempered with professionalism, Kristin appeared to have a cruel streak a mile wide and would administer punishments for no reason other than that she had grown bored or irritated.

However, as time passed a tacit understanding was reached, unspoken, but nevertheless adhered to. Rose never interfered with anything that went on in Kristin's domain, including the various cells and dungeons in the cellars of the house, and Kristin left the running of the stable blocks and their various inmates to Rose.

At least, that was how it had been up until now, Rose thought, furrowing her brow. The arrival of the new pony girl was threatening to upset the longstanding status quo and, if Kristin were to be believed, this Tits, as she was now called, was only to be the first of many similar creatures.

Rose knew the woman had reputedly been the leader of the team of women who had raided Dennison Hall, and could understand Master Rafe's desire to get even with her. So if he decreed that Kristin should play a role in effecting that revenge, Rose was not disposed to raise any objections. However, it appeared that the pair of them were determined to ensnare the entire raiding party and, from what little Rose could remember of that night, there had been the better part of twenty of them. They would need more than half her available stall accommodation for that number and that would mean Kristin, the sour-faced blonde bitch, strutting about in *her* stables, giving orders and taking over the entire show.

Not only that, but if they really did intend going through

with what Rose had overheard Rafe and Kristin discussing, she could but pity the poor fillies and, from what had been done to Tits already, it appeared that they were determined to exact an awful retribution. Removing back teeth from a few volunteer pony girls who received plenty of financial reward for their subsequent services, that was one thing, but the former commando girl was certainly no volunteer and the enforced dentistry was, apparently, only the beginning.

In fact, Rose thought, drawing the curtains and turning away to find the light switch, the bloody vet man was due to return early in the morning, and though Kristin had not deigned to inform her of the purpose of the visit, Rose did not for a moment think it boded anything but further suffering for her latest charge. The days of home made whipping benches and rubber dog bones as bit gags were long gone, she reflected grimly, and it didn't help matters that the upstart blonde bitch, Phoebe, seemed content to be in Kristin's pocket and carry out her slightest whim.

'And there's still been no further contact from them?' Alison pursed her lips and looked across at Ruth, who was sitting in the passenger seat of Alison's Mini Cooper. Ruth shook her head.

'There won't be,' she said, 'not yet for a while. They've got people watching, following, trying to establish where we all are at the moment.'

Alison jerked around automatically, looking back across the nearly deserted seafront car park. 'Were you followed here?' she asked, her eyes darting back and forth between the ten or so vehicles that were scattered around the windswept site. Ruth laid a hand on her arm.

'Take it easy,' she cautioned. 'We don't want to give the game away, do we? Yes, I was followed here, as I expect you were too, but you need to know what to look for. I take it you've got some company with you?'

Alison nodded. 'Mike Hallet and this bloke called Douglas. I think Douglas is carrying a gun, too. They're in that Morgan sports car, just by the entrance where you came in.'

'Good.' Ruth paused, gazing out across the empty promenade and across the white flecked waves. 'But don't get over confident just because your guy's carrying a gun. Hancock's now using professionals, I suspect. His original bloke was a complete idiot, but since I gave him the run-around, the replacements have been a whole lot better.

'They're shadowing me and then putting an observer to follow anyone I visit. When they think they've located the entire team, that's when they'll start moving in, but not before.'

'And when will they have located all of you?' Alison asked. 'I mean, aren't you just playing into their hands, calling on all your friends like that?'

'If I didn't do something along the lines of what they anticipate,' Ruth replied, 'then they'll know I'm on to them and they may just have a crack at me and those of us they think they have pinned. They'll get more than they bargained for if they do, but that isn't the point.

'Six of the girls aren't in the country just now, although four I've contacted by phone are making their way back. I've had a few meets, just to make things look good, but the real contacts are being made by phone, from public boxes and by two way radios, though the range of those is a bit limited.

'Meanwhile, we're pulling in a bit of extra help and every time they stick a tail on one of us we put a tail on him, once we have him identified. So far that hasn't brought us much. They may well be using radios for communication as well, plus the phone-boxes, same as us, but eventually there will have to be physical meetings and then, hopefully, whoever they meet will lead us further.'

'Back to Hancock, you mean?'

'Eventually,' Ruth said, 'if we're really lucky. My guess is that he'll have someone else controlling operations in the field, and whoever it is he must be pretty thorough, especially if he was the one behind kidnapping Hannah.

'The thing is, no matter how good the generals are, or how good their crack troops are, when a battlefield spreads, they have to use the conscripts. The more we can run these people around, the more they'll have to go back to relying on idiots like the guy I nearly piled through a tank on Salisbury Plain the other night. And the more of those they put in the field, the more likely they are to make slip-ups.'

'You seem pretty confident,' Alison said, but Ruth shook her head again.

'No,' she said quietly, 'I'm not confident at all, but we have to do what we can when we can, and these bastards have Hannah. It could all go terribly wrong at any stage. We know next to fuck all right now, which is the only reason I agreed to give your little plan some thought.'

'Well, at least it's something,' Alison retorted. 'I went back through all the notes I made last year and checked the address to make sure the dozy bitch still lives there.'

'But what makes you so sure she'll know where Hancock's new base is?'

'I'm not,' Alison said, 'but she may well have some sort of contact number. She appeared to have been a particularly valued guest at Dennison Hall, probably because her father is worth around forty million quid and in his late seventies. With no other siblings and a real mother who died fifteen years ago, apart from some sort of bequest to the second wife and *her* daughter, little miss inbred stands to inherit the lot shortly and Hancock would love to get his hands on some of it, regardless of how much he's got at the moment.'

'Sound thinking,' Ruth agreed, 'but what if she doesn't

want to play ball?'

Alison smiled grimly. 'From what I know about her and what I saw of her during my little stay at Dennison Hall, I think I know just how to get through to her,' she said. 'And I also know just the man to do it. The only problem is, we'll need to lose anyone who's following us, otherwise they'll suss what we're up to and blow the whole thing.'

'That,' Ruth said, reaching for the door handle, 'should be easy enough to arrange. Go back home, watch your back and wait for me to call you.' She reached inside her jacket pocket and pulled out a compact portable transceiver.

'Keep it switched off till I ring you,' she said. 'I haven't got a spare battery charger, but we'll only need radio contact for a short time.'

'And when will this all happen?'

'Maybe tonight,' Ruth said, opening the door. 'Tomorrow night at the latest. Got to carry out a few more checks and assemble a small team without anyone realising it.'

2.5

Hannah paced slowly back and forth across the narrow stall, her steel shod hooves grating on the uneven flagstone surface beneath the thin covering of straw, her heavy breasts rising and falling in time with her laboured breathing, the recently readjusted corset girth biting cruelly into her ribs.

Her arms, as ever, were linked helplessly to her sides, her neck encircled by the regulation posture collar that kept her head permanently high, and her head was enmeshed in the intricate webbing of yet another bridle. The bit hung down across the top of her bosom. Phoebe had informed her that, in future, it would only be put back in place when she was to be taken outside, but now its function was little more than ornamental and, even without it between her jaws, she could not speak.

The metal strip felt huge inside her mouth and Hannah wished she could feel it with her fingers, for from the glimpse she'd had of it before the so called vet screwed it to her lower back molars, it had not looked that big. However, large or small, it was a cruelly efficient device, holding her tongue down and making intelligent articulation totally impossible.

'Cheer up, Tits,' Phoebe had said, seeing her obvious distaste and discomfort when she was returned from the vet's barn, 'at least you'll be able to eat and drink properly now, once you've got used to sucking up your oats, that is.'

The blonde bitch was enjoying each new humiliation as it was visited upon her charge, relishing seeing her offering herself to Hercules while the silent brute pumped his massive organ in and out of her three times a day.

Then, each evening before locking Hannah in for the night, Phoebe was there again, leading her out into the paddock, bending her over the hitching rail in front of the stables, tying off her bridle rein to prevent her from rising and then lashing her rump with crop or whip, counting the strokes with slow deliberation and then throwing cold water on the burning flesh and leaving her to dry in the cool air.

And through it all, throughout all the days Hannah had been kept in this hellhole, not once had they let their guard slip; not once had Hannah seen even the briefest glimmer of hope of escape. Stifling a moan of angry frustration, she turned and shuffled across to where the metal trough was riveted to the timber wall. The mash it contained was awful and half of it would end up smeared around her face, but as Phoebe had pointed out, it was all she was getting.

2.6

Not even her closest friends would have described Emma Barrington as particularly bright, but then, they would reflect, she was never likely to find herself in the position of having to use her brains. Unless, of course, one counted making a decision as to which invitations she should accept and which she would have to regrettably decline, and even then she usually left such matters to her stepsister, Philippa.

Philippa also chose most of Emma's clothes for her, picked out likely men, drove them both everywhere in her car, and generally ran most of her admittedly idle life, with a little extra help from their long-time former school friend, Daphne Horrocks.

As far as Emma was concerned this arrangement was ideal. In fact she was not even aware that it existed, nor that she herself would have been totally useless without the support of the other two, assuming that it was in some way her right to the devotion they apparently showed. After all, she reasoned, neither Philippa nor Daphne was anything special: Daphne was a plain girl, the youngest of six and without any great expectations in life, whilst poor Philippa would have little after daddy was gone, apart from what she, Emma, would give her from the vast fortune that daddy and poppa – his father before him – had built up over the past sixty odd years.

Philippa was prettier than Daphne, but not so much fun and could be a regular old dry stick at times. Why, she had even seemed glad that the weekends at Dennison Hall, to which the girls had been introduced by Bunty Horrocks, Daphne's mother, had been brought to such an abrupt end the summer before.

Such a goose, Emma thought, turning down the chance to drive all those pretty boys and girls in their lovely harnesses and then to be able to choose any one of them – two, if you wanted – and take them to bed, still all nicely strapped up and obedient, willing to do just about anything to please. Philippa had gone with them, of course, and had kept her mouth shut about it in front of daddy and their mother, but for some reason Emma just could not fathom, she had never seemed to enjoy the experience.

Which was why, when the message had come through that Ralphie and his chums had set up house in a nice new place, Emma had decided it best not to tell her stepsibling. Of course it wasn't easy, trying to get away for a few days at a time without arousing Philippa's suspicions, but Daffers was good at those sort of things and always managed to think up a good excuse.

Take this coming weekend, for example. It had been a brilliant ruse to get Toby Fanshawe to invite Philippa to go sailing in the Solent. Emma had suffered from seasickness for as long as anyone could remember, and so Philly had been truly grateful for Daphne's offer to keep poor old Emma company, rather than go along as well.

With daddy in the south of France for the month, that left only the housekeeper, the part-time cook and one maid at the house, and when Emma had informed them she'd also be away for a few days, they were quick to accept her suggestion of a few days off themselves, leaving the house completely empty.

Which left Emma with a whole glorious day to herself, making preparations, sorting out her growing secret wardrobe, ready for Daphne to help choose what she should wear for the trip down to wherever the place was now. That was one of Emma's favourite parts of the whole adventure, though she was careful not to let on to Daphne about it, for Daffers hated the blindfold hoods that the driver always insisted they now wear, while Emma found she could use that period of enforced sensory deprivation to imagine all sorts of lovely things.

She walked through to her dressing room, took the key to the special closet from where it hung on its thin gold chain between her generous cleavage, and began to hum a tuneless little air. As she unlocked the door and drew aside the first row of everyday dresses and coats, the wonderful aromas of leather and latex wafted out and began to fill her nostrils. And her mind began to fill with images of pony girls in impossible boots, pony boys with huge phalluses and another pony girl being led meekly to the bridle; a pony girl who looked remarkably like herself.

Perhaps this trip, she told herself. Perhaps this trip she'd summon up the nerve to ask Ralphie if she could spend a day in the stables like that… just to see what it felt like, of course.

'I think she's almost ready to be transferred to regular duties.' Phoebe ran a hand down and across Hannah's bare shoulder, and then moved her gloved fingers across to stroke the base of her neck beneath the artificial blonde mane. With her other hand she cupped Hannah's right breast, better displaying the prominent nipple with its attached ring and bell. Ralph Hancock nodded his appreciation and turned to Rose, who stood quietly just behind him.

'You've done well,' he said, 'all of you. And how long before her breasts can be enlarged another stage?'

Rose hesitated and cleared her throat. 'The vet says another week or two, once the flesh has fully acclimatised to the initial implants. However,' she continued, pausing to cough again, 'I was wondering whether that was really necessary. At the moment she makes a perfect pony girl and the breasts bounce beautifully when she canters.'

Hancock glared at her, eyes burning with venom. 'Whether they bounce beautifully or not is not the point of the exercise,' he snapped. 'The whole point of the exercise is to teach this slut – and her damned friends when we finally have them – that their arrogance has been their downfall. They dared to interfere with something I've been working on for years, and now they'll pay.

'I don't want this mare to run away with any fancy ideas. She may not be very happy with her present situation, but I know these animals and eventually she'll be proud of the fact that our guests want her, believe me.

'No, this one – and the others – they'll be workhorses, nothing more. They can draw the carts, pull the guests around the grounds, keep the stallions happy, at least until they're too slack even for that, and they'll be available completely free to anyone who wants their services, from the most respected guest to the lowest stable hand.

'Eventually, we may even sell off a few of them to our Arab friends. They seem to like their mares just a bit more on the fleshy side and they'll pay a decent fee to use them for breeding purposes. The sultana has expressed an interest in having her own little stable bred from scratch, especially given the pedigree of these sluts. She derives a certain amount of humour from the prospect.'

Hannah shuddered and closed her eyes. That Hancock was mad had never really been in doubt, but it was the magnitude and scope of his madness that was so horrific. Not content with what he had already inflicted upon her, he was preparing to sell her off to a high-ranking woman in a country that was the sworn enemy of her own nation, a country which she, Hannah, had herself fought against and helped defeat with such humiliating efficiency.

Life for a Jewish pony girl in an Arab stable did not bear contemplating, especially for a pony girl who had been deliberately reduced to a state where she would become an object of derision. If they ever gave her the slightest chance, she vowed she would kill herself rather than face that prospect.

Everything had happened so quickly Emma still was not totally sure where these people, these women, had appeared from, nor what it was they wanted with Daphne and herself. They moved silently, working with ruthless efficiency, straps and chains deployed to render their two captives completely helpless before they knew it was happening. So that now the two girls lay side by side, wriggling on the carpet of the library like two black snakes, surrounded by a circle of six sinister masked faces, from which twelve eyes glittered with menacing purpose.

Yet the day had all progressed so normally until a few minutes before. Daphne arrived in mid-afternoon, by which time Emma had laid out a selection of her personal rubberwear. Ralphie liked the girls to arrive ready dressed, and Emma loved the feeling of being swathed in latex, ever since she had seen the pony girls running in similar outfits during the winter months and acquired a rubber catsuit similar to the ones used to keep the worst of the seasonal extremes at bay.

In the case of the ponies, of course, the suits were coloured, emulating the natural looks of their four-legged counterparts: roans, bays, dapples, greys. Ralphie had even been experimenting with fitted headpieces that looked amazingly like the real thing, complete with manes to match the tails that were fixed strategically at their other ends.

She really would have to have a word with Ralphie about that stables thing, though she wasn't sure how Daffers would react. Daffers was too like Bunty, too keen on using the whip and not at all sensuous. They could be a simply horrid pair and they just didn't know how to appreciate real beauty. Pony girls were beautiful, Emma thought, and it would be fun to be a beautiful filly, with all those admiring looks. Just so long as they kept their riding crops for the fillies who were supposed to be fillies full-time, that was.

Wriggling into the latex catsuit was one of Emma's favourite moments, the odour of the rubber mingling with the scent of the talcum-powder and her own sweet, clean after-bath fragrance. To stand, flexing feet and fingers inside their black skins, listening to the zip purr up her spine as Daffers closed the suit up to the nape of the neck, ready for the driver to mate the eyeless rubber hood in which she would travel. Oh, so delicious to be led out, blind and sensuous, tottering on the heels that made her beautiful legs look even longer and more desirable.

Just like a pony girl should, she thought idly, but dismissed the looming daydream before it could take a proper hold, for now it was time to prepare Daphne. And tonight, just for a change, Emma felt like making a decision. Daffers could forget her jodhpurs and riding boots, the silk shirt and leather waistcoat. She could wear Emma's spare black catsuit and a pair of boots with proper heels.

Maybe then, after they had been driven the two hours to Ralphie's latest place, she might not think Emma's pony girl idea such a stupid one. In fact, if Emma asked Ralphie especially nicely, he might help her play a little trick on Daffers and the two of them could be pony girls together for a little while, whether Daffers liked it or not.

Yes, Emma mused as she helped her reluctant friend ease the tight latex up over her shoulders, that could be really fun. She could hardly wait to see Daffer's face with a bit in her mouth and, she thought as she ran a moist tongue over lips that had suddenly become dry, she could almost feel the bit between her own teeth.

The woman looked to be in her mid-forties, overly made-up, but still what Hannah had seen described as 'handsome'. She was tallish, squarely built and, despite the high heels, walked with a mannish stride. She wore white leather riding breeches tucked neatly into the highly polished black boots, a red silk shirt open at the throat to reveal her generous cleavage, and a tightly laced waist cincher that shone to match her footwear. Her hands were encased in black kid gloves, the long fingers curling and uncurling about the handle of a particularly long riding crop, and her slender neck was encircled by a thin studded collar made of more highly gleaming black leather.

As she approached Hannah, who had been left tethered to a stake in the middle of the paddock, away from the stallions, she rapped her right boot with the crop and tossed her mane of auburn hair, the bright red lips curving into a smile of satisfaction at what she saw.

'By golly, old gel!' she exclaimed. 'Rafe was damned right. A bloody thoroughbred if ever I saw one.' She stopped a pace short of Hannah and looked her up and down, reaching out with the end of the crop to tap the side of Hannah's girth corset, where her sleeved arm was joined to it.

'Nice tight belly,' she commented. 'And good flanks.' She stepped sideways, running the tip down Hannah's buttocks, which were still burning from her daily whipping at Phoebe's hands. 'Decent quarters,' she muttered. 'Bit more development and you'd make a promising hurdler.' She continued to circle Hannah until she finally returned to her starting point.

'They tell me your name is Tits,' she said, 'and I can see why, but I don't like it much. Far too coarse for my liking. So, I shall call you Star of the Nile. Star for short. My name is Bunty. Mistress Bunty to you.' The woman smiled again. 'Of course, that hardly matters, does it?' she laughed. 'Master Rafe tells me you're a proper dumb animal, even without your bit. Open and let me see.'

She stepped forward, reaching out to prise Hannah's jaws further apart. Hannah's first reaction was to try to bite the probing fingers; with the extracted molars at the back, the bit did not prevent her bringing the remaining teeth together. However, such a show of rebellion, especially one that inflicted actual harm on a guest, could only lead to punishments so severe they did not bear thinking about. Dutifully, trying not to look into Bunty's eyes, she let her lower jaw go slack, affording the woman a view of her mouth obstructed only by the bit itself.

'Interesting arrangement,' Bunty mused. 'Simple but efficient.' She released her grip on Hannah's jaw and stepped back, her gaze dropping to the heavily belled nipples.

'Fine animal all round,' she concluded. 'Shame they're intending to ruin you. Especially these.' She tapped Hannah's left breast lightly. 'Of course, I understand Rafe's position, but it seems a dreadful waste. I'd rather see you as a competition pony. Maybe I'll try talking to him.'

Hannah tried not to show the relief this statement gave her and, at the same time, hated herself for the wave of gratitude she was suddenly feeling towards this crazy woman. After all, even she seemed to regard Hannah as nothing more than a beast, even if her intervention might mean a reprieve from the fate Hancock had planned for her.

'Right then,' Bunty said, stooping to untie the trailing end of Hannah's tether, 'we'll go hitch you up to one of the lightweights and then see what you can do. I'll drive you through the woods to the new circuit and see if we can't get one of the stable hands to time a few trial laps.'

As she straightened up she seemed to notice the tiny labial locks for the first time. 'Got a shaft in there, Star?' she asked. Hannah hesitated and then nodded, feeling her cheeks redden, but seeing the possibility of relief from the monstrous dildo, albeit temporary. Her hopes, however, were dashed almost before they had formed.

'That's good,' Bunty said, wrapping the leather rein around her left fist. 'No good timing you otherwise. Race rules and all that,' she added, revealing a row of white teeth that looked a little too perfect to be real. 'Of course,' she said, jerking gently on the rein to indicate that she wanted Hannah to turn and follow, 'I don't suppose anyone will have explained the finer points to you, not with what Rafe was intending. But I'm sure you'll be a quick learner.'

'They'd done most of the work themselves before we got here,' Ruth said, grinning behind her newly acquired leather mask and nodding at the two helpless female forms on the carpet. 'Can't see what they find so fascinating about all that rubber stuff myself, but then each to his own – *her* own in this case,' she added.

Behind her mask Alison felt herself blushing, but she wisely decided not to say anything. 'Those hoods were theirs as well, were they?' she asked, stooping down to examine the nearer head more closely. She could see that the all-enveloping masks were eyeless, though there were openings for mouth and nostrils, the former currently filled by large red rubber ball-gags, held in place by leather straps that had been buckled cruelly tight. From what she remembered of the two stupid girls who had visited her in the stables at Dennison Hall, the hoods seemed out of place, the sort of items reserved for submissive types, whether voluntary participants or, as in her own case, otherwise.

'Well, they had them laying on the bed upstairs,' Ruth replied, 'so I reckon they intended to use them at some stage, though the gags were in a drawer inside a huge wardrobe full of this stuff. Rebecca decided to use them, just so we could have a bit of peace and quiet while we were waiting for you.'

Alison grinned. The Israeli girl might not be totally appreciative of the finer nuances of the bondage and discipline scenario, but her practicality and thoroughness of approach certainly rivalled anything she had encountered with either Marcia or Ralph Hancock.

'Have you managed to find out anything yet?' she asked.

'Haven't bothered even asking yet,' Ruth said. 'This is your shout and you're the expert in this particular field, so we thought it best to wait for you, rather than waste time going over the same ground twice.'

'Fair comment,' Alison agreed. She reached into the bag she had brought with her and withdrew the envelope containing the two photographs.

'Which is which?' she said, passing them to Ruth.

Ruth studied the two faces briefly and jabbed a toe into the rump of the nearer prone figure. 'This one's Emma,' she said. 'That's her diary over there on the reading table. There are several names and phone numbers there, including a couple I think are what we're after. However, there's probably some sort of password involved.'

'Or just whoever is on the other end recognising the voice,' Alison said. 'I doubt it'd be anything too complex, not for these bird brains.' She looked about the library, her eyes lighting on a particularly fine carved chair, probably from the Jacobean period.

'Let's have her up on that,' she decided. 'Strap her arms and legs down and run a nice tight strap around her chest. I've brought a load of stuff with me,' she added, kicking the bag at her feet. 'And while you're doing that I'll pop outside and see where Douglas has got to. He should be here by now, especially the way Mike drives.'

'Fair enough,' Ruth said, 'but we don't want to waste too much time. Unless this pair like playing snakes together, I'd say they were expecting visitors before too much longer. I've posted guards at the end of the driveway, but if your idea is going to have the slightest chance of working, we can't afford to tip anyone off.'

2.7

It wasn't the first time Hannah had been hard driven – Phoebe had been gradually increasing the pace of their daily drives – but it was certainly her most extended period of activity and Bunty seemed keen to push her to the limits.

The circuit had been laid out in a large clearing, about half a mile through the woods from the stable block that had been Hannah's home for the past several days. It was an oval of closely mown and heavily rolled grass that stood out from the lusher pasture from which it had been cut, providing a track some fifteen feet in width and a lap distance of about a quarter of a mile.

Underfoot – *hoof*, Hannah found herself correcting – the ground was hard from many days of summer sunshine, the last appreciable rainfall having been a fortnight since, as far as she could remember. The surface was also remarkably even, testimony to a lot of care and attention from someone who understood grass and soil conditions, reminding Hannah of the many typically English village cricket grounds she had visited over the years, where the pitch was always kept like a billiard table.

Of course, she told herself idly as she plodded around the circuit for the fourth time, it made sense to lavish so much attention to the surface. Presumably, not all Hancock's human ponies had been pressed into service and even then, it would be foolish to risk injury to people who were the product of a lot of time and training.

Hannah was no expert on these matters, but from paperwork found in the Dennison raid and from odd snatches of conversation she had caught since her arrival in this place, she was learning fast, and human pony racing was taken very seriously by its devotees. They had cups, classes, league tables and even international matches, and a champion pony was a valued asset.

So much so, she thought as the ground rolled by beneath her pounding hooves, her nipple bells jangling their taunting rhythm, that it would be in her best interests to do her utmost to impress this Bunty woman. Hancock was psychotic, beyond a doubt, a neo-Nazi who craved revenge for what Hannah and her girls had dared do to his schemes, but he was also a realist in matters pecuniary and even he might consider his original plans for her to be a waste of potential.

Douglas dropped the long grip bag onto the floor of the library, the contents clanking and jangling, the floorboards vibrating from the weight of the impact. Both blindfolded figures jumped at the sudden noise, but no one else in the room moved.

'Just give me a few minutes to get organised,' Douglas said, grinning around the small circle of waiting faces. 'I thought we'd do this properly, rather than mess around with half measures.' He shrugged the jacket from his shoulders, tossing it into a corner and revealing bare arms and a lot of chest around a tight leather vest. He wore skin-tight leather trousers with calf-length boots laced tightly, the laces threaded through gold-coloured D-rings. He cut an imposing figure.

He turned, opened the grip and began extracting various lengths of metal tubing, slotting them into each other with bewildering speed.

'Just a little something I knocked up some time ago,' he explained, as still more lengths were added to the confusing assemblage. 'It started life as one of those garden swing frames, the sort you buy for kiddies, but I could see the possibilities from the word go.'

'We have to watch the time,' Ruth warned, as he lifted the first A-framed side and leaned it against the bookcase.

'No problem.' He nodded from the seated figure of Emma to the prone figure of Daphne. 'My guess is that these two were getting ready to be picked up, though whether they were going to our friend's place is something we don't yet know.

'They were already dressed, apart from the hoods, you say, so it would seem they were supposed to travel in mode. Now, even assuming that the car has blacked out windows,' he paused to raise the second side section and clip a crossbar between the two apexes. 'Even assuming that, which I think we can safely do, the odds are that they wouldn't want to be travelling like that during the busy period.

'One idiot pranging the wing of their car and Old Bill is

crawling all over the place.' He added a bracing section at the top of the frame. 'So, if you want my opinion, I reckon these two Cinderellas weren't expecting their coach to arrive much before eight this evening and, if one of you wants to check, I'd bet you'll find at least a couple of bottles of bubbly chilling in the fridge, wherever that is.

'I've met the type before. Love the ritual, spend ages getting ready, then slowly get as pissed as they dare and probably get their jollies just thinking about what's to come. They probably even love the idea of the journey to wherever they're going. You said those hoods were ready and waiting, so I'd say they were to prevent them knowing where they were going.

'Our friend is too careful to reveal too much to a couple of dopey debs, I'd say, but we can check that very shortly. Once I get started I think they'll be quick enough to tell us what we need to know.'

'These times really are something, I agree Bunty.' Ralph Hancock looked up from the sheet of paper, his features concentrated in deep thought. 'They are accurate, I take it?' he added.

Bunty Horrocks gave him a withering look. 'Whatever else you may think of me,' she said, 'I can read a damned stopwatch. Besides, I had one of the stable boys running a check watch at the same time.'

'Hmmm.' Hancock's expression remained contemplative, his eyes flickering up and down the column of hand printed figures once more. 'If that's the case,' he said at last, 'then the bitch is two seconds inside Fantasia's best ever mile time and she was the best European filly ever to run in competition.'

'I know,' Bunty said. 'I drove her in three races and she was something special. But then so is Star.'

'And you think I ought to race her, rather than carry on with my original plan, is that it?'

Bunty nodded. 'I do,' she confirmed, 'and I'd like to drive her, if you wouldn't mind. I don't mind contributing towards the cost of her upkeep and training, either.'

'That's not the point,' Hancock snapped. 'The money side is completely immaterial and she can earn her keep whilst training anyway.'

'Listen,' Bunty urged, laying a hand on his forearm and leaning towards him, 'I know how you feel about the filly, I really do. You'd like to turn her into some top-heavy brood mare and sell her to the Arabs, but this way could be even better.

'Think of it, Rafe,' she continued, her tone earnest, 'it would be an even greater humiliation for the little slut. Every time she races, every time she wins, she's adding to your – our – kudos. Let me have charge of her for three months, with Rose handling her day to day training, and I promise you she'll be unbeatable. Even those African fillies won't be a match for her.'

'Not even Khaled's much vaunted Sable?'

'No,' Bunty said emphatically, 'not once Star is fully trained. I've seen Sable run a few times now and she's past her best. She must be thirty-five if she's a day, whereas Star is no more than thirty at best.'

She paused, turning to glance out of the window to where the shadows were lengthening across the manicured lawn onto which Hancock's study faced.

'And think about it,' she urged. 'You can still bag the rest of them, the same as you intended. Except before you make them all top-heavy fodder for the Arabs, let's have a look at what they can do too. These girls have fought alongside men; they're trained to endure almost anything.

'You could end up with a stable of fillies that would be the envy of the racing world, Rafe. They'd be worth millions, especially if you bred from them.'

'You're right, of course,' Hancock sighed, his expression softening at last. 'First rule of business, never let personal feelings get in the way of a good proposition.' He clapped his hands together and grinned. 'Thank you, Bunty,' he said. 'I owe you one.'

'At the very least,' Bunty said. 'And you can start this weekend. My Daphne is due down tonight, with her friend, Emma. Mind you, this is as much doing yourself a favour, considering how much the silly mare is going to be worth shortly.'

'I'm listening,' Hancock said. 'What is it you want?'

'Ah well, my dear old thing,' Bunty said, 'that's the point. It's not what I want, but what Emma wants. And also,' she added, 'though she doesn't realise it as such, I think the same thing would do my gel a bit of good – with certain restrictions, of course,' she added hastily.

The atmosphere in the library was suddenly very heavy. Alison finished securing the second wrist strap and stepped back, Douglas released his supporting grip about Daphne's waist, and the black shiny figure hung from the crossbar of the frame, the high heels of her boots waving inches above the carpet.

'Better secure her ankles,' Douglas growled. Alison nodded and stepped forward, the pair of them seizing a leg each, drawing the limbs wide and fastening another pair of the padded straps, snapping the short connecting chains to links bolted to the rear uprights of the A-frame supports, so that now the helpless figure hung, legs splayed, her body tilted slightly forward. Wordlessly, Douglas reached out, seized the zip tag and drew it backwards between Daphne's thighs, the latex parting to reveal the girl's sex.

Behind him, Ruth coughed. 'Is that really necessary,' she said between clenched teeth.

Alison gripped Ruth's arm and drew her away. 'He knows what he's doing,' she whispered, leaning close and speaking directly into Ruth's ear. 'If anyone can get what we need out of this pair, I'd put my money on Douglas.'

'It's barbaric,' Ruth hissed, shaking her head.

'And what they're doing to Hannah isn't, I suppose?'

'These two aren't involved in that,' Ruth protested, 'not directly, at least.'

'Maybe not, but they're our only hope of getting to her and it's their type that Hancock exploits. The one in the chair there will be only too pleased to give him great chunks of her daddy's fortune the moment he pegs it, and you don't think she'll show any sympathy for Hannah, do you?

'I met this pair of sweethearts last year,' Alison continued. 'They've scarcely got a live brain-cell between them, but that makes them more dangerous, if anything, not less. They probably think Hancock's capable of walking on water and they'd do anything he told them, but we can turn that to our advantage.

'The one in the chair, Emma – I remember what she said, the stupid cow: wanted to have a go at playing pony herself, of all things. It's just a great big laugh to her kind, so let's see if she's still laughing when she sees her friend.' Alison paused and drew in a deep breath. In truth, she was not completely happy with all this herself, but there was no time for niceties and the direct approach was their only hope.

She nodded to the commando girl who stood behind the bound and seated figure of Emma, the girl's mask obscuring her identity. A moment later the sightless hood was yanked from Emma's sweating head, revealing a tangle of blonde hair and wild staring eyes in a red and blotchy face. The moment her eyes readjusted to the sudden incursion of light, they focused on the hanging black figure and a low wail forced its way past her tightly drawn lips.

Alison stepped forward in front of her. 'Just shut up and listen!' she snapped and, on impulse, reached forward and seized a hank of Emma's hair, jerking her head back and forcing her to look up into her masked features.

'I want some answers,' she said, 'and you're going to give them to me, otherwise your little friend over there is going to suffer. Not only that, but my *big* friend, the one standing behind her, will fuck the lights out of her, got that?' The seated girl swallowed and nodded, her head bobbing frantically. Alison, however, was not in the mood to take chances.

'Before I start asking,' she said, letting go of the tousled blonde mane, 'I think it might save time in the long run if you witnessed a small demonstration of the seriousness of our intent.' She turned, looked at Douglas, and nodded.

The short, multi-thonged whip had appeared in his hand as if by magic, and he stepped back, measuring the distance.

'Her rubber suit will prevent her flesh from being cut,' Alison said, trying to ignore her fast beating heart and keep her voice authoritative. 'However, the whip my friend is using at the moment is just a plaything, compared to some of the other things he's got in his bag. So, if you think you can fuck me about, think again, missy.'

The final word was hardly out of Alison's mouth before the whip hissed around in an arc, the braided thongs slapping a resounding impact that spread from Daphne's shoulders down to her buttocks. Her entire body jerked and bucked, the metal frame creaking and rocking in response and a muffled shriek exploded from around the ball-gag. Emma's eyes widened and a gasp of horror bubbled in the back of her throat.

Again the whip descended, and again.

'No!' Emma's shriek was ear-splitting and the heavy Jacobean chair rocked forward as she tried to throw her weight towards Alison. 'No!' she wailed. 'I'll tell you anything you want to know, just stop what you're doing to her, please!' She broke off, her head slumping forward, sobbing and choking. Douglas paused, arm drawn back in readiness to strike again, his eyes glinting from behind the mask, watching Alison for the next cue. With a sigh of relief she half raised her left hand and then turned back to the near hysterical figure in the chair.

'Right,' she said, her voice steadier than she could believe, 'let's get down to business.' She once more grabbed a handful of hair, trying to ignore the whispered conversation that was now taking place behind her, or the fact that, according to the two astonished female speakers, Daphne Horrocks had apparently come before the third stroke of the whip had even touched her!

2.8

Rose made her way back along the cart track without hurrying, a faint smile of satisfaction tweaking at the edges of her mouth. She could hardly wait to see Phoebe's reaction to what she had just overheard, but discretion was the watchword now, for if the blonde bitch ever realised that Rose had been deliberately eavesdropping on Master Ralph's conversation with the Horrocks woman, she would lose no time in turning that to her advantage. Besides, Rose reasoned, it would be better for Phoebe to hear it directly from Kristin, and that was another blonde cow who needed taking down a peg or two.

Rose had liked Bunty Horrocks since their first meeting five years before, for Bunty, despite her affectedly superior air, was a true connoisseur, appreciating Rose's pony girls in a way that few of the other visitors did or could, deriving a deep-seated satisfaction that went far beyond anything that either Kristin or Phoebe could ever hope to understand. Cruelty for cruelty's sake had never held much appeal for Rose, and her experienced eye had jaundiced at the thought of what wasteful plans had been laid for the unfortunate Tits.

Tits. Rose shook her head and smiled to herself. Star – now that was a far more appropriate name and the filly would soon justify it, of that Rose had no doubt whatsoever. A physique like that was rare, her stamina unbelievable and everything about her screamed thoroughbred, even if her pedigree was not one that met with Master Ralph's immediate approval. Rose had thought about trying to intercede, but had known from the start that any such attempt would have been doomed to failure. With Kristin above and Phoebe below, she would have had no chance of convincing Hancock, whereas Bunty Horrocks...

Rose paused, saw the fallen tree trunk where it had lain for at least a decade, peered up at the gathering evening sky and chuckled. With a shake of her head she made her way across the mossy grass, sat down on the trunk and closed her eyes.

It had been a masterstroke, phoning Bunty and telling her about the new filly. She had been careful not to say too much and had also elicited a promise from Bunty not to mention Rose's intervention, but there had been little danger and even less doubt as to the outcome. From the moment Bunty had first set eyes upon her newest protégée, the unfortunate filly's immediate future had been secured.

Bunty would drive her to triumphs never before seen in the fraternity, Ralph Hancock would gloat that his Jewish whore was winning him money and recognition, but Rose would be happy in the knowledge that Star of the Nile would be returned to her sole charge. Kristin had her useful points, as did Phoebe, but when it came to nurturing human horseflesh, Rose was in a league of her own and Ralph Hancock knew that only too well.

'How's everything going in there?' Marcia emerged from the shadows to the side of the front door with such unexpected suddenness that Mike almost bit through the end of his cigarette. Coughing, he whirled around to the sound of her voice, blinking back smoke-induced tears.

'Jeez!' he exclaimed. 'I didn't hear you coming. Where's your car?' Marcia jerked her head in the direction of the gates, hidden in the darkness of the trees that overhung the far end of the drive.

'I left it a little way down the road,' she said. 'No point in drawing unnecessary attention – never know who might be turning up here later.'

'Well, there's a driver from Hancock's place at the very least,' Mike said. 'Apparently he's due just before midnight. Our two daffy debutantes were getting themselves all prettied up for the trip.'

'Well, well,' Marcia mused. 'That's very convenient – saves coercing them into phoning out of the blue. Do they know where the place actually is?'

Mike shook his head and dropped the glowing cigarette butt onto the gravel, grinding it out with his heel. 'No, it's much as we suspected,' he said. 'Apparently, not even the other one's mother knows exactly where to find it. Hancock sends a car – a helicopter even, for the mother, but then they live further out into the country with room for it to land – and the passengers have to put on what you call a discipline hood, though it doesn't have a gag.'

'Typically thorough,' Marcia grunted. 'No chance of peeking, as there would be with a conventional blindfold.'

'Also interestingly,' Mike added, 'quite a few of the guests travel in costume, if you get my meaning. This pair are wearing latex catsuits and rather impractical boots and Alley Cat tells me that the one, Emma, had fitted herself with a bloody dildo.' Mike shook his head again. Despite twelve months spent with Honey, he felt he would never truly understand the masochistic fetishist's mind, besides which, from what Alison told him of her previous encounter with the two girls inside the house, he had assumed that they preferred to play dominant roles.

'Inside almost every dominant,' Marcia said, as if reading his mind, 'there's a latent submissive.' She paused, stroking her chin. 'We could turn that to our advantage. How much time have we got.'

Mike raised his left arm, shaking back the sleeve of his jacket to reveal the luminous face of his wristwatch. 'Less than two hours,' he said. 'An hour and a half to be on the safe side.' There was a glint of white teeth in the half-light from the hallway.

'In which case,' Marcia said, brushing past Mike and heading towards it, 'we'd better get a move on. If this works it could save us trying to get the information out of the driver, assuming the Alley Cat is up for a bit of playacting. By the way, where's Teddy?'

'At home,' Mike said. 'She still doesn't want him to know anything about all this; reckons he'd insist on taking her to America or something.'

'Maybe we should all think about going there,' Marcia retorted grimly. 'It'd be a lot less risky than all this.'

Hannah had been back in her stall for what seemed like a long time and, through the tiny skylight in the roof she could see it was dark outside, when Rose appeared. The pony mistress swung open the top half of the split door and leaned over the lower section, studying Hannah as she lay sprawled on the floor, by the dim light of the oil lantern she held.

'This won't do, pretty pony,' she said softly. 'I can see I shall have to have words with Mistress Phoebe. All ponies should sleep in the proper suspension harnesses, not in untidy heaps in damp straw.' She opened the remaining door section, stepped inside and hung the lantern on a hook just inside the door.

'You're to be moved to the proper racing stable, anyway,' she said, as Hannah finished scrambling to her feet.

Hannah stared back at her, trying to figure what was different about her this evening. It wasn't the way she was dressed: she wore her customary high boots and breeches and a lace-up top that emphasised her heavy breasts as ever, and her dark hair was in its normal businesslike chignon. Even her makeup was as severe and dramatic as ever, yet there was something in her eyes, something about the expression on her face.

'You're our first permanently non-talking pony girl,' she said, raising one hand to touch Hannah gently on the cheek. 'It suits you, with those great big dumb eyes, especially now you have proper-sized tits. Of course, inflating them the way they were talking of doing, that would have been a waste.

'Oh yes,' she continued, seeing the questioning look in Hannah's eyes, 'you're not going to be turned into some monstrosity now, not after the way you ran earlier today. Would you like to keep your shape, Star?'

Solemnly, Hannah nodded, guessing that Rose wanted something more from her.

'Then let me hear you say please, pretty pony.' Confused, Hannah continued to stand before her, until Rose began to chuckle. 'Poor pony,' she said, 'you don't understand very much, do you? You have to snort and snicker, silly thing. Your tongue may not be much use any more, but you can still make suitable noises.'

To her chagrin, Hannah heard herself attempting a guttural whimper, something she would never have thought herself capable of mere days ago. But the thought of further cosmetic surgery was too horrific to bear, and if this slightly crazy female could help prevent that, Hannah was prepared to do almost anything she asked. Slightly crazy was, after all, a huge improvement on the manic cruelty displayed by Phoebe.

'Not bad, Star,' Rose said, smiling. 'But you'll have to practice until you can whinny properly. If the master sees you are really making an effort he might feel a bit better disposed towards you.'

Hannah tried again. The sound that came out was dreadful and not at all equine, but Rose seemed pleased at the effort.

'It'll take a bit of time, my sweet,' she said. A hand was suddenly on Hannah's left breast, gloved fingers kneading gently, and her face drew closer to Hannah's. 'But then,' she added, speaking very softly, 'you've been returned to my personal charge and my personal quarters are at the end of the racing block, right next door to your new stall.

'So you see, Star, my beauty,' she said, toying with the nipple, which was swelling rapidly beneath the touch, 'time is something we shall have plenty of.'

'You understand what will happen if you try to fuck about, don't you?' Douglas told the quivering Emma. 'Alison will be sitting next to you all the way and if you give any indication that everything's not as it seems, she's got a tiny alarm in her belt that will have us to you within seconds.'

'Even if you struggle,' Alison added, 'the driver will just think it's part of our new game. And you'll be securely gagged, naturally, so you won't be able to speak to him anyway.'

Still securely strapped to the heavy chair, Emma stared

up at her through rounded eyes. 'Promise you won't whip Daphne again?' she begged. The gagged and hooded figure of her friend still hung limply in her spread-eagled bonds.

Alison nodded. 'Not if you behave yourself,' she said. 'When this driver gets here I'm going to be Daphne, as far as anyone's concerned. I'll leave the gag out until he gets here, so he can hear you speak, but all you say is "Yes, mistress". Got that?'

Emma swallowed hard and blinked. 'Yes, mistress,' she replied dutifully.

'And you're certain he doesn't know either of you that well?'

'No, mistress,' Emma whispered. 'There are five or six different drivers and we seldom get the same one twice running. Daffers and I usually wear our own masks under the blindfold hoods and there's only one of the men who has ever seen our faces. The cars are fitted with glass screens between the front seat and the passengers, so we never talk to them either.'

'Well, once he's heard your voice you won't be talking to anyone,' Marcia cut in. 'And remember, we'll be in here with Dolly Daydream over there. You tip him off and the girls will shoot him before he can even think about getting to the front door. Then they'll shoot her and you can watch.'

'I'll do as you say,' Emma croaked.

'I still think I should be the one to go in the car with her,' Ruth interrupted. 'Same as you say, in a rubber catsuit and mask who's to know the difference?'

'It's not that simple,' Alison retorted. 'Look at the heels on their boots, for a start. Just standing up in those takes practice, let alone walking in them. And breathing in a tight corset is an art in itself. Also, spending a couple of hours in a blindfold you can't remove can be disorienting for a beginner. People have been known to panic – even people like you,' she added, deliberately.

'Well, why don't I take *her* place?' Ruth persisted. 'That way we don't have to go through this rigmarole of Emma suddenly wanting to play slave girl, and there'll be two of us in the car if anything goes wrong.'

'Yeah,' Alison said, 'two of us wearing locked blindfold hoods and one of us wearing stuff she won't be able to move about in, even if she could see where she's going. You'll be better off in one of the following vehicles. I'll be okay. Like I said, I'm used to walking in high heels, wearing a tight corset and being blindfolded for hours on end.

'Once we get to where we're going the driver will remove our blindfolds and I'll just keep Fanny here neatly gagged and cuffed until you all make your move.'

'You'll have to make sure that either Hancock or his girlfriend are on the plot first,' Ruth reminded her. 'Or signal if you see Hannah, of course, but there's no good us charging in if none of the important players is up for grabs.'

'Indeed,' Marcia confirmed. 'Dear Rafe is very good at abandoning his minions. I'm not even sure he'd hang about for Kristin, let alone exchange her for Hannah afterwards, so it's better to forget about her and wait until you see either Hannah or the man himself.'

'And don't panic if we don't come straight in when you trigger your signal,' Ruth said. 'We'll need a little while to scout the place and get into position. I'm assuming the defences will be better than they were at Dennison Hall. Hancock doesn't strike me as the sort of man to be caught out twice.'

As long as those defences aren't *too* good, Alison thought, but she decided to keep that particular observation to herself.

2.9

The block that held the racing stables was much nearer the house, though screened from that building by an area of dense woodland, so that it, and the narrow paddock that adjoined it, seemed to be set in a world of their own; a world illuminated at night by yellow electric lamps set on slender poles, with bright white lamps inside the block itself.

Following demurely in Rose's footsteps, the tether between them hanging slackly, Hannah observed everything with her trained eye, noting the mesh fencing that was mostly hidden within the undergrowth that grew beneath the surrounding trees, the metal ramps that were set among various other obstacles, the heavy timber pillories set by one end of the building, and the small brick hut set by the side of the track that led on to the house, through the open door of which a lone sentry was just visible in the gloom within.

Every window in the stable block was heavily barred, the metal struts painted white, matching the frameworks of those windows and the various doors. The roof was tiled, a single chimney stack rising from it at one gable end, two small dormers projecting from the nearer slope at the other, presumably upper rooms above Rose's quarters, Hannah guessed.

All in all, compared with the two stables in which she had been housed since her arrival, this place looked a whole lot more modern, well cared for and professional. Clearly, whilst the majority of the pony girls here were kept for sexual purposes, the business of actually racing the better performers was taken seriously.

Hannah's new stall was much larger than either of the first two, the walls brighter, brickwork and timber alike painted a soft white, tack racks a gleaming black in contrast. The flagstones, both in the outer passageway and within the stall itself, were even and well scrubbed, the straw that covered one side of the stall floor area clean and laid thickly.

'Your new home, Star,' Rose announced, leading Hannah inside. She pointed out the two food troughs along one side wall, and a curious cylindrical affair that was fixed to the partition next to them. From the bottom of this, just below head height, a narrow tube projected, first down and then up, forming a U-shape. From the back a steel rod ran down to the floor, attached by some sort of pivotal mechanism to a wide flat pedal.

'Press down on that with your hoof,' Rose explained, 'and you can suck water out of the nozzle. It saves all that business of slopping water over your face and getting your bridle damp. Racing tack is much more expensive than the ordinary harnesses.' She went on to explain that Hannah was not expected to eat from the second trough, which was currently empty. The first contained a dried mixture, which appeared to be a crushed cereal mix, whereas the second was for 'wet' food.

'That has to be sucked up by a special tube,' Rose told her, 'which will be strapped to you whenever a wet meal is brought in. It's really a sort of wide straw and works like the drinking tube, to keep the mash from splattering your bridle.'

Having completed the brief guided tour, Rose lost no time in setting about changing Hannah's tack. First she replaced the dark leather bridle harness with a lighter version, the leather itself white, the studs and rivets a gold colour. A matching collar followed and then a thin chain was clipped to the stout ring in the very crown of the bridle and hooked up to a thicker chain that hung from one of the overhead beams. Crossing to a small panel in the wall, Rose flipped open the cover-plate and pressed one of the switches inside.

There was a low whirring noise from above and Hannah found herself being pulled erect as the main chain ascended. For a moment she thought that Rose intended to lift her clean off her feet, but she flipped the switch back just before that happened.

'This is just for retacking,' she said, returning to stand alongside Hannah. 'Some silly ponies have been known to try to make a bolt for it once their arms are free. It's impossible to escape, of course, but this way saves such a lot of wasted time and effort.'

She quickly detached Hannah's sleeved arms from her girth corset, but left the sleeves themselves laced to the limbs until after changing the girth for a longer version, once again in white. The relief as the plain dark corset was loosened was indescribable, but short-lived, and its successor was no less constricting. If anything, the boning was even more severe and now Hannah felt as if the top half of her body was completely separate from the lower.

The new white leather sleeves ended in blank mitts, forcing Hannah's hands into tightly balled fists, virtually useless even before the tight tubes were snapped to the sides of the girth. Finally came the hoof boots, identical to the first pair apart from the colour and the fact that they felt even heavier. Experimentally, Hannah shuffled her feet.

'There are three grades of horseshoe attached to various hooves,' Rose explained. 'The normal workaday shoes are what you've been used to. These are training shoes. They are twenty-four ounces heavier and help to build up the leg muscles. Yours are already excellent, but we'll develop them even further.

'When you actually race it will be in hooves fitted with what are known as racing plates. They are thinner, made of alloy and weigh less than ten percent of the weight of those you are now standing in. As a result, you will feel as if you're running on air.' She crossed back to the wall panel and lowered the chain, returning to detach it from the top of Hannah's bridle harness.

'It's getting late now, pretty pony,' she said. 'I really should bed you down for the night, but I'll stay with you for a little while afterwards. Come, stand over here.'

She manoeuvred Hannah a few paces sideways and returned to the electrical controls once again. This time the chain that descended appeared to be split into several smaller chains of differing lengths, and their purpose soon became clear.

Snap links were fastened to the back of Hannah's collar, to either side of the top of her girth and to small rings set into the top of each sleeve at the back. Rose made a few adjustments and then operated the winch motor one final time. Now, as the slack disappeared into the roof, Hannah found herself held in an upright standing position, her weight barely on her feet and as unable to slump in posture as she had been when the tacking up chain had been attached to the top of her head. The one difference was that with this arrangement there was no additional strain on her neck muscles and, to her surprise, the position was not uncomfortable. Not uncomfortable, that was, given that her feet were perched on near tiptoe inside the hoof boots and her waist felt as if it had been trapped between two charging bull elephants.

'This is how you will sleep from now on,' Rose said, 'except for very special circumstances.' She gave Hannah a sly grin, leaving little room for her to doubt the inference. Her prize pony was to receive her close attention in more than one way, it seemed, and if Hannah needed any confirmation of that summation, it was very quick in coming.

Stooping, Rose unlocked the curved bar that held

Hannah's labial rings together and slowly withdrew it. With extravagant care she turned and placed it on the narrow shelf that ran at shoulder height along most of the length of the wall nearest to where they were now standing. Then, with studied deliberation, she stooped again, prised Hannah's lower lips apart and carefully withdrew the fat dildo that Phoebe had delighted in inserting there at first light that morning.

'Far too wide for a racing pony,' she muttered, throwing it into the straw. 'You have to wear one for racing, but the rules stipulate a maximum width much more practical than that.' She remained almost kneeling and craned her head forward, her mouth closing in on Hannah's sex. The heat of her lips, when they touched the tender flesh, brought an involuntary groan from Hannah.

'Such a sweet pony,' Rose said, her voice muffled. 'Such a sweet, tender morsel.' She pressed forward again and began to gently suck, drawing Hannah's swollen clitoris forward and between her soft lips. Hannah groaned again and closed her eyes, but made no attempt to close her legs together. Rather, shuffling awkwardly, she moved her booted feet even wider, thrusting her hips forward eagerly.

If Rose was to become her mentor and her only chance of protection against the more savage excesses of this place, she thought dimly, then they might just as well both enjoy the experience as much as possible.

Hancock's driver proved to be an unremarkable fellow in his late thirties, neither ugly nor particularly good looking. He seemed quite at ease with the fact that both Emma and Alison were already masked when they greeted him in the wide hallway, and greeted Emma's confirmation that she wanted to act as her friend's slave for the weekend without apparent interest. His only concern was to see that the blindfolding hoods were locked on to both of them before he led them out to the car, and he simply stood by and waited patiently while Alison first gagged Emma and adjusted the complex arrangement of thin straps that would prevent her spitting out the penis-shaped rubber plug, and then manacled her hands to either side of the narrow corset belt that now confined her waist.

The interior of the car smelt of polished leather, the door felt heavy and solid as the driver closed it behind them. Quality, Alison thought, sitting back in the enforced darkness; Rolls Royce, Bentley, maybe even a Mercedes, but definitely quality, for the engine, when it purred into life, was barely audible.

Sitting in almost total silence, listening to the sound of her own heartbeat and breathing, it was all Alison could do to stop her fingers wandering up to check that the tiny bug transmitter was where Ruth had placed it, slipped inside the lacing of her corset belt. Of course, she told herself, she was being silly: she could feel the hard plastic digging into her flesh through the thin latex of the catsuit.

But what if the driver could see it? No, that was also stupid. Ruth had checked it, Alison had checked it in the mirror herself and there was no perceptible bulge, no telltale wrinkling of the leather. So why did it now suddenly feel so huge? Surely he would see it. Was he looking at her in the mirror now? Was he maybe even turning around, peering at her directly, guessing there was something not right?

No, she told herself fiercely. No. He was just a driver and he was driving. The sound of her heart grew louder, faster. Stifling the urge to scream out, Alison dug her fingers into the upholstery on either side of her thighs, willing herself not to panic. It had all seemed so straightforward back there in the house, surrounded by Ruth, the other girls, Marcia, Douglas.

What if they lost track of the car? What if the little tracking device one of the girls had attached to the bumper while the driver was in the house wasn't working? What if…?

As the powerful car slid through the night, Alison promised herself that this was the last time she'd ever volunteer for anything, the last time she'd ever complain to Teddy about being bored.

Hannah finally drifted off into a light sleep, waking with a start at the sound of voices outside her stall, surprised that she had been able to doze off in her standing position. On the other hand, she thought, fatigue worked wonders when it came to being able to sleep in the most unlikely circumstances.

The stall itself had been in darkness since Rose's departure, but a thin chink of light showed under the bottom of the door and it was via this gap that most of the sound of conversation was coming.

Straining her ears, Hannah recognised Rose's voice and the higher-pitched tones of Phoebe, who was apparently upset about something. Hannah caught the word 'bitch' several times and then Rose shouting something about treachery and back-stabbing, but she could not really follow the argument closely. She surmised, however, that her own change of fortunes was somehow involved.

Being elevated to the status of racing pony and transferred back into Rose's direct control, Hannah was for the time being at least out of Phoebe's more sinister clutches. Rose was the senior and Phoebe clearly did not like that, and probably thought that Rose had interceded in a deliberate attempt to put her firmly back in her place.

Maybe Rose had, Hannah thought, but it was more likely down to the influence of the woman, Bunty, who clearly shared Rose's enthusiasm for a more aesthetic and less brutal approach to their mutual interest. Bunty had to be some sort of friend to Hancock to even be there at all, so maybe she was more than that, which would not sit well with Kristin, for a start.

Phoebe was supposed to be Kristin's protégée, from the little titbits Hannah had gleaned, so maybe that had something to do with it, too. On the other hand, maybe Phoebe was ambitious enough to think she could supersede not just Rose, but Kristin herself.

As the voices at last began to fade away, Hannah grinned to herself in the darkness. Despite her predicament, she could see the funnier side of the developing situation, even if the humour was of a very black variety. It was the first sign of real hope since she had been there, apart from being temporarily spared from Hancock's original plans for her.

The three women were among Hancock's most senior and trusted aids and yet, so it seemed, they did not trust one another, and Hannah suspected any one of them would probably be prepared to go to almost any lengths to discredit either, or both, of the others. They were all crazy in their different ways – dangerously so – but at least the friction between them offered possibilities. Maybe it could be turned to Hannah's advantage; divide and conquer, divide and rule.

Except, she thought ruefully, trying to wiggle her tongue beneath the unyielding metal plate, it was going to be bloody difficult sewing seeds of further discontent and dividing anything, not when she looked like being deprived of the power of speech, at least for the foreseeable future.

As the car bumped onto the rougher ground, Alison suddenly found herself jerked back to full consciousness, though there was a period of several confused seconds before she realised what was happening and remembered where she was. Unbelievably, she had actually dozed off. For how long she had no idea, and certainly no way of telling.

Instinctively her hand flew up to confirm that the tiny

transmitter alarm was still in place, before she remembered the driver. At least, she thought, as the car lurched again, he was probably more concerned with the road they had turned onto and, assuming Emma's assertion that the road journey took a couple of hours, by now he had probably all but forgotten his passengers.

Emma!

Cautiously, Alison stretched out her right hand and found the solid, rubber-covered thigh of her captive companion. She let out a sigh of relief, for the contact induced no reaction, which probably meant that Emma, too, had fallen asleep and even the transition to the poorer surface had not yet wakened her.

Uneven road surfaces meant only one thing: they had to be getting close to their destination. Silently, Alison offered up a little prayer that Ruth, Douglas and the rest of them were still out there somewhere, preferably not too far behind, and that they still remained in contact with the car.

Any minute, she thought. Any minute and they'd be there, wherever 'there' actually was. Not that the precise location mattered; 'there' would be a reincarnation of Dennison Hall, or a close copy, with all that that meant and all the horrific memories of Alison's brief yet seemingly interminable stay there.

The prospect of facing Ralph Hancock and his psychotic girlfriend again, especially if they discovered her true identity, was not something Alison wanted to dwell on. Crossing her fingers, she willed herself to remain still, fighting back the feeling of panic that she knew would overwhelm her the moment she lost control.

2.10

By day, the lay-by apparently served as a picnic area for holiday travellers, the mixture of gravel and tarmac that provided the main parking area set well back from the road itself, partially screened by the row of scrubby bushes that ran along the verge.

At one end of the area a new caravanette stood in darkness, holidaymakers taking advantage of a free overnight stay on their way to whatever destination they were heading for, and a battered Ford van keeping it company at a respectful distance. Four of the five vehicles in which the pursuit party had been following the black Bentley stood clustered together at the other end, the various occupants waiting expectantly, some still inside their transports, some standing around in the darkness, smoking or simply exercising cramped leg muscles.

At last the dipped headlights of Ruth's MG appeared, swinging back in off the road, the little sports car sounding even noisier than usual in the stillness of the night air. The engine had scarcely died before Ruth was out, striding purposefully towards the waiting groups, which now began to coagulate into one large knot.

'The place is about a mile and a half further on,' she said, getting straight to the point. 'Can't see any buildings from the road, but it's definitely there. I've left Becky watching; she'll radio back if there's any further movement.'

'It's a big place then,' Mike said.

Ruth nodded. 'We'll need to do a proper recce before dawn, to find out just how far the grounds extend, but from what we saw I'd say they've got to be at least as big as Dennison Hall. Trouble is, the perimeter fences are even tougher; double row of chain-link fences, barbed wire on the tops and alarm wires woven through both lots, probably vibration sensitive.'

'You'd think something like that would attract attention,' Douglas muttered. 'People tend to get nosy when other people get too private.'

'Well, the gate and outer fence are set well back with plenty of cover, and the track up to it isn't exactly vehicle friendly. Plus, they've got a bloody great sign up warning that it's supposed to be some sort of agricultural disease testing establishment, complete with a very official looking logo.'

'With Rafe's contacts,' Marcia said, still leaning against the bonnet of her car, 'it probably is officially sanctioned, though I doubt any real officials ever come here on legitimate business. That'd be just like him. It wouldn't surprise me if he didn't even get some government funding for the place.'

'If it is an official establishment,' Mike said, 'then we'll have to go very carefully. Whatever the bastard is up to in there, breaking into government premises is a very serious offence. Did you see any sign of guards, by the way?'

Ruth nodded. 'Plenty, I'm afraid,' she said. 'Two on the gate and two lots patrolling the wire, both with dogs and all looking very official and smart. Plus,' she added, 'they're armed with what look like automatic rifles. And that's only in the small area we *could* see. Compared to what we had to face at Dennison, this lot could be some sort of small army.'

'Which lets out a direct assault,' Mike said.

'Definitely. We're seriously under strength tonight, and apart from a couple of Brownings, all we've got are the dart guns.' Ruth looked pensive. 'I think we might have made a terrible mistake trying this.'

'Then we'll have to call in the proper authorities,' Mike

said.

'And tell them what?' Marcia snorted. 'You know what Rafe is like. Firstly, we've got no real evidence, other than that Alison was taken inside there in a car. But she went voluntarily, remember? The other girl, Emma, she was the prisoner if either of them was, and she's a regular guest anyway.

'Rafe will also have enough clout in the relevant departments to delay any police interference for long enough to get shot of any evidence, including Hannah. You heard what that Emma said about a helicopter. All he has to do is bundle in Hannah, Alison and anyone else he doesn't want found there, lift them off and transfer them to another vehicle, far enough away from here that we can't follow by road, and what are we left with?'

'We should have thought of all this before,' Mike growled, 'before we let Alley stick her head in the noose.'

'There is a possibility,' Ruth cut in. 'I've been thinking about it all the way down here. That Bentley is the key to it. We wait until it comes back out next time, set up some sort of official looking roadblock and grab the driver.

'The rear windows are tinted so no one can see inside, and the passenger area will hold six of us easily, plus another in the boot. Stick a nine millimetre Browning in the ear of the driver and he'll be more than happy to take us back inside again.'

'And what if the car doesn't come back out for another two or three days?' Douglas snapped. 'I suppose we just hang around out here and do nothing?'

'It won't come to that,' Ruth assured him. 'For a start, I'm willing to bet that there are two or three cars used for ferrying in visitors and this is the weekend starting, so they'll probably be busy. This may have been the last trip tonight, but you can be sure they'll be active again in the morning.

'As a back-up plan, we know the car and its registration,

so if I nip back to that last village and use the public telephone, there's someone in London I know could have us a ringer vehicle down here in six or seven hours.'

'And you think they'll fall for that on the gate?' Douglas sneered derisively.

Ruth gave him a withering look, her eyes flashing in the moonlight. 'They'll change those guards on a regular basis,' she said coldly. 'Probably the night shift will finish around six in the morning, maybe seven. After that they'll work four or five hour watches. Gate duty is boring, so they'll probably swap them all around to stop them falling asleep.

'All we have to do is drive up to the gate just after a shift change and whoever's on there will assume the car went out during an earlier shift.'

'It could work,' Douglas admitted, grudgingly. 'But it would have to be done very efficiently.'

'Efficiently we can do,' Ruth smiled. 'We train for efficiency. We'll have those gate guards in the bag before they know what's hit them, and the dart guns will see off the dogs and the nearest perimeter patrols. We can even take out one of those patrols from this side of the wire, though we'll be stretching our main attack party a bit thin for my liking.'

'I can shoot as straight as anyone,' Douglas asserted. He patted his jacket. 'This is also a Browning automatic,' he added grimly, 'and I can hit a man at forty yards, three times out of four. I did my time out in Korea.'

'That'll help,' Ruth said, 'but actual firearms tend to leave somewhat permanent results, so we should only use them as a last resort. There are spare dart guns in the Hillman; I'll get one of the girls to show you how they work. They're pretty straightforward.

'Now,' she added, addressing the entire party once again, 'I suggest we straggle these vehicles about a bit and get some of you under cover, just in case. This part of Somerset is probably pretty quiet at night, but we don't want to take chances.

'I'm going to drive back to that village and make a couple of phone calls, so please, no one do anything until I get back, whatever happens. We still need to wait for Alison's signal.'

'Sod the signal,' Mike snapped. 'I think we should go in anyway. The less time she spends in there the better, in my opinion.'

'Obviously,' Ruth replied patiently, 'but it's a very large area and there are only ten of us at the moment. I can maybe have another three or four here by first light, but even that's not enough to search the entire place in the time we'll have available, so we'll need Alison to know when we're about to make our move.

'Hopefully she'll find us and, if Hannah's in there, lead us straight to her.'

'And if she doesn't?' Mike persisted.

Ruth shook her head. 'Just hope she does,' she replied tersely.

When the car finally stopped everything happened so quickly that Alison barely had time to react.

She had expected the blindfold hood to be removed once the journey was complete, and then be shown to a room. She was fairly confident she could manage a passable imitation of Daphne's strangulated cut-glass accent, and with the rubber inner mask still in place, would be safe enough from immediate detection. As long as she stuck with the pretence about Emma wishing to play the role of slave and kept the girl gagged and cuffed, she would not be in a position to betray her and any struggles would be interpreted as part of the role play.

Given an hour or two, Alison should then be able to confirm the presence of either Hancock, Hannah, or better still both, trigger the signal button and wait for the cavalry to arrive.

Presuming, she reminded herself, that Ruth and company could find a way in and bearing in mind, as Ruth had pointed out, that they were well below the strength of the previous summer's raiding party. The plan this time would have to involve moving directly on Hancock, or on Kristin if the man himself was not present.

'In and out quickly,' Ruth had specified. Smoke grenades, flashes and maximum confusion as a diversion, and a surgical incision straight to the nerve centre, once Alison had established where it actually was. She made it sound easy, talking about it with the confidence born of training and several previous raids made in genuine wartime conditions, but the events that followed from the moment the car crunched to a halt had not been part of the plan.

No sooner had Alison stepped out onto the gravel surface than her arms were seized, dragged behind her back and cuffed there. Strong hands grasped her shoulders, spinning her around and pushing her towards she knew not what.

'Hey!' she exclaimed, remembering just in time to clip her vowel sounds. 'Hey! You've got the wrong gel. It's Emma who – ummphhh!' The unseen gag was forced between her teeth before she had time to react and she felt the strap being buckled behind her neck by quick and experienced fingers. Panic-stricken, she tried to kick out, but her assailant avoided her clumsy attempts long enough to force her to her knees and snare her ankles with a short hobble chain. As she was being dragged back to her feet again a female voice cut through the confusion of male oaths and mutterings that had accompanied her submission.

'Daphne dear,' it said, the accent a slightly more mature version of the girl Alison was impersonating, 'do calm down and stop wearing your silly self out. It's only a bit of fun and it'll do you good to see things from the other side of the bit, as it were.

'No one's going to harm you, I promise, but I do know Emma wanted to find out what it was like to act out the part of a pony girl, so I thought it only fair for you both to have a stint at it. Don't worry,' she trilled, as blandly as if she were explaining the rules at a school sports day, 'you won't have to do *all* the things a real pony girl is expected to do. I've had a word with Ralphie and he's given strict instructions to all the handlers.

'Now, I've got a few things to see to, but you'll be safe enough. You'll even be stabled in the racing section, so you'll be as comfortable as any pony girl could want. And in the morning I'm even going to drive you myself, as a pair, just until you get used to the routine.

'When Emma let her little secret slip a few weeks ago, I must admit I thought it was a jolly silly idea. But the more I thought about it the more I started to think what a terrific wheeze it might be. And you'll even be able to train with a future world champion. How about that, eh?'

Alison was dumbfounded, as well as dumb. These people were madder than even she had realised, though she did now recall, when Emma and Daphne had visited her in her stall last summer, how Emma had then been musing about what it might be like to be in her situation.

As the unseen hands dragged Alison away, she had one major problem. Even assuming that the stable hands left their rubber masks in place – and she had seen the so called volunteer pony girls masked before, presumably to keep their real identities a secret – it was unlikely that she would be returned the use of her hands, so the little transmitter could not be activated, nor could she get rid of it.

And that spelled bad trouble, for even if her mask wasn't removed, the little waist cincher inside which the device was hidden would certainly be changed in favour of the regulation corset girth that all the pony girls wore. If the handlers recognised the alarm for what it really was the game would be well and truly up, and whether Ruth and her team would move without the signal, she had no idea.

Presumably, if they didn't hear from her, eventually they'd have to realise that something had gone wrong, but how long would they wait and what would Hancock and his pals do to her in the meantime? Closing her eyes under the leather blindfold mask, Alison began to pray like she had never prayed before.

'It's starting to get light,' Mike said. Beside him, in the front seat of the powerful Morgan, Marcia gave a quiet sigh and nodded. 'This waiting is really getting to me,' he continued, fumbling in his jacket for his cigarettes. Between them, the ashtray was already threatening to overflow, the extinguished butts piled high.

'It'll be okay,' Marcia whispered, laying a hand on his thigh. 'You heard what Ruth said, there are actually five more of their girls on the way here now. They should arrive within the hour.'

'If I've let anything happen to the Alley Cat,' Mike said, 'I shan't be able to look Teddy in the eye ever again, nor Honey, for that matter. I mean, I wouldn't even let her come on this little jaunt and she'd have been safe back here with us. Alley's in there, with lord knows what happening.'

'She'll be fine,' Marcia assured him. 'That Alley Cat is a tougher cookie than you'd think. I saw some of the things they did to her at Dennison and she still bounced back, didn't she?'

'But your ex is out for revenge now,' Mike pointed out. 'He could do anything to her.'

'He could and did, last year,' Marcia retorted darkly, 'and he's not the only one with a long memory.'

When the inner rubber mask was pulled off following the

removal of the outer blindfold hood, Alison steeled herself for the worst. But to her relief the blonde who confronted her was not Kristin, but a complete stranger, similar in appearance but clearly a few years younger.

'Welcome to pony world, slut,' the woman said cheerfully. 'My name is Mistress Phoebe and it will be my pleasure to show you just what we do with errant fillies in these stables. The fact that you both volunteered – well, one of you, anyway – won't make much difference, except that the male stable hands won't be allowed to fuck either of you, not unless I receive orders to the contrary.'

With a start of horror Alison remembered Emma. The moment her gag was removed she would surely give the game away, or would the threat of what might happen to her friend, the real Daphne, be enough to still her tongue? Being turned into a pony girl for the weekend wouldn't worry her, not if what Daphne's mother had said was true. In fact, it would be quite the opposite.

Hopefully the stupid bubble-headed creature would hold her tongue until a bit held it for her. She'd probably even get off on the whole thing even more. Alison remembered her own early experiences, both at Marcia's and after her arrival at Dennison Hall. To her everlasting shame there had been times, even amidst the very real danger on the latter occasion, when she too had surrendered to a power and longing she had never dreamed lurked within her.

Maybe, she thought grimly, Emma wasn't the only bubble-headed blonde around the place.

'Can I ask where my friend is?' she asked meekly, hoping she sounded upper class enough. Evidently this woman had either not met the real Daphne, or else she'd had so little contact with her that she'd forgotten what she really looked like.

Phoebe smirked. 'In the next stable, being prepared by your mother. We thought it best that I took care of you; family connection and all that.'

'How – how is she?'

Phoebe looked surprised at the question. 'How would you expect her to be? After all, this was her idea, according to Mistress Bunty.'

'So I understand,' Alison said. 'But please, this isn't really my thing. Let Em play if she wants, but I didn't come down here for that.'

'Sorry,' Phoebe said, grinning. 'I've got my instructions, not just from your mother, but from the boss man himself. He says you're a pony – you're a pony.'

'He's here then?'

'Of course,' Phoebe snapped, suddenly sounding impatient, 'but it won't do you any good appealing to him. Once he makes up his mind…'

'I see.' The tiny transmitter box seemed to be growing bigger with every passing second and Alison knew she had to either activate it, or at least find some way of getting rid of it, and quickly.

'I – I wonder if I could use the toilet,' she stammered. 'Before we get started, I mean?'

Phoebe laughed. 'You can do that once I've finished preparing you,' she said. 'Ponies don't have the luxury of toilets. Ponies pee on the floor and dump where they stand, only make sure you keep your boots out of the line of fire.'

'Please?' Alison persisted. 'Only I don't think this will wait and you don't want me fouling up the floor in here, do you? After all, I'll have the rest of the weekend to do it the other way.'

Phoebe sighed. 'Okay. It takes a good hour to get you fitted out the way I've been told to, so a couple of minutes extra won't hurt, I suppose. Mistress Rose has a toilet in her quarters. She's out trotting her new pet, so you can use that.'

'Can you just release my hands then?' Alison asked, offering her wrists. Phoebe's sigh was even more pronounced, but she fumbled in her belt pouch.

'Make it quick,' she said gruffly, 'and get shucked out of that suit while you're at it. You won't need that while you're here. I've got a nice new pony skin for you, there, on the rack, see?' Alison looked, saw, and her mouth started to feel very dry indeed. But for now her main concern was getting rid of the one thing that would immediately arouse Phoebe's suspicions – to get rid of it, and to activate the signal that would let her intended rescuers know that their quarry was in the trap.

2.11

The relief Alison felt at having been able to hide the signalling device behind the toilet cistern in Rose's quarters was rapidly replaced by a returning apprehension, for Phoebe wasted no time in getting to work on her once she was back in the stall. For the few minutes she had been relatively free she considered making a break for it, perhaps finding a hiding place until the rescue party appeared, but a quick inspection showed that every window was barred and the door from Rose's section of the building to the outside world was securely locked.

'You took your time,' Phoebe remarked, standing in the wide corridor outside the stall, and effectively blocking any route of escape in that direction. She nodded towards the waiting chamber. 'Get your arse in there and stop wasting any more of my time.'

Alison held up the rubber suit that was now draped over her arm, together with the waist cincher. In her other hand she held the boots she'd arrived in.

'I'm sorry,' she said, 'but it's a bit of a struggle getting out of something like this on my own. Emma usually helps me,' she added, by way of further explanation.

'Well, she won't be much use to you for a while,' Phoebe said. Alison cast a sideways glance at the two closed stalls she had passed. From inside the second she'd heard the sounds of movement and her biggest fear was that Bunty Horrocks would suddenly open the door and see her without her mask. She needed no further encouragement to scuttle into the open stall, and relaxed again only when the two sections of the door were pulled shut behind them.

'Now,' Phoebe said, taking her things and tossing them into a corner, 'as I said, neither of you will be available to the stable lads. In that respect, you'll be treated like the competition ponies. They don't get screwed by anyone, not without sanction from either me or Mistress Rose.

'However, in all other respects you are to be treated the same. That means no talking – though you'll be bitted most of the time anyway – no alcohol, no smoking, no sleeping lying down and no disobedience, not unless you want to feel the whip on your hindquarters.

'You'll be exercised, paraded and trained to draw various carts, and you'll also be expected to perform certain other functions for selected guests, as directed either by myself or Mistress Rose.'

'Other functions?' Alison echoed.

Phoebe smiled again, but it was not a pleasant smile. 'Use your imagination,' she leered. 'You've got more than one suitable orifice and, like I said, you'll be bitted *most* of the time, not all of it.'

'Oh,' Alison murmured, 'I see.'

'Got any problems with that, pony girl?' she grated. 'Not that it matters if you have, of course. Pony girls aren't permitted choices, as you probably realise.'

'Of course,' Alison said, lowering her gaze. 'It's just that – well, this wasn't any of my idea.'

'Not my problem,' Phoebe sniggered. 'Just be grateful it's only for a day or two.'

The 'pony skin' Phoebe had referred to earlier turned out to be another latex catsuit, though, Alison realised, as Phoebe began to put her into it, to describe it as 'just another' catsuit was not doing justice either to it, or to whoever designed and made it. And it was immediately obvious that Hancock's enthusiastic cohorts had not been idle in the twelve months since she had last fallen foul of them. Someone, or several someone's, had put a lot of thought and creativity into the refinements that had been made in the past year, and the suit was perfect testimony to their efforts.

Firstly, the rubber itself – dappled brown and cream in appearance – appeared to have been pierced all over by a series of tiny needles, so that the surface was covered in thousands of tiny holes. A neat idea, Alison admitted grudgingly, especially if it was intended to be worn for long periods, for a body contained within an impervious skin of the fabric would perspire alarmingly before long, especially if required to undertake any great exertions. Making the skin porous would reduce this problem considerably.

Phoebe fitted hoof boots to Alison's legs and feet, and then stepped back and examined her charge critically, nodding her approval. Alison was only too aware of the picture she now presented, with her breasts bulging proudly out through the restrictive circular openings in the chest of the suit, her denuded sex forced into prominence by the tight rubber at either side of the opening between her legs. The dappled skin covered more than

199

ninety percent of her body from the neck down, but in leaving the most intimate parts so lewdly displayed and accessible, made her look and feel even more vulnerable than if she had been left completely naked.

'Not bad for a start,' Phoebe commented. 'With sufficient training you might even make a decent competition pony, in the amateur fillies class, anyway. The real professional thoroughbreds are a class apart, of course.'

She turned and took the white leather girth corset from the rack and proceeded to wrap it around Alison's midriff, hooking the front together with the sturdy steel snaps, forcing Alison to suck in her stomach as she proceeded down the entire front busk. When she had finished it felt tight and restrictive, but Alison was experienced enough to know that she was far from finished.

The gap between the two halves at the rear of the corset was a good three inches, but that, she knew, was only a temporary state of affairs, and Phoebe went to work on the thick laces, using her powerful fingers at first and then employing a wicked looking, wooden handled hook when the whole thing became too tight to force even one finger between the laces and the rubber skin beneath. Gradually the gap narrowed, forcing Alison's waist into a smaller and smaller diameter, driving the breath from all but the very top part of her lungs in a fashion more severe than any corset she had encountered before.

'There,' Phoebe announced at last, 'that should keep you nicely under control. You know the routine for breathing now, don't you?' Red-faced, Alison nodded, concentrating on taking in short shallow breaths; it was a technique she thought she had perfected long since, but this vicious leather vice taxed even her experience to its limits.

Phoebe, meanwhile, was more concerned with other matters. Firstly, she took down a long tail made from brown horsehair. The base had been braided to form a stiffened stem and this was now slotted and twisted into some sort of receptor in the rear of the pony skin, set just in the top divide of Alison's buttocks, where it was impossible for her to see it.

Next came what Alison initially assumed was a dildo, except that, as Phoebe made ready to insert it into her, she saw it was hollow at its centre and that there was a series of oval openings along one side. Furthermore, Phoebe seemed to take an inordinate amount of care in ensuring that the rubber shaft entered in a particular plane, so that when she added the intricate harness straps that prevented its expulsion, they also linked up to holes on the flanged base, thus preventing it from rotating.

'You can pee with this in,' Phoebe explained curtly. 'And the straps at the back here,' she continued, adjusting them sideways and around underneath each buttock, 'leave you free to take a dump, too. Just watch out you don't foul your tail, or you'll feel the crop. You'll have to adjust your stance a bit.'

Alison was horrified: her initial introduction to the world of pony girls had not lasted very long, although it had felt longer at the time, and the question of toilet arrangements had never arisen. 'But I can't!' she protested, ignoring Phoebe's immediately raised eyebrows. 'I mean, I'll just splash everywhere if I do it standing up!'

Phoebe snorted. 'A fussy filly, eh? Well don't worry, pony girl, it's all taken care of. See, I'll show you.' She reached up to the rack and this time took down a curiously curved metallic object. With deft fingers she clipped one end of it to the two front straps that secured the dildo. Quite how this was effected, Alison could not see, but the result was that the curving chute-shaped piece was held so that it jutted down beneath the opening in the centre of the rubber shaft.

'When you pee now,' Phoebe told her with clear relish,

'it should all be deflected backwards, which saves splattering your boots and hooves. It's quite a new idea and is very popular among certain of the guests.'

'That sounds sick,' Alison muttered.

'I thought I told you there was to be no talking?' Phoebe snarled.

Alison tensed for the blow she was sure was about to come, wondering if perhaps she should retaliate while she still had her arms free. After all, she reasoned, one decent kick from the weighted boots would inflict considerable damage, maybe even break a leg. However, Phoebe's immediate anger abated as quickly as it had appeared and the moment of decision was past. A few minutes later the opportunity was also gone, Alison's arms laced into mitten-ended sleeves, her wrists snapped together behind her back.

'And now,' Phoebe announced with an air of triumph, 'it's time for your head, pony. I think you'll appreciate this, even if you do find it a bit uncomfortable. Look at it this way, if there are any of your friends out there, they certainly won't recognise you.'

Indeed, Alison thought, as the complicated piece was lowered over her head, they certainly would not recognise her: not friends, not family, not even Teddy. The mask left only her eyes and mouth exposed, the former behind strange shaped tinted lenses, the latter all but hidden by the elongated snout that now projected from the bridge of her nose, forming astonishingly horse-like jaws and ending in the stiff collar to which the entire ensemble was affixed.

'Superb,' Phoebe declared, snapping the collar fastenings shut beneath the mane of horsehair that descended from the back of the head. 'All we need now is to get you a bridle and fix your bit. And I see you've already had your nipples pierced, so I can fix you up with reins the way the full-time pony girls wear them, down from either end of the bit and through nipple rings. You'll soon learn to respond properly like that, I can tell you.'

The substitute Bentley arrived with the rising sun, bringing with it six more people – five more of Hannah and Ruth's female commandos and a shallow-faced young man with greasy black hair and badly pockmarked face. His name, Ruth told Mike and Marcia, was Pieter, an orphan refugee from wartime Poland whose uncle was responsible for supplying the car.

'He doesn't ever say a lot,' she explained, 'but he's very reliable and has got more guts than any man I've ever met.' She smiled grimly but refused to elaborate and, at that moment, one of the original group of girls called over from the car in which she had been sitting.

'I'm getting the signal, captain,' she announced. 'Loud and clear.'

Ruth raised a hand in acknowledgement. 'Good for Alison,' she muttered. 'Now we can start getting ourselves properly organised. The moment that car comes out of there we'll be ready to go in.'

'And what if it's a different car?' Mike demanded.

'As long as it's another Bentley,' Ruth said, 'I don't give a shit. There should be a number-plate kit in the boot of ours, so we can change the number accordingly.'

'And if it's not a Bentley?'

'Then we wait until it is,' Ruth replied firmly, 'and hope we don't have to wait too long.'

Phoebe completed the task of fitting the bridle and bit and then, collecting up Alison's discarded travelling outfit, stepped outside into the corridor and kicked the lower section of the stable door closed. With her free hand she slid a heavy bolt across and stood looking back into the stall for several seconds.

'Normally,' she said, 'I'd hitch you up to a sleeping harness, but I don't think I need bother. Those boots are so new I doubt you'll be able to bend your knees, and even if you do manage to sit or lie down, you won't get up again on your own. If you're found lying down without express permission, that's a whipping offence.'

Alison stared back at her through the tinted lenses, the wide spacing of which made direct forward vision almost impossible, and bit into the rubber bar between her teeth, which at the same time pinned her tongue flat by means of a small projecting metal plate. She had encountered a similar device at Dennison Hall and knew that a smart tug on the reins, which now led down from either corner of her artificial outer mouth, via the rings in her nipples, would cause the plate to swivel upwards, driving a stud hard against her palate with painful results.

As Phoebe turned and stalked off down the corridor, Alison found herself hoping fervently that Emma had been subjected to the same design of bit. The stupid little cow next door was responsible for her present predicament, after all, and had even been stupid enough to wish this sort of treatment on herself.

But then, Alison mused, as she turned and paced slowly back and forth across the confined floor space, hadn't she done something not dissimilar herself? Not that she would have volunteered to become a pony girl in the hands of these maniacs, but then, as far as Emma and Daphne were concerned, Hancock and company were no more a real danger than Marcia and Douglas were to Alison, Honey, or any of the other girls who regularly placed themselves at their mercy.

To her horror she realised the slow pacing was producing a steady friction from the dildo-catheter that could have only one result if she kept it up. She had to keep her mind on the job. Not, she realised, that it would make very much difference what she did at that moment. Trapped inside the dappled skin, the pony head locked as securely in place as the fetters that held her wrists and the bridle that kept the bit forced deep inside her mouth, Alison's part in the coming events would be nothing more than a passive one. Assuming Ruth and her team moved soon, the first she would know about it was when it was all over.

Trapped inside the pony skin and head also meant *safe* inside the pony skin and head. Given that neither she, nor presumably, Emma, had been allowed any sleep since they had been collected the evening before, it was most likely they would be left alone for a while, neatly packaged little fetish icons, harmless, unconsidered, waiting on the convenience of whomever finally decided to avail themselves of their uncomplaining services.

Backing into a corner, Alison leaned into the angle of wall and partition, carefully balancing her weight against the L-shaped support it offered, and tested the hoof boots for flexibility. True to Phoebe's assertion, there was almost none at the knee joint.

Bracing her legs, feet slightly apart, Alison sighed and closed her eyes. It was unlikely she would be able to sleep like this, but at least, she reasoned, she could catnap after a fashion and, if she ended up on the floor, well, she would tackle that problem when the time came. Meantime, she was beginning to feel very tired – very tired indeed.

2.12

'If I said I didn't have a bad feeling about all this,' Ruth said, 'I'd be lying. But then I guess you all feel the same way.' She looked around the semi-circle of sombre faces and then back again, until her gaze met Mike's.

'In case anyone didn't recognise the number,' she continued, 'the car we followed down here has diplomatic plates; diplomatic plates from the embassy of a country very unfriendly towards my own – our own, in the majority case here – and very powerful. Whatever we do here, if it involves any of their so called diplomatic personnel, there will be some pretty heavy repercussions. But as far as I'm concerned, that's somebody else's problem, right?'

The arc of heads nodded, to the accompaniment of a general mumble of agreement.

'So,' Ruth said, drawing in a deep breath, 'all we need to worry about is here and now. God knows, that's enough worry on its own.' She extended the piece of branch she had picked up from the nearby verge and drew a rough circle in the dusty mud between her and the rest of the party.

'Perimeter fences,' she said curtly. 'Not to scale, because we don't have the first idea how big this place really is. The recces we've done, however, suggest it's a big area, partly wooded, though we can't find a vantage point to tell any more. The gate is here,' she said, marking a small cross, 'and what passes for a road runs straight in this way.' She added another line.

'We have to assume some sort of main building, possibly an old house that's been converted, possibly a new purpose-built structure, we don't know. Odds are that there will be more than just a single building and Hannah and Alison could be in any of them. Therefore, the main target has to be Hancock, if he's here, or his bitch of a sidekick if not.

'What we don't want to do is tip them to our presence before we really need to, otherwise our friends could suffer for it. So, we don't just go storming in, okay?' She looked around again, waiting for nods of comprehension.

'The gatehouse seems to be in communication with the rest of the place by means of a telephone landline,' she continued. 'There are poles leading back from behind the building carrying two cables. One appears to be power, the other a single telegraph wire.

'That wire must be a prime objective. As soon as we jump the guards one person will go for the wire and cut it, in case there are other guards inside.'

'And what if they've got a radio link?' Douglas interrupted.

'There's no antenna on the building and none of the guards observed were carrying handsets, not on the gate, anyway. The patrols seem to have walkie-talkies, but it looks as if they report back to the main building, or some sort of control centre further in. So, as soon as the car enters the gate, Sarah T and her section will take out the patrol in this sector.' Again the twig stabbed down.

'The nearest patrol in the other direction can't see the gatehouse unless they're almost on top of it. There's a heavy screen of trees and large bushes all along here, and here, and here.' She looked up again.

'Once we're in and the first patrol has been taken out,' she said, 'we spread out and tackle the perimeter patrols as we encounter them. Sarah's group, having taken care of the first patrol, will enter and secure the gate and gatehouse.'

'Surely,' Douglas pointed out, 'trying to take out all the perimeter patrols is going to take time? Shouldn't we just go for our main objective?'

'If you're going to be a part of this operation,' Ruth retorted testily, 'then just listen and keep your mouth shut. I'll ask for questions in a minute.

'However,' she said, smiling coldly, 'as you've asked, I'll explain. If we just crash ahead we leave ourselves open to being trapped, hemmed in on all sides. We've no real way of knowing how many patrols there are, any more than we know how long the perimeter actually is. But if they're following the usual procedures, each patrol will cover a sector that slightly overlaps the next and if any one patrol fails to meet up with its neighbour, then the balloon will go up pretty quickly.

'Therefore, even though it'll take time, our best strategy is to clear that perimeter so we know we don't have to watch our backs. If any other visitors arrive at the gate meanwhile, Sarah and her girls will deal with them. We have our own radio contact on very secure frequencies, so everyone should be in the picture.

'Once we've cleared the patrols we can move in on whatever main centre there is in there.'

'And what if anything goes wrong with your plan?' Mike asked gently.

Ruth looked at him for several seconds, before finally replying. 'It depends on exactly what goes wrong,' she said at last. 'We can probably handle the odd mishap, but if the worst comes to the worst, then it's a case of get the fuck out of there as fast as possible.'

'And Hannah and Alison?' Marcia said, speaking for the first time.

Ruth stared down at her rough mud map. 'Like I said,' she replied, her voice barely audible, 'we get the fuck out of there, even if it means leaving them behind. They've already got two of us – let's not give them any more, okay?'

To her surprise, Alison realised she had actually dozed off in her standing position, jammed tightly into the corner of the stall, and it was only the ringing sound of steel shod boots on the bare paving outside the door that brought her jarring back to the world of wakefulness and reality. Instantly she was alert, pushing herself upright and clear of the supporting walls, preparing to face whatever fresh indignities the callous Phoebe had in store for her.

Except…

The two sections of the door swung back as one, to reveal the awesome bulk of Ralph Hancock himself. Alison felt her stomach somersault, cramping inside the vicious confines of her corset girth, her knees melting so that only the rigidity of the hoof boots kept her from crumpling to the straw covered floor. It had seemed easy enough from the outside, something she felt confident she could confront again. But now the moment had come the unexpected confrontation tripped the treacherous safety catches of her self-control, leaving only fear and a sequence of memories that thrust past the barricades of a year to present themselves in full glory.

Slowly, Hancock stepped forward. He was dressed simply; leather slacks tucked into heavy ankle boots, and an open fronted silk shirt that hid little of his powerfully muscled chest. His hair was fairer than she remembered, and slightly longer, though still fairly close-cropped, and his complexion showed evidence of many hours spent in the sun. He raised his right hand, crooked his index finger and made a beckoning movement.

Alison moved forward hesitantly, praying her legs would not betray her. Her iron hooves scraped on the stone beneath the straw, her left foot catching on a slight unevenness that threatened to propel her headlong, but with a supreme effort she recovered her balance, took one more faltering step, and stopped, an arm's length before him.

'I see you've remembered something of what Mistress Rose had started to teach you,' he drawled. Alison blinked. Rose? She had not seen Rose since the previous summer at Dennison Hall, which was fortunate, for had the pony mistress, rather than Phoebe, been the one to see her without her mask, she must surely have recognised her.

'You seem a little confused, pony girl,' Hancock said. 'Hardly surprising, I suppose. This isn't quite what you had in mind, is it?' he reached out, seized Alison's left nipple roughly between finger and thumb and squeezed it brutally. Alison chewed deeply into the bit and tried not to make any sound, but it was a challenge she only just met. Her breasts rose and fell in heavy unison, but Hancock maintained his grip and simply allowed his hand to move with the inflamed teat.

'Let me guess,' he continued, speaking quietly, almost lazily. 'You thought you'd get in here and have a look around, see if you could find the Jewish bitch, is that it?' Alison froze, even the pain in her nipple suddenly gone. Hancock threw back his head and roared with laughter.

'Stupid little slut!' he cried. 'Did you think Bunty wouldn't recognise her own daughter, even under a mask and discipline hood?' He released his grip and shoved Alison between her breasts with such force that she back-pedalled into the rear wall with a rib-jarring crash, the impact on her bound elbows sending shock waves up to her shoulders.

'Well, Miss Katt,' Hancock sneered, 'you've saved me a lot of trouble in the long run. Oh yes, I know you've got a whole load of friends out there somewhere – we spoke to the silly bitch, Emma, and she told us what she knew.

'I suppose you thought it would just be a case of poking around for an hour or two and then sending for the cavalry, eh? Well, my dear little Miss Katt, I'm afraid not. Your interference at Dennison Hall was an inconvenience, to say the least, but it did serve a valuable purpose, believe me. The security there was a joke – I see that now, which is why the defences of this place have been so much better prepared.

'You wouldn't have had the chance to see on your way in, of course, but there's a double fence, the inner of which is electrified, with floodlights at regular intervals. There are many more security personnel than before, many of whom are funded by the taxpayer, which I find quite amusing. Not only that, but there are concrete pillboxes hidden in the undergrowth, from which they can fire upon any would-be attackers. And this time we are forewarned, of course.

'So you see, your friends out there will find a very unpleasant reception waiting for them when – and I say when, not if – they attempt to repeat their tactics of last summer. Of course, it may well be necessary to kill a few of the Jewish sluts, which would be a great waste, but those who do happen to survive will find we have stable accommodation aplenty waiting for them.'

Hancock stepped forward, grasped the rein dangling from Alison's bridle and hauled her back towards him.

'Meanwhile, you meddling little baggage, there will be plenty of time for us to renew acquaintance. I have been promising myself a few extravagances since our last encounter, and right now would seem as good a time as any to begin.' He moved back towards the door, dragging Alison in his wake.

'First things first,' he growled, stepping out into the passageway. 'You came here looking for the Jewess, so the least I can do is let you see her. Then she can watch and see for herself just how futile your pathetic attempts to cross me really are!'

'Gold one from gold two – we have two male targets in sight. Ready to go on your word.'

'Roger, gold two. Target vehicle has just left and we are

211

now mobile. Repeat – we are now mobile. Stand by.'

'Roger, gold one. Standing by.'

Ruth lowered her radio and looked around the cramped rear of the Bentley, the knuckles of her other hand white on the stock of her dart rifle.

'Remember,' she said levelly, 'quickly and quietly, and those of you with actual firearms, they're only as a last resort in life-threatening situations, okay?'

'Gold one from gold two – hold up there a moment, we have a problem.'

'Shit! Roger, gold two, what's the nature of your problem?'

'Targets have disappeared back into the bushes and there seems to be some sort of structure in there, maybe a sentry box or something.'

'Damn! Why didn't we know about this before, gold two?'

'Search me, captain. It's well hidden and we wouldn't have seen it now, not if they hadn't headed straight for it.'

'Roger, gold two, fair enough. Maintain your position and get ready to take them if they show any signs of making for the gate.'

'Roger that, gold one.'

'Something's up,' Mike said, licking lips that had just become even drier than before. 'Maybe we should hold off for a bit and think about this.'

'I just did,' Ruth said curtly. 'And we go ahead as planned. Sarah and her team are in position further along the fence, out of sight of the gatehouse, though only just. If they're opposite this pillbox, or whatever it is, then whoever's inside it can't see the gate either. Odds are, the two guards have just sloped off for a crafty fag and a cup of tea.'

'But if not and they hear us they can radio in,' Mike pointed out.

'*If* they hear us,' she said. 'If not, then nothing's changed, except that we'll have to take them out ourselves. Sarah and company can keep an eye on them in case they come out meantime, but if not, they'll be watching the fence. They won't expect us to come at them from the inside.'

'I hope you're right,' Mike replied.

So did Ruth, but decided that sentiment would be best left unvoiced.

By the time Rose finally dragged Hannah out into the paddock again, the wheeled covering frame had once more been positioned directly in front of the stable block and its intended victim stood beside it, held on a short rein by Hancock. Hannah stared at the hapless female figure in horrified fascination: if she had not been told that this was Alison Katt, the girl she had rescued the previous summer, she would never have known it, for her head was encased in one of the bizarre pony heads, rendering her as anonymous as Hercules or any of the other stud stallions.

Hancock seemed so pleased with himself that any lingering doubts Hannah might have entertained as to whether this really was Alison Katt were immediately banished; besides, she reasoned, there would be no reason for these swine to lie to her. No, somehow or other they had managed to capture the poor girl, and Hancock lost no time in explaining how.

'No doubt the slut has friends on the outside,' he said. 'Probably they're your friends – yet again – and they think they're going to rescue the pair of you. I imagine she was only sent in to check whether you were actually here and that the device we found secreted in the toilet is some sort of signalling equipment. Oh yes, Miss Katt,' he went on, turning to address Alison, 'we've found it all right.

'Not that it took a great deal of detective work. As soon as Mistress Phoebe said she had allowed you to go to the toilet on your own, I guessed you might have been up to

213

something. Well, you had no way of knowing if this bitch was here before we secured you, but there's always the chance you did activate the thing anyway, so we haven't interfered with it at all – wouldn't want to tip your friends that we're on to you, would we?

'Not that it will make the slightest difference. As I said, the security here is first rate, and now we're alerted they won't get in. Wherever they are, it won't be long before we have a fix on them.' He turned back towards the stable block as Phoebe emerged, strutting with her usual arrogance.

'Did you contact Cameron?' he snapped.

'As you instructed,' she replied. 'The chopper needs warming for a few minutes and they have to fit the gun anyway, but he reckons to be here within twenty minutes or so and then he says he'll need another fifteen minutes to quarter the area for likely targets.'

'Excellent.' Hancock's smile grew wider than ever and he turned his attention back to the two captives. 'Air supremacy,' he said smugly. 'The key factor in all modern warfare. Assuming your friends are out there in numbers they should be easy enough to spot. And then we can deal with them when necessary.

'Repeat the alert warning to all security stations,' he added, this time to Phoebe once again. 'Have them all report status back to control at five minute intervals and have the central security put on to maximum. All guests are confined to the main house until further notice – all slaves and ponies are to be moved to the cellar stables.'

Phoebe nodded, spun elegantly on her high heel and disappeared rapidly back inside the block. Almost before she had started moving, Hancock seemed to have forgotten all thoughts of problems. He jerked on Alison's lead rein, almost pulling her off her feet.

'Meanwhile,' he said, nodding to the waiting frame, 'I think we can teach you a few valuable lessons.'

'You wanna coffee?' Charlie Doyle flicked the switch on the electric kettle and moved two clean mugs across the small work surface that covered most of the back wall of the cramped gatehouse. Ronnie, his twin brother and the younger by almost ten minutes, looked up from the crumpled remnants of the morning racing page and grunted acceptance.

'You wanna try looking a bit more on the ball,' Charlie advised. 'Whatever's going down has got them on bricks up at the house, and I wouldn't be surprised if they didn't send someone down here to check up on us.'

'Nah.' Ronnie returned his main interest to the big race form and shook his head. 'They won't stir themselves,' he asserted. 'Besides, I'm only passing the time, ain't I? I mean, look at these fucking great gates, will you?' He raised his head momentarily, nodding pointedly to where the heavy steel and mesh barriers rose up only a few feet from the observation window. 'What the fuck's gonna get through that lot without us opening 'em, eh? You couldn't ram through them with a ten ton truck.'

'Maybe not,' Charlie said, scratching absently at his receding hairline, 'but they said to be on our toes. You checked your gun, by the way?'

'What's to check?' Ronnie patted the breast of his uniform jacket, his fingers caressing the reassuring bulge just forward of his left armpit. 'It's still fully loaded, the safety catch is on and it'll probably stay that way until the end of the shift.'

'Let's hope so,' Charlie said, ladling instant coffee into the first mug. 'I don't mind being tooled up for any job, you know, but actually shooting at someone is a bit different.'

'We shot at people out in Malaya,' his twin reminded him, smirking.

Charlie sniffed and spooned coffee into the second mug. 'That was different,' he asserted. 'They was Chinks and they was shooting at us first, ungrateful little slitty-eyed fuckers.'

'Well, same as I said, it won't come to that,' Ronnie said. 'This is probably just some sort of exercise drill. Maybe they've got some bigwig coming down.'

'Who knows?' Charlie replied. He flicked off the power to the kettle and unplugged the cord. 'I gave up wondering about this lot months ago. It's a bloody weird set-up.'

'And definitely not as kosher as it's supposed to look from the outside.' Ronnie grinned. 'But who cares, so long as they keep paying the dosh?'

'And letting you fuck the odd bird, eh?' Charlie retorted. 'Can't see how you can do that myself. Give me a nice London bird with big knockers and a comfy bed. All those straps and things don't do bugger all for me.' He grinned and splashed boiling water across the tops of the two mugs. 'Sometimes,' he said, 'I wonder if you really are my brother, the things that turn you on. Ain't natural.'

'Maybe I'm just the dark side of us,' Ronnie sniggered. 'I was reading something in a Sunday magazine last week, I think it was. Bloke reckons some twins are like that: chalk and cheese, good and bad, light and dark. Reckon maybe I'm the devil's side of the family.'

'Reckon you are,' Charlie agreed, banging the kettle back down again. 'Got any fags on you, by the way? I forgot to pick up a packet on the way in this morning.'

'Not again.' Ronnie folded the paper untidily and tossed it onto the small desk that stood beneath the observation window, where it sat crookedly atop the clipboard and the cellophane wrapped sandwiches he had bought at the transport cafe two hours earlier. He reached inside his jacket and withdrew a fresh pack of cigarettes.

'I'm going to start keeping a record of all these,' he said. 'Reckon you must owe me about… 'ullo, we've got visitors.' He started to stand up, but as the sleek black limousine finished rounding the bend in the track, he relaxed back into his seat again and reached instead for the lever that controlled the electrically powered gates.

'As you were, soldier,' he muttered. 'It's one of ours.'

'Jerry,' Charlie said, turning to peer over his brother's shoulder. 'He must have been up and about bright and early.'

'This is probably the visitor all the fuss is about.'

'No one said there actually *was* a visitor,' Charlie said. 'Anyway, there's *always* fucking visitors here. Tell me a day there isn't.' He moved towards the door, pausing to retrieve the clipboard from beneath the gathering detritus. 'But, seeing as how we're supposed to be looking efficient today, I guess we'd better do this by the rules. Open the gates.'

Tethered to the rail in front of the stable block, Hannah could do nothing but watch in silence as Hancock and Rose forced Alison onto the covering frame, securing her hands and neck in the manner to which Hannah had become so accustomed, so that she was left in the same helpless bent posture, her buttocks thrust invitingly upwards and outwards. In such a position the stallions were offered no resistance, as Hannah knew only too well.

However, on this occasion it seemed Hancock was not intending to put his newest prisoner to the ordeal of Hercules' inordinately proportioned manhood, but simply to administer a thrashing on the rubber clad rump. He picked up a long riding crop from the decking of the frame, flexed it between his hands, and nodded approvingly.

'The two of you have, in one way or another, been the cause of a considerable amount of inconvenience to me,' he said, swishing the braided leather through the air. 'One meddling little slut and one arrogant whore.' He looked from Alison to Hannah and then back again. 'And now look at the pair of you. Good for one thing and one thing only.

'By the time I'm through with the pair of you, you'll regret the day you ever heard my name. And you'll be begging to do anything I ask. You, Miss Katt, saw only a hint of what we can do, whereas the Jewess here has already been here long enough to understand her new position.

'So, miss reporter of the year, perhaps you should start taking notes. Oh, silly me, you don't have a notebook and pencil, do you? Never mind, my dear, I can assure you I have my own methods of making sure you never forget a single second.' He stepped back, flexed his elbow and drew back his arm, the crop hanging, quivering, for a second or two.

'One!' he cried, swinging into the first stroke. The crop hissed through the air like a firework, the leather exploding against the thin rubber skin covering Alison's buttocks, the report sharp, like a ricocheting bullet, the thin scream renting the morning air a split second later.

Hannah flinched, and every welt on her own skin seemed to come alive again in tortured sympathy.

'Two!' Again the crop seared through the air and this time the shriek it invoked was even louder. Hannah closed her eyes, blinking away tears. It was bad enough being whipped herself, but in a way that she could never explain, this was even worse, to be forced to watch a fellow human being made to endure the same pain, misery and anguish without being able to lift a hand against it.

2.13

Ruth stood just inside the small gatehouse, staring down at the two near identical unconscious figures, the dart rifle cradled across one arm, radio held poised in her other hand. The dark-haired figure of the other Sarah, Sergeant Levinski, appeared in the doorway behind her.

'Perimeter incursion squads away, captain,' she said quietly. 'Sarah T's squad are on standby to rejoin us.'

Ruth looked down at her radio and nodded. 'I heard,' she said. She pushed a booted toe against the nearest recumbent guard. 'Better secure these two jokers and set up a dummy guard. Ask Douglas and Mike to come in, would you? Best get them to do it; I doubt Hancock is the type to employ women as guards.'

'Will do,' Sarah confirmed. 'What about the rest of us?'

'Get the Bentley out of sight and make sure the other cars are well away and hidden in the woods off the lane outside. Then, two in here with me and Miss Davenport, you and the other two get under cover in those bushes at the rear of the building, where you can see anyone coming back down the track from the inside, okay? No one moves except on my word, or unless you're seen and in immediate danger, got that?'

'Got it.' Sarah Levinski saluted, spun on her heel and was gone, leaving Ruth alone for a few seconds. Slowly, she let out a deep sigh of relief. So far, so good. These two clowns had proved to be about as efficient as the way they wore their so-called uniforms, the cluttered and grimy interior of the small room evidence enough of a general lack of discipline and enthusiasm. If the rest of Hancock's forces proved to be of a similar calibre, then maybe this venture might turn out not to be such a disaster as she had been beginning to fear.

Maybe. But Ruth Goldman was an experienced enough campaigner not to put too much faith in uncertainties, and the biggest of those was that they still had no idea of the size of the forces they were now pitted against.

The dreadful beating had finally come to an end, but Alison's buttocks still felt as if they were on fire and Hancock, it seemed, was far from finished with her. Tossing the crop aside, he walked slowly around to stand in front of her, one hand grasping the ears of her rubber head, the other resting suggestively on the prominent bulge in the crotch of his tight leather breeches.

'I don't think I need to tell you what's coming next, do I?' he leered. 'I leave the Jew girl to the animals, but you're something else again. We'll keep you nice and tight for now and let you earn your keep, though I reckon Mistress Rose can train you with the whore in between times. She seems to think you've got potential as a racer, too, even though you'll probably never be as fast as the other one.

'Still, we can't have everything, can we?' he said, letting Alison's head flop down again. 'So, I'll just have to see what your other attributes are worth.' He drew down the heavy zipper, pulled apart the front of his breeches and withdrew an organ that was already well on the way to achieving a full and very daunting erection. Once again, he grasped one of the rubber ears and yanked Alison's head up, ensuring that she had a full and perfect view of what was coming.

'I might even have you as my personal filly, once you're fully broken in and trained,' he said. 'I've never really bothered too much with the ponies, but I have to admit the thought of these pretty legs and their hooves stretched out on my bed is quite appealing.'

This time he lowered Alison's head less dismissively,

but she hardly noticed the difference. Stretched out over the cunningly adjustable frame, all she could think of was that she was being presented to him like a mare in season, thighs held wide, her exposed sex stretched and, even worse, despite the beating – or even because of it – already well lubricated. And Hancock was not slow to notice the fact.

'Hah!' he exclaimed. 'Some things never change, eh my pretty pony?' She felt his gloved fingers pricing apart her saturated entrance and tried to draw away, but without any success. And then, as the first two fingers pushed their way inside her pulsating tunnel, she suddenly found that her treacherous body was trying to respond by pushing down harder against the invading digits. Desperately, she chewed into the bit and willed herself to fight against the urge to surrender to the inevitability of emotions of which she was so ashamed.

Less than ten minutes had elapsed since the capture of the gatehouse, although the time seemed to stretch interminably in the stuffy interior of the tiny building. Crouched down by the rear wall, out of sight of any vehicles approaching from the outside world, Ruth clutched her walkie-talkie in one hand and counted away the seconds on her wristwatch.

'Outside party coming in, captain.' The girl seated just behind Douglas, whose massive bulk filled most of the observation window, relayed the message back in flat monotone. Mike, wearing the jacket taken from one of the unconscious guards, stepped outside the door, looked to either side and nodded back to Ruth.

'All clear out here,' he said, a slight quaver in his voice betraying the tension he felt. 'Let them in?'

'Of course,' Ruth snapped. 'Get that gate open and closed again as quickly as possible.'

Sergeant Sarah Testeyev, a solid blonde whose slightly

flattened nose spoiled what claims to beauty she might otherwise have had, ducked inside the gatehouse, followed by the other two members of her team. She threw up a half salute.

'They've taken out that blockhouse, ma'am,' she reported, 'and they're moving on down the perimeter. Do you want for us to go after them?'

Ruth shook her head. 'No. There's enough of them to accomplish what needs to be done and we need to concentrate our forces here now, until we get status reports back. Meanwhile, I want you to scout ahead and see if you can get a better idea of what's waiting for us in there, okay? Don't engage unless you're forced to and report back on the radio anything you do see that looks relevant.'

'I've never seen anything quite like you girls,' Mike said admiringly, when Sarah had gone again. Ruth smiled, but the smile did not reach her eyes.

'I suppose,' she said, 'if we were all men you wouldn't have felt the need to say something like that?'

Mike looked flustered. 'Well, no, I mean, yes,' he stammered. 'Look, I was just trying to pay you a compliment, okay?'

'Women who act like they've got balls make me nervous,' Douglas muttered. Ruth pointedly ignored him.

'Compliment accepted,' she said. 'But thank the Israeli army, plus your own commando school. We've had good teachers, believe me.'

Hancock slipped easily inside Alison's throbbing vagina, pushing forward until his pubic bone jarred firmly against the underside of her buttocks, the leather covering his lower stomach abrading her tortured flesh. Alison heard the grunt of satisfaction and bit into the hard rubber even deeper, screwing her eyes tightly shut and trying to blot out the reality of what was happening, concentrating on the pain, rather than the sensations that his entry were

222

already beginning to produce.

'Still a nice tight fit, pony whore,' he grated, slapping her thigh, 'so we shan't give you to Hercules just yet, I think.' He withdrew a few inches, paused, and then drove fully home again. Despite herself, Alison gasped and moaned, the fingers on her pilloried hands clenching and unclenching. Behind her, Hancock guffawed with pleasure.

'And still as hot as ever, I see!' he cried, repeating the in and out motion once again. Alison blinked furiously, her vision blurred by tears of shame, frustration and horror, but she knew there was no escaping, neither Hancock, nor herself.

Salt tears trickled down between the soft flesh of her cheeks and the thick rubber of the pony mask that covered them. Little rivulets seeped towards the corners of her bitted mouth and this time, as Hancock withdrew and poised himself to renew his invasion of her, Alison thrust backwards in time with his advance and screamed unintelligibly into the warm morning air.

'How much longer, Ruth?' Marcia shifted her cramped squatting position slightly and resumed drumming her fingers on her knee.

Ruth shrugged. 'How long's a piece of string?' she said. 'That's a total of seven of their pillboxes taken care of now, but we don't know how big the perimeter is. The girls reckon they're spaced at between seventy and a hundred yards and if this place is anywhere near the size of the estate at Dennison, that could mean a hundred more still to go.'

'A hundred?' Marcia gasped. 'But that could take hours.'

'I know,' Ruth acknowledged grimly. 'And we don't have hours. My bet is that all these sentry positions are supposed to report back by radio every fifteen minutes or so. They're all equipped with walkie-talkies, apparently, so someone is going to start getting a bit suspicious before too much longer.

'It's taking an average of three minutes for each team to get to and take out each position. So if their control centre gets suspicious they'll alert them to the possibility of an attack and that will slow things up considerably, at best. At worst, it could mean we start taking casualties.'

'It seems an awful risk,' Marcia muttered. 'Perhaps we should call it off before someone gets seriously hurt. We could inform the police, surely?'

'And they wouldn't move without much higher authority,' Mike said, turning around from his position just inside the doorway. 'You know your ex-husband and his influential friends. This whole place is down as some sort of official establishment, whatever else they get up to here, so by the time the police did move – assuming they even bothered – Hancock will have cleared out anything incriminating.'

'He's right,' Ruth said. 'We have to go in, whether we like it or not. I'm going to give the girls as long as possible. They've got the captured radios with them, and we've got the telephone over there, so we'll know as soon as anyone starts getting twitchy and that's when we move.

'At least we're whittling down the odds while we can and we'll have some sort of clear retreat line back to here.'

'Captain!' The dark-haired girl crouching in the corner beneath the front window interrupted the discussion. Ruth looked up. The girl raised the small black box she had been holding for several minutes.

'Ah!' Ruth exclaimed. 'The tracker on the original Bentley. It must be coming back into range.'

'Is that good, or bad?' Marcia demanded.

'Good,' Ruth smiled, 'so long as we can take out the occupants without any fuss. The car will give us cover to get up to whatever house, or houses, are being used as their centre. We could have used our ringer car, but I was working on the fact that they might just get suspicious if their Bentley returned too early.

'The two idiots here probably had no idea as to when it was expected back, which was why we were able to surprise them so easily, but whoever's in charge up there won't be so easily fooled. That car was obviously sent out to collect someone and they'll have a good idea of how long that would take.'

'So we can't delay much longer anyway,' Mike pointed out.

'We won't,' Ruth assured him. 'Just as soon as we've got the vehicle secured, I think we can start to make a move. If there are perimeter guards left out there, they won't want to leave their posts without direct instructions, so we'll have a bit of leeway. Ideally we could do with a proper jamming device, but if the girls tape down the transmission keys on the radios they've captured, that should effectively block the air on their frequency.'

'Neat idea,' Douglas muttered appreciatively. He turned and looked down at the girl holding the tracking receiver. 'How long till that car gets here?'

'About two minutes,' she said, studying the small display panel. 'Maybe three, depending upon what speed they maintain over this last stretch.'

'The sooner the better as far as I'm concerned,' Douglas said. 'All this waiting is starting to get on my nerves.'

2.14

It seemed a lifetime before Hancock finally reached his climax, but by then Alison was only dimly aware of him ejaculating deep inside her and she continued to spasm and tremble weakly long after he had withdrawn from her. Vaguely, she heard his voice as he gave orders, but it wasn't until the woman spoke that Alison realised Kristin had returned to witness the final stages of her humiliating ordeal.

'I think it would be a good idea to remove both of these sluts to the main cellar dungeons,' she said. 'I've given your instructions to security and also organised two extra patrols within the grounds, but if the whores are about out there, we ought not to take chances.'

'Chances, no,' Hancock agreed, 'but there's no need to overreact. You and Rose take them inside and stable them and I'll ring through and get one of the patrols to reinforce us here. The stable block is easily defendable and there's more space for the helicopter to land in this paddock. Any attack is likely to be directed at the house first, in any case, so that will give us more time.'

'You intend taking these two out of here?' Kristin asked.

'For a little while,' he confirmed. 'They're our only problem, after all,' he went on. 'The girls in the cellars are all on the payroll, or volunteer visitors, so they can quickly be dressed normally and the hidden doors sealed off until this is sorted out. I wouldn't put it past our friends out there to try to involve official agencies and, whilst I can delay any unwanted visits for so long, it would be easier to just let the police come in and see for themselves that there's nothing wrong here.' He walked around and stood in front of Alison, his softening organ still dangling incongruously from the front of his breeches.

'We wouldn't like to lose you again, would we?' he sneered. 'Not after all the trouble you've gone to in order to renew our association. A short air journey north into South Wales and we can have you installed in a nice new stable. Not as roomy as the facilities here, of course, but warm and dry and enough space for what I have in mind for the time being.'

As the now unconscious occupants of the second Bentley were being dragged into the rapidly overcrowding gatehouse, Sarah Levinski reappeared and huddled in urgent conversation with Ruth.

'What's the score then?' Douglas demanded impatiently.

Ruth pursed her lips thoughtfully. 'Well,' she said, 'there's a largish old house, together with a couple of barns and some smaller outbuildings, about four hundred yards up this main track. There are also several men wandering around, all armed with rifles. They're not too much of a problem, not out in the open like that, but we don't know who, or what, is inside the buildings, nor whether there are other potential strong points inside the grounds.'

'The house sounds the most likely place for their control centre,' Douglas retorted, 'so why don't we just load up into the car and try to take it out by direct assault, while a few snipers take out the ones outside?'

'That's about the only plan I've come up with,' Ruth agreed, 'but I'd like to give our perimeter squads as long as possible to neutralise more of their sentry positions.'

'And if they realise they haven't had any radio reports and try to raise them in return?' Douglas pointed out. 'That'll put them right on their guard at the house.'

'Unless we try to blank out their radio frequency now,' Ruth suggested. 'Four or five of the captured sets with their transmit keys taped down and scattered around that part of the perimeter we've already secured would be enough to do it. They might just be fooled into thinking that either their main set is faulty, or else that one of the fence guards has got his radio key stuck down my mistake.'

'In which case,' Mike put in, 'they'd be bound to send out some sort of party, or parties, to investigate.'

'Except that they'd possibly be looking for a careless idiot, rather than a force that's actually penetrated their outer defence ring,' Ruth replied. 'They'd also need to send out more than one party, given that there are a number of possible places the faulty set could be. And unless Hancock's got a major army here, assuming he'd need to keep a reserve to protect his nerve centre, those parties would have to be quite small.'

'And easy enough to pick off,' Sarah Levinski said, grinning. 'From what I've seen these aren't exactly crack troops we're up against. There are a few that look like they could be ex-servicemen, but the majority are little more than thugs with guns. Easy pickings,' she finished, confidently.

Hancock released Alison from the frame and led her, unprotesting and unsteady on the steepling hoof boots, back inside the stable block, thrusting her inside the stall in which she had originally been outfitted. Without speaking he grasped her bridle, began unbuckling it and shortly tossed it aside. A few moments later the rubber pony mask followed. Red-faced and still breathing heavily, Alison stood before him.

'Still as pretty as ever, I see,' he taunted, flicking one cheek with an extended finger. With her hands not yet resecured to her sides, Alison was tempted to retaliate, but his sheer size and presence dissuaded her. Outside somewhere, she knew, were Kristin, Rose and any number of guards and other associates and, even if she managed to get past Hancock and then them, she had no idea which way lay escape, nor whatever obstacles lay in the way.

'Such beautifully natural breasts, too,' Hancock smiled, transferring his attention to the ringed nipples that, due to the constriction forced about the base of her breasts by the tight rubber pony outfit, were standing proud and erect still. 'You don't realise how much I've waited to meet you again, my dear,' he said softly. 'I've thought about you every day for a year now, and visualised this day in so many different ways.'

'Well, make the most of it,' Alison snapped defiantly. 'By now this place is probably surrounded, so you may as well give yourself up.'

Hancock looked at her, eyes widening in mock surprise. 'My dear Miss Katt,' he said, with exaggerated politeness, 'you really should pay more attention to what I say, especially as our renewed friendship is likely to be such an extended one. Unless your friends have an entire army brigade out there, which I somehow doubt, then this place is quite impregnable. And besides, as I told you, I intend to take you and the Jew slut out of here for a few days, maybe even a few weeks, until all the fuss has died down.

'By that time my people will have dealt with the whore's so-called soldiers and your other friends will mysteriously disappear, or meet with unfortunate accidents one by one. Of course, my dear former wife will eventually join you in your new stable; it would be such a waste to have her killed, and I think I'd rather watch her grow old disgracefully, in harness, as a plaything for my own people.

'You, on the other hand, will make good breeding stock. The new order will need as much good Aryan stock as we can produce. Ten years from now, when this drug-induced hippie culture has wreaked its carnage on the world, people will turn back to look for the one true path, and by then we shall have stables filled with pedigree mares and stallions all over the world, not just in this country.'

'You're barking mad!' Alison spat. 'Completely off your

trolley. Besides,' she added, seizing on even the slenderest opportunity to delay Hancock with conversation, 'if you're so all-fired keen on establishing a pure race, how come you allow the likes of your Arab friends to have their way with your precious brood stock, eh?'

'My so-called Arab friends are nothing more than a means to an end,' he replied. 'They have money – lots of money, more money than you could hope to count in a hundred lifetimes. So, we keep them happy and if we give them a few whores to play with, so what? The pure stock will remain just that and our breeding programme will be strictly controlled and monitored.'

'And then what?' Alison challenged. 'You think the world hasn't learned from what Hitler and his cronies did? You really think you can repopulate the world with a load of children who are, to all intents and purposes, laboratory orphans?'

'There will be other children,' Hancock said levelly. 'The breeding programme is just an additional insurance, something which will, over many decades, help to expedite the creation of a truly pure race. The first generation of these children will never know any life beyond their stable, trained to unquestioning obedience, happy enough when their time comes to be the mothers and fathers of each succeeding generation.'

'But that would be pointless,' Alison protested. 'All you'd have is a whole load of unthinking, uneducated, completely dependent non-individuals.'

'Not all, Miss Katt,' Hancock said, with total assurance. 'There would still be leaders, though it is unlikely that they would come from within any stable. We aren't talking about a second coming here, you know,' he added, with an amused smile. 'In fact, for many generations the stables will serve only to produce pure breeding stock for the real elite, releasing a lot of the female population from the chores of motherhood and enabling them to play a more productive role in the economy of the new order.'

'It'll never work,' Alison retorted. 'Ordinary people won't go along with that sort of crap.'

'In the same way they didn't go along with things in Nazi Germany, you mean?' Hancock said. 'You'd be astonished at what "ordinary people" can be persuaded to believe in, especially if it happens to be the only true alternative to decadence, destruction, civil wars, famine and any number of other horrors. The western world is heading for a crisis that will approach Armageddon.

'The third world turns its eyes to us and sees everything it doesn't have, everything it believes it should be entitled to. Before long they'll be thinking they can take from us by force, but long before they have the power we shall make sure that our western world recognises the danger signs and meets force with force, overwhelmingly.

'However, unlike Herr Hitler and his misguided friends, we will not be taking on the world alone. We have already established networks in the United States, the white Commonwealth, in Germany, France, Spain, Italy, Scandinavia and even Russia. When the time comes, the power will be ours and the people will follow without question. Our sons and daughters will grow up to a much better world, I can assure you.'

'*Our* sons and daughters?' Alison echoed, horrified. 'I'd rather die than give birth to anything that came from your bloody sperm!'

'Unfortunately, my dear,' Hancock said, 'your life will never be yours to take. After today you will be kept as a helpless pony girl until you are beyond the age of breeding. You will have the very best medical care, comfortable quarters, regular exercise and the best diet science can produce.

'I shall be the only one to impregnate you for several years at least, and you will dutifully produce, I am sure, the most perfect offspring. Surely, even you must realise that you will be helpless to do anything to prevent this.'

'You're hideous!' Alison shrieked. 'You're filthy, perverted, unspeakable!'

'And you are insolent, in need of proper training and discipline,' Hancock replied, coolly. 'I'd have thought the taste of the whip you've had already would have taught you to guard your tongue, but then, perhaps you enjoy pain, eh?'

'Enjoy it?' Alison said. 'You think I'm as sick as you?'

'I'm not suggesting you're sick,' he replied, 'but I think you do enjoy the pain, in the same way you appear to enjoy being helpless.'

'Rubbish!'

'Is it? Can you deny how easily you are aroused when you are bound and gagged, or in this case, bridled and bitted. Even before I touched you your body was receptive and eager. It was the same a year ago, or had you forgotten? The whip, with you, serves only to unlock your deepest passions.' He reached out, grasped her nipple rings again, and pulled Alison to him.

'Shall I string you up against the wall and give you further proof?' he hissed. 'Or shall I simply take you in the straw now? That hot little cunt is almost certainly still twitching and, as you can probably feel, I am already beginning to rise to the prospect once again.'

The two man patrol appeared out of the undergrowth without warning, but before they could even raise their rifles two dull reports from the Israeli girls' dart weapons sent them toppling backwards, drugged needles embedded in their necks, arms and legs twitching spasmodically as the fast acting anaesthetic did its work.

'Someone's getting suspicious up there,' Ruth muttered, 'otherwise they'd have tried to phone the gatehouse first. Helen!' She swivelled about, calling to the redhead who'd been given the task of communications before the party had finally moved out from the building.

'Helen, let all units know we're moving on the main house now. Tell them to take care of their next objective and then start to head inwards. We're going to need to concentrate everything now. And warn them we've got active bandits now, okay?'

Helen nodded and immediately began muttering quietly into her walkie-talkie. Douglas, carrying one of the dart rifles as if it were a toy, came racing up to Ruth.

'Listen,' he said, 'this is starting to get serious, and these things,' he added, waving the rifle, 'don't necessarily drop a target immediately. I reckon we should use proper weapons now and stop pissing about.'

'You may have a point,' Ruth replied, 'but I can't sanction a full-blooded shoot-out, not here. The repercussions of a heap of corpses in a British government establishment... it doesn't bear thinking about.'

'So, you'd rather risk your own people?' Douglas demanded.

'No,' she said impatiently, 'but there are limits. Let's just get as many inside the Bentley as we can and get up to the house, okay? If we hurry we may still have the element of surprise. Right now they're just a bit suspicious, but you've seen how bloody inept they are, so if we can hit them before they've got time to organise themselves, we can still do this.'

Pressed against the wall of the stall, legs astride and braced, Alison could feel the hard heat between her thighs, the huge head of Hancock's penis probing the entrance to her sex. Desperately she fought to subdue the raging tide that threatened to engulf her, biting into her lip. Hancock looked down into her upturned face and a sneering smile spread across his features.

'You see?' he taunted. 'This is what you really want, isn't it? You need to be controlled, to be humiliated, to be used.'

Alison groaned and summoned one final effort. 'Yes,' she gasped. 'Yes, you're probably right. But is this what *you* really want? Do you really want a Jewish baby, you bastard?'

Hancock seemed to freeze and a strange expression overrode the lecherous smile.

'What?' he demanded. 'What are you talking about?' He pulled back, his right hand coming up so that his fingers and thumb encircled Alison's throat. Staring back up at him, Alison suddenly felt cold and the coldness instantly swept aside everything else that had been threatening to betray her.

'You heard, you bastard,' she hissed. 'So go ahead, shoot your fucking seed into me and see what it gets you.'

Hancock recoiled visibly. 'No!' he rasped. 'It can't be true. You're lying!'

'Why?' Alison felt a new strength rising through her body. 'Why should I lie? You've already whipped me and fucked me and yes, you're right, I get off on it, but I can be stronger than that. I'm worth far more than that, too. So go ahead; screw me again, but all you'll be is the father of a Jewish bastard!'

'It's not true,' Hancock said. He relaxed his grip about Alison's throat and stepped backwards, looking at her in disbelief. 'It *can't* be true.'

'Why not?' Alison sneered. 'Because I'm blonde, is that it? Because I'm blonde I can't possibly be a Jew? Well, have I got news for you, mister.'

'Secure the house, now!' Kristin whirled around to the two men sitting in front of the control console. 'Whatever's going on out there I don't want any chances taken, okay?' The older man, his jacket gaping open, his dark blue tie hanging loosely about his throat, nodded.

'Yes ma'am,' he said. 'What about sending out more

patrols?'

'Forget it!' Kristin snapped. 'That's two patrols already and nothing heard from them since they left here, according to you. And all the radios seem to have gone on the blink at the same time? I tell you now, those bitches are inside the perimeter. Phone the number one stable block and let the boss know what's going on.'

'Line's dead,' the second man intoned. 'I just tried and suddenly there was nothing.'

'Shit!' Kristin hesitated, but only for a moment. 'Give me a gun,' she ordered. 'I'll go and find him myself. In the meantime, one of you get up top and see to it that the emergency clearance procedures are started. I want this entire building cleared of anything that might cause unwanted questions. And get on the radio to that fucking chopper and find out where he's got to, or is his radio out as well?'

'No,' the second man said. 'The chopper's on a totally different frequency. It's just the handsets that seem to be out. All we're getting is white noise and a sort of hum, as if someone's keying over and jamming out the normal channel.'

'Yes,' Kristin said, taking the pistol he offered her as he spoke. 'All just a little too coincidental. Alert the chopper and tell him to stand off until he's certain of what he's looking at. I'm going to take two men with me, right? The rest of you will hold this place regardless, until you have a direct order to the contrary, either from me, or from Mr Hancock himself. Understand?'

'Down!' Ruth screamed, throwing herself flat on the ground and immediately wriggling towards the back of the Bentley. Three more shots rang out, this time a bullet ricocheting off the roof of the car. 'Get out!' she yelled. 'Get out of the car and get away. Douglas, get the fucking thing back, for God's sake. If they hit the petrol tank…!'

235

Mike dived out of the car door on the far side from the house and rolled and scrabbled towards the slight hollow at the base of the nearest clump of bushes. From the house, not fifty yards away, another two sharp reports echoed and a fountain of earth erupted mere inches from his head. He continued to roll sideways, stopping only when the undergrowth was between him and whoever was doing the shooting.

The Bentley's engine roared, gears crunched and screamed and the heavy car slued backwards, but not before the offside headlight had exploded in a shower of glass shards. Two more bullets ploughed into the ground, sending up more earth and stones and then, quite as suddenly as the action had started, everything was once again quiet. Mike raised his head and looked across to where Ruth was lying behind a flowerbed, the impressive blooms affording her cover, if not protection.

'They're on to us!' he called.

Ruth rolled her eyes and looked up towards the sky. 'I had noticed,' she replied. 'I didn't think this was the standard reception for guests.' She turned her head, looking across to where two more of her girls were lying behind a bush that looked far too small to offer even a hope of camouflage. 'You both okay?' she called. The two women nodded, their attention still focused on the house.

'Just keep your heads down then,' Ruth instructed them. 'We can't risk rushing the place, not in daylight, but Becky should be back up here with smoke grenades in a few moments. I want everyone back then, and no heroics.'

'What about Hannah and Alison?' Mike demanded.

Ruth groaned and rolled over onto her back. 'If they're in the house,' she said, 'then we've blown it. Right now I'm more worried about avoiding casualties, okay?'

'Yeah, understood,' Mike nodded. 'You think they are in there?'

Ruth opened her mouth to reply, but suddenly stopped, head raised, listening intently.

'Helicopter!' she hissed. 'Hear it?'

Mike turned his head on one side, ears pricked, and in the distance he too heard the faint *thwicka-thwicka* sound.

'It's a Huey!' Ruth said. 'That rotor signature is unmistakable.'

Mike's eyes narrowed. 'That's a US machine, isn't it?'

Ruth nodded. 'Yeah, it's a Yankee chopper all right. Workhorse of the Vietnam effort, but they sell them to almost any so-called friendly power that can afford the price. Yeah, look, there it is!' She jabbed a finger towards the northern horizon, where a dark speck had suddenly materialised against the clear blue sky.

'You think it's one of theirs?' Mike asked.

Ruth regarded him levelly across the twenty yards that separated them. 'Well,' she said at last, 'it definitely ain't one of *ours*!'

2.15

The restraining device was as simple as it was effective. A two inch wide steel collar locked about Alison's neck, from either side of which projected an eighteen inch long tubular steel strut, terminating in lockable steel fetters, into which Hancock quickly secured her wrists. Its function was identical to the ancient Chinese chang, but it was much lighter than its heavy timber predecessor, and by the simple expedient of turning sideways, its wearer could negotiate even the narrowest of doorways.

'I suggest you get used to this,' Hancock said, pocketing the key. 'You could now be spending most of your miserable life wearing it.' His attitude had changed dramatically following Alison's revelation of her ancestry: where he had been almost solicitous and clearly relishing the prospect of taking Alison as his personal mate, now he was cold, detached, and it seemed, intent on punishing her for something that was beyond her ability to control.

He selected a length of fine chain from the tack rack, threaded it through both her nipple rings and linked the two loose ends in his left hand, jerking the makeshift leash cruelly to demonstrate its effectiveness.

'You'll discover that we have our own methods for dealing with treacherous bitches!' he snarled. 'You and the other whore will make a fine racing pair, though we'll have to enlarge your tits to match hers now, of course. Come – I'll show you what delights await you.'

He yanked the chain again, forcing Alison to follow after him, stumbling in his wake as he led the way out into the corridor, along and in through the last stall door. Inside the light level was much lower, and it took Alison several seconds before her eyes adjusted and she was able to make out the figure that stood in the centre of the floor, held up, it appeared, by a series of chains attached to her intricate body harness.

'Hannah!' she gasped, when she finally realised the blonde creature's true identity. The girl stared mutely back at her and did not attempt to communicate, other than with her eyes, despite the obvious lack of either bit or other form of gag.

'Yes, Hannah,' Hancock said. 'A pretty sight now, isn't she? Such succulent tits we've given her, and she can even

238

take a bit without distorting her features too much. See?' He dropped Alison's chain and took a step towards the silent figure, prising open her mouth to display the missing back teeth. Alison gasped in horror.

'And of course,' Hancock continued, 'she no longer has the power of speech.' He forced Hannah's jaws even wider, moving his fingers to afford Alison a clear view of the thin steel strap that was secured to her teeth and pressing down on her tongue.

'Simple, but effective,' Hancock said, releasing his grip and stepping back again. 'We considered surgery to the vocal cords, but that has a tendency to prevent all sounds, which we don't really want. And the other option, removal of the tongue, tends to reduce the efficiency and value of a pony girl in other directions.'

'I think you need help,' Alison muttered. 'You're one very sick cookie.' Her captor bridled for a moment, tensing, a dark cloud moving rapidly across his features, and Alison steeled herself for the anticipated reaction. But before Hancock had time to move on her the sound of Rose's urgent tones in the corridor beyond brought him a more immediate problem on which to concentrate his energies.

'There are intruders inside the grounds, sir,' Rose stammered, appearing in the doorway. 'They're outside the house, apparently pinned down for the moment, though no one can be sure of numbers. Kristin is on her way down here now and I can see the helicopter coming in, so I brought you this.' She extended a hand, holding out a handgun. 'I think we should get these two out of here without delay,' she added.

Hancock took the gun, nodding agreement. 'Yes,' he said. He looked at the weapon for a few seconds, as if trying to make up his mind about something, and then passed it back to Rose.

'You get the pair of them to the outer door,' he said,

'but remain inside until I get back. I need to phone through to the house and make sure they follow the emergency procedures. There were two guns in your room, I believe?'

Rose, who was plainly ill at ease with the gun she was holding, nodded. 'Yes, the other one is still in the bedside locker,' she said. 'I didn't think to bring it—'

'The problem with women,' Hancock rasped, 'is that they never do think. Why do you think you were issued with those guns and given training in their use?' He pushed his way roughly past her without waiting for a reply. 'Just do as you're told for once and, if anyone shows up you don't recognise, fucking well shoot at them, okay? And make sure they get a clear view of these two beauties at the same time,' he added. 'That should make them think twice about shooting back.'

'It's coming down over there, beyond that patch of woodland,' Ruth said, as the grey helicopter continued its circling descent. She crouched behind the bonnet of the Bentley, one hand held up to shield her eyes from the sun.

'It's a UH-1H,' she said, talking to herself as much as to Mike. 'It's one of the newer models, capable of adapting to almost any requirement.'

'But that's a US insignia on the side, surely?' Mike said, pointing.

Ruth shot him a sideways glance. 'And a bloody machinegun slung on one side, too,' she said. 'Unfortunately, the bullets it fires don't ask for birth certificates or passports.'

'But how come an American military chopper—?'

'What does it matter?' Ruth demanded. 'Anyway, we know Hancock has friends in all sorts of high places, so why not the use of an American helicopter? There are scores of the damned things flying about all over the place in this country, half of them involved in secret training stuff, so the civil aviation authorities don't bother even asking most of the time. It's a perfect cover.'

'Yeah,' Mike agreed. 'Too bloody perfect, but what's it doing here?'

'Evacuation, possibly,' Ruth said. 'Your friend and mine isn't renowned for staying around and fighting, is he? My bet is that he keeps that Huey somewhere close enough to get him out, though I expect it's normally used for ferrying people and supplies in and out.'

'Maybe that's all it's doing today?' Mike suggested.

'It's possible,' she conceded, 'but it's turned up just too conveniently for my liking.'

'Can we stop it taking off again?'

'Not with what we've got,' she said. 'But we might just be able to stop Hancock reaching it.'

'Why not just let him go?' Mike suggested. 'Once he's out the way, maybe we can persuade his goons it isn't worth trying to resist?'

'And maybe not,' Ruth retorted. 'Besides, it isn't likely he's going to leave here empty-handed. Hannah is a witness against him, and so is Alison, if they've rumbled who she really is. He'll be wanting to get them out of here – that way there won't be anything to prove what he's really been up to.'

She scrambled into a more upright stance, moving back along the length of the car to keep her head below the roof level.

'Sarah!' she yelled towards the bushes where the square-featured Sergeant Testeyev and several other girls lay hidden from the house. 'Smoke grenades to cover. Four with me and the rest to remain here with you, in case they try to break out and follow us. When the perimeter parties return send another two after us. We're going to try to stop them getting to that chopper!'

If the sight of the gun in Rose's hand had not been enough, the obvious fact that she was uneasy with it certainly convinced Alison that any attempt to resist was fraught with danger. Guns were bad enough at the best of times: in the hands of the inexperienced and frightened, they could be even worse.

But if Rose's handling of the gun was suspect, she had lost none of her expertise in the controlling of her beloved pony girls. A second length of chain was quickly threaded through Hannah's nipple rings and then a short chain leash was used to clip all the loose ends of chain together, so that with one hand Rose was able to lead and direct the two helpless girls. As they tottered along the corridor in her wake, Alison heard the first sounds of the approaching helicopter and, as they halted in the open doorway, she saw it slowly beginning to settle at the far side of the paddock, the down draft from the beating rotors flattening and rippling the grass all around it.

'Stand!' Rose commanded, peering out. She held the gun before her, but the muzzle was wavering and Alison could see the nerves twitching beneath her jaw. Whether she was remembering Dennison Hall and the first rescue, the confusion of falling bodies, screaming and yelling guests, staff and slaves, the unnerving efficiency of Hannah's commando squad, Alison could not tell, but this latest sudden chain of events had certainly disturbed her usual composure.

'Right!' Hancock yelled, clumping up the corridor behind them. 'We'll take one each. I'll go first. Kristin will be here in a few seconds and the two of you can bring the Jew whore as soon as I give the word.' He snatched the leash from Rose's hand, separated the two sets of chains and took Alison's himself. In his free hand he now held a pistol identical to Rose's, which he jammed viciously beneath Alison's exposed armpit.

'Mystery tour time,' he said, looping the chain over

Alison's other shoulder and shortening it so that the hand holding it rested against the side of her neck. 'Just start walking and do exactly what I tell you, and believe me when I tell you that I won't have the slightest compunction about blowing your stupid brains out if anyone tries anything clever!'

The three smoke grenades provided a perfect screen between the house and the small party that set off towards the site of the helicopter landing, and although someone inside the building let off a couple of speculative shots, they were aimed well away from the danger area. Once the group had gained the cover of the trees Ruth paused, holding up a hand.

'Fan out,' she ordered. 'See, there are three different tracks from here, so let's divide our forces. There may well be guards somewhere in these woods, but I doubt they can cover all the paths.' She slung her dart rifle over her shoulder and drew a businesslike looking automatic from her belt.

'Fuck the consequences,' she snarled, giving Douglas a meaningful glare. 'It'll be someone else's problem later, okay?'

Douglas nodded and drew his own pistol from inside his jacket. 'Suits me,' he said. Ruth jabbed a finger at the various girls, detailing them into two separate parties, leaving her, Mike, Douglas and the breathless Marcia as the third group.

'Stay behind me,' she instructed. 'Keep in to the undergrowth and get ready to flatten yourself at the first sign of trouble.'

Taking the left-hand path she set off at a fast lope and Mike, trailing behind Douglas, soon found himself falling further and further behind. Marcia, her heels completely unsuited to the uneven terrain, stumbled headlong twice, but gamely struggled back to her feet.

'Go on!' she urged Mike, whose immediate reaction had been to stop to help her. 'I won't be much use anyway, so just get after them. If that bastard gets Alison on that helicopter we may never see her again.'

They ran out into the clearing almost without warning. Ahead of Mike Ruth had already swerved to one side, dropping into a crouch as she surveyed the scene ahead of them. Mike hesitated and then stepped back, pressing hard against one of the trees that formed the perimeter of the open space. The dart rifle felt awkward in his hands, but too light, and he was only too well aware that these people were armed with weapons that could kill at a considerable range.

Forcing himself to concentrate, he quickly took in the situation as he saw it. Straight ahead, perhaps a hundred and fifty yards away on the far side of the clearing, the helicopter sat, rotors beating the air, grass rippling and flattening beneath the down draft. To his left, nestling against the tree screen, stood a small stone complex, part single storey, part double storey, from which had just emerged two figures, one clearly male, the other female, but dressed in the most bizarre fashion, her wrists apparently locked to some sort of device that encircled her neck.

For a second or so the unexpected sight threw Mike completely, but then, as he recognised the powerful figure of Ralph Hancock, he suddenly realised who his squirming captive really was.

'It's Alison!' he yelled before he had time to think and his cry, intended for Ruth and Douglas, served only to warn their intended quarry. Hancock halted, pulling Alison closer to him, and whirled around to face the new threat.

'That's far enough!' he shouted. His left arm snaked about Alison's throat, the gun in his right hand jammed hard into her side. Ruth held up her arm and Douglas immediately flattened himself, his pistol extended in front of him. Fifty yards to the right three of the Israeli girls broke cover, but came immediately to a halt as they saw what was happening.

'You all think you've been quite clever, don't you?' Hancock sneered. 'Well, enjoy your little victory while it lasts. Even if you do persuade the police to take an interest here, I'll have it screwed down tighter than a drum before they can get a warrant to search. Local plods tend to obey orders when they come direct from Whitehall.

'And don't think I've forgotten about any of you Zionist whores,' he snarled. 'I've got a very long reach and I always repay debts. Each and every one of you will wind up as a bloody workhorse for some fat Arab prince. Next time I shan't bother holding onto any of you here, nor anywhere else. You'll be shipped straight out, same as the other bitch is going to be now.' He paused, raising his head and craning his neck.

From his left came the sound of wild snorting, followed by the high-pitched crack of leather striking flesh, and from around the end of the stable block appeared another pony girl, also blonde, bound and struggling against the efforts of a powerfully built woman in a bizarre parody of riding gear. Behind them, pointing a long-barrelled pistol, came the unmistakable figure of Kristin, face set with grim determination.

'Get back and let them through!' Hancock shouted. 'Anyone tries to stop them, you know what will happen.'

'Let her go, Hancock!' Mike yelled, pushing his way past Ruth. 'If you want a hostage then take me with you.'

Hancock stared back at him, cold-eyed. 'Quite the hero, eh?' he sneered. 'Well, you'll get your chance too, all in good time. But if you think I'm letting either of these sluts go, you've got another think coming. You can have your one back in forty-eight hours, just so long as no one tries to contact the police in the meantime.'

'During which,' Mike retorted, 'you'll make sure your

friends in high places pull all the necessary strings. On the other hand, if you do shoot Alison you won't find that so easy to hush up.'

'Maybe not,' Hancock agreed, 'but it'll be too late to do her any good, won't it? If you don't think I mean it, just take one step nearer,' he added. 'I'll also shoot you, too, and Kristin will put a bullet through the Jewess's spine. That's not a very pleasant way to die, so I'm told.'

'How do we know we can trust you, Rafe?' Marcia demanded, appearing at Mike's elbow.

Hancock shrugged. 'You don't, my sweet,' he said, 'but then you do know me enough to know I will carry out my threat if you do try to stop us leaving. Now, stop fuck-arsing about. Kristin, Rose – get the bitch over to the chopper.'

'Better do as he says,' Marcia grated. 'He's totally mad, worse than ever before and he *will* kill them both. This way, at least there's a chance of getting Alison back in more or less one piece.'

'But what about Hannah?' Mike protested.

Ruth's hand fell on his elbow. 'Let them take her,' she whispered. 'They'll both be dead if we try anything here, so leave it. If he doesn't release your friend we'll hunt the bastard down later. And if he harms either of them, I'll take the greatest pleasure in disembowelling him personally.

'First rule of warfare,' she growled. 'Never carry on a losing battle, not when you're outnumbered, nor when the enemy holds the high ground. Just fall back, regroup and make sure you win the war itself, next time around.'

'You're the expert,' Mike said. 'I only ever made corporal during my national service, and that was in the pay corps.' He turned back to Hancock, who was continuing to edge backwards towards the waiting helicopter.

'Okay,' he conceded, 'you can leave, but if anything

happens to Alison I'll make it my personal business to see that you rot in hell.'

'Very commendable sentiments, I'm sure,' Hancock laughed. 'I'll send the stupid filly back in a couple of days, don't worry. I can find her again any time I want. Come to that,' he said, grinning broadly, 'it seems I only have to wait around somewhere and she comes to me anyway. Must be down to my personal charisma, I guess.' He half turned towards the advancing Kristin and Rose, who now had hold of Hannah between them.

'Move it!' he snapped. 'Keep close together and let's get the pair of them aboard.'

'He's lying,' Marcia muttered between clenched teeth. 'He has no intention of releasing Alley. He knows we don't have any proof without her. The goons inside the house will have destroyed anything that might be evidence. That's why he came out here, to buy them the time. He'll just dump the two girls off somewhere temporarily, then come back here when we've all gone.'

'There has to be someone in the police force who'll listen to the truth,' Mike said. 'He can't have them all on his payroll.'

'And he doesn't need to,' Marcia replied. 'It'll be our word against his, and his cronies will soon find something they can blacken our names with, whether it's true or not. In my case it'd probably be true anyway, and you're a newspaperman, so you'd have a vested interest. Besides, all the time he holds onto Alley we daren't go to the law, and he knows it.'

'I'll find a way,' Mike said. 'Believe me, I'll find a way!'

The retreating quintet had arrived at the helicopter and Kristin was first up and through the open doorway. Reaching down, she took the bridle rein from Rose and used it to force Hannah to turn, so that the powerful Rose could lift her up into the machine. Rose then took hold of Alison and Hancock leapt up to join Kristin, taking

Hannah's rein from her so that she and Rose could lift Alison.

A moment later they were all inside and the steady *thrup-thrup-thrup* of the Huey's rotors began to pick up in time to the increasing pitch of the whining engine. For a brief second the whole airframe seemed to shudder and then the helicopter was lifting clear of the ground, spinning around in a graceful backward semi-circle as it gained height.

'Shit!' Mike pounded his fist into the palm of his hand, face burning with frustration and helpless anger. 'We should have done something and now it's too late.'

The Huey was climbing swiftly, turning towards the north and tilting slightly as it banked against the crosswinds. Within seconds it was shrinking against the sky, picking up speed, but suddenly it began to turn, arcing around in a long turn and heading back towards them at increasing speed.

'Get down!' Ruth screamed. 'Everyone get under cover. That's not a dummy gun under there!' One of the remaining female guests let out an ear-piercing shriek, turned and fell headlong, but the Israeli women were made of much sterner stuff. They split into three separate groups, running for the ditch, the stable block and the nearest trees, rather than offer a single target if the helicopter did open fire.

Mike found himself running alongside Marcia, keeping her upright as she struggled to cover the uneven grass in her high heels, looking back over his shoulder as the chattering machine came speeding towards the paddock. The solid stonework of the stable block looked further away than ever and his feet seemed to have become weighted down. Any second now, he thought, a hail of bullets would rip through them, long before they got within twenty yards of cover.

But the engine note suddenly changed again, and when

Mike looked back he saw the helicopter was hovering over the far edge of the paddock, some two hundred feet or so above them and too close for the fixed machinegun to be deployed, unless the pilot dipped the nose dramatically.

'Keep going,' he urged Marcia. 'Just get inside and get down on the floor.'

'He's taking the piss!' Ruth growled, whirling around and stopping. Defiantly, she stood her ground, hands on hips, challenging the helicopter and its occupants. 'Yes,' she shouted, raising two fingers in a V-sign, 'gloat all you want, for now.'

'Ruthie!' one of the other Israeli girls shrieked. 'Ruthie, for fuck's sake get over here! They can pick you off any time they want from there!'

'No,' Ruth said, her voice almost drowned out by the roar of the engine and the whirring rotors. 'No, he won't do that; I won't be any fun to him dead.'

'Oh shit! No! *No*!' Marcia's shriek split the air almost before the blonde figure emerged from the open doorway of the Huey, arms and legs flailing as it tumbled over and over in dreadful, slow-motion descent. From above, as all eyes on the ground were glued to the falling marionette with horrified fascination, came a different sound, a sharp report and then another figure tumbled backwards and was falling even as the first figure thudded into the bushes at the far side of the clearing.

Mike found himself sprinting and was only dimly aware of the hurtling figures to either side of him, only that the second figure had landed only yards from where the first had fallen…

And then they were all standing around the crushed bushes, staring down at the two broken and twisted figures, discarded dolls with drained faces, staring eyes and, in the case of Ralph Hancock, a bullet hole drilled neatly in the centre of his forehead.

Clearly he had been dead long before he hit the ground, but a few yards away, head bent at a crazy angle, blood oozing from one corner of her gaping mouth, Kristin's fall had ended in a broken neck and the terror of her impending doom was etched into her twisted features even after death.

For fully half a minute no one spoke, but then the sound of the helicopter beginning to descend broke the trance. Whirling around Mike saw the Huey settling back into the middle of the clearing and then, almost before the skids had touched the grass, two female figures, reins trailing, legs flailing, were leaping out and hurtling towards them.

'R-Rose!' Alison gasped, as Mike ripped the bit from between her teeth. 'Rose threw Kristin out and then shot Hancock. He was going to toss Hannah out.'

Mike turned towards the Huey, to where Rose had stepped down onto the grass. In her hand she held what he presumed had been Kristin's gun, and behind him he heard a volley of sharp clicks as the Israeli girls brought their weapons back to readiness.

'Hold your fire!' Ruth snapped out the order and stepped forward, holding out her free hand. 'Lower the weapon and pass it to me, butt first!' she called out, but Rose did not seem to hear her. The big woman paused, looked back at the idling helicopter and then down at her feet.

'He was going to throw Star out,' she said dully, her voice barely audible over the engine noise. 'He was going to throw her out, to kill her.'

'I understand,' Ruth said, with commendable calmness. 'He deserved what he got and you were only preventing a murder. We'll all testify to that.'

Rose looked up and seemed to see her for the first time. 'Murder?' she echoed. 'Oh yes, murder. You can't go around killing pony girls, especially not champions like Star. That would be such a waste.' She shook her head and stared down at her boots again.

'Such a waste!' she repeated and then, before any of them could react, calmly lifted the gun, placed the muzzle into her mouth and blew the top of her head off in a display that none of those who witnessed it would ever forget.

'Oh fuck!' Ruth breathed, lowering her own gun. 'What a fucking mess.' To one side of her Douglas doubled over and was violently sick.

Epilogue

The atmosphere in Marcia's lounge was sombre, the heavy curtains closed against the late afternoon sunshine. Marcia herself sat in her usual fireside armchair; the remainder of the party scattered between the two ancient sofas, the second armchair and the thick carpet. Alison, wrapped in a quilted dressing gown, sat on the floor at Marcia's feet, her knees drawn up to her chin, arms wrapped about them. Hannah, minus the blonde wig, her black hair resembling a velvet skullcap, had changed into a khaki jump-suit, and stood leaning against the wall by the window, as if the events of the past days had never happened.

'I still don't think we should just walk away from all this,' Mike said. 'Okay, so Hancock's dead, but surely he's just the tip of the iceberg? Besides, the police are sure to ask questions. We left three dead bodies back there, don't forget.'

'I doubt they'll be calling in the law,' Ruth said. 'With Hancock gone, plus Kristin and that Rose woman, all that's left down there is the chaff. We know Hancock had friends in high places, friends who had the same warped principles as him, so no doubt they'll be called in to sort it out.'

'You mean they'll just do some sort of whitewash?' Alison protested. 'We didn't ought to just sit back and let them get away with it.'

'There's not much else we can do,' Hannah said. 'These people have money, influence and power. And besides, what proof do we have? If we say anything they'll just turn it around so that we get the blame for everything and, given the current delicate political situation surrounding our country,' she added, 'that's not a risk we can afford to take.'

'No,' Mike agreed, 'I can understand that, but there ought to be something we can do.'

'There's something everyone can do,' Hannah said sombrely. 'The trouble is, there's *always* something everyone can do, but everyone just sits back and leaves it to someone else. It happened thirty odd years ago and it'll happen again, believe me. People only ever believe what they want to believe.'

'Well,' Alison said, looking up at the circle of faces, 'at least *we* did something this time. We stopped the pig, if nothing else.'

'Yeah,' Hannah replied, staring down at the carpet. 'We stopped one pig, no question about it. Problem is,' she continued, reaching out and pulling the curtain to one side, so that a thin shaft of sunlight fell across the dark carpet, 'that's one very big pigsty out there – one very big pigsty indeed.'

Exciting titles available from Chimera

All **Chimera** titles are/will be available from your local bookshop or newsagent, or direct from our mail order department. Please send your order with a cheque or postal order (made payable to *Chimera Publishing Ltd*) to: **Chimera Publishing Ltd., PO Box 152, Waterlooville, Hants, PO8 9FS**. If you would prefer to pay by credit card, email us at: **chimera@fdn.co.uk** or call our **24 hour telephone/fax credit card hotline: +44 (0)23 92 783037** (Visa, Mastercard, Switch, JCB and Solo only).

To order, send: Title, author, ISBN number and price for each book ordered, your full name and address, cheque or postal order for the total amount, and include the following for postage and packing:
UK and BFPO: £1.00 for the first book, and 50p for each additional book to a maximum of £3.50.
Overseas and Eire: £2.00 for the first book, £1.00 for the second and 50p for each additional book.

*Titles £5.99. All others £4.99

For a copy of our free catalogue please write to:

Chimera Publishing Ltd
Readers' Services
PO Box 152
Waterlooville
Hants
PO8 9FS

Or visit our **new** Website for details of all our superb titles and secure ordering
www.chimerabooks.co.uk